"BY THE EDICTS OF THE CALIF DON CARLUS...

"...and his fathers before him, and the word of Calif Don Felipe, there is to be no disruption of the peace on matters of conscience in Al-Andalus or in any lands ruled by Al-Andalus! No Jihad! No Crusade!"

He repeated the words loudly in Arabi and then again in Erse for the benefit of anyone who did not understand Arabi.

"Islim rules, but the followers of the Redeemer may worship as they will, and the Yehudit are allowed to settle where they will, so long as they observe the calif's laws, pay their tolls, and do not disturb the general peace. Prester Nicodemus, if you continue to disturb the Calif's Peace, you and your followers will be subject to the calif's displeasure."

"And who are you to tell me what I can and cannot do?" Prester Nicodemus sneered.

Halvar raised his head and glared across the plaza at the crowd.

"I am Halvar Danske, the Calif's Hireling, and his personal representative in Manatas. I carry the calif's own seal, and what I do is by his orders. Right now, I order all of you to go about your business and allow us to do the same!"

There was an ugly muttering from the crowd. Ruiz stepped forward, one hand on the cudgel at his belt. The Guards behind him unhooked the cudgels from their belts and held them ready to enforce the calif's will on anyone who dared defy it.

"The mullah will hear of this," the imam said as he retreated to the muskat at the entrance to the plaza.

"This is not over," threatened Prester Nicodemus, with a nod to Jehan.

Halvar was suddenly aware of a sharp pain in his side. He pressed his hand to his back and realized that it was wet and, when he looked at it, red.

"You're bleeding," Ruiz observed.

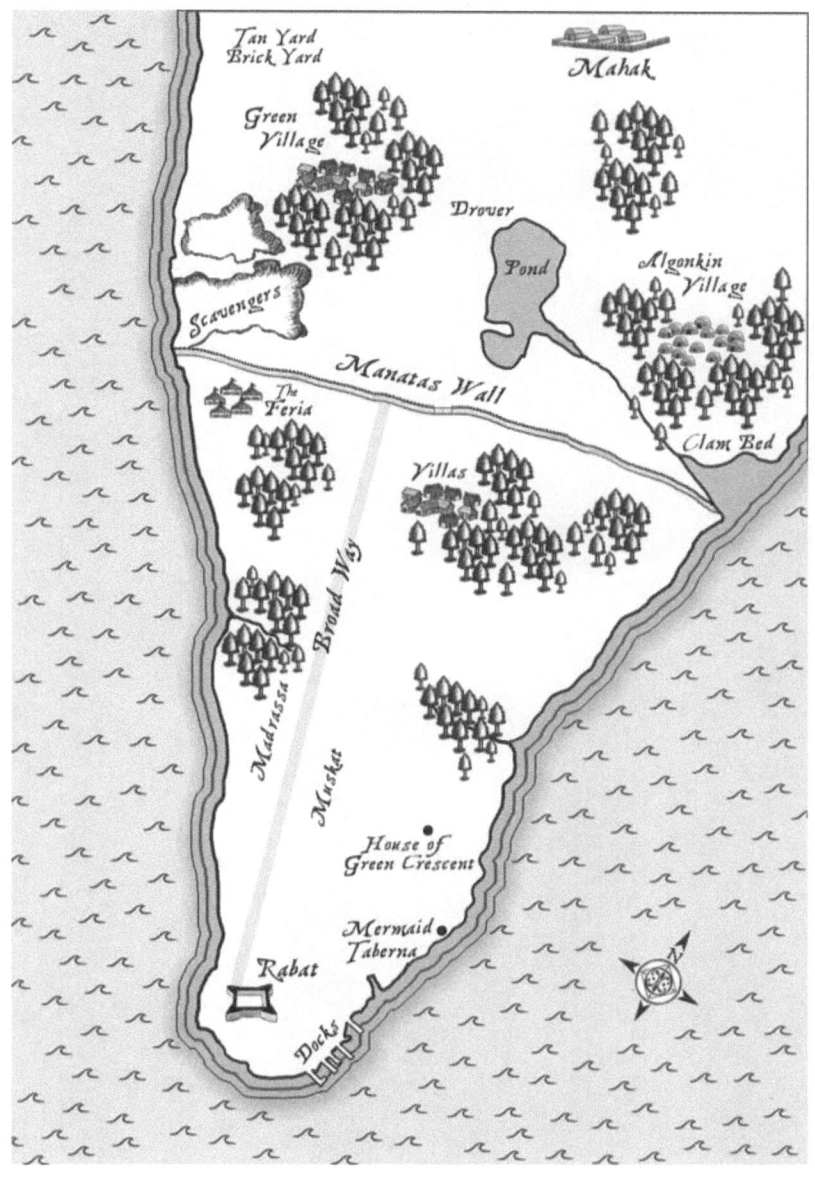

Manatas Island

MAYHEM
IN
MANATAS

The Saga of Halvar the Hireling
Book 2

ROBERTA ROGOW

ZUMAYA OTHERWORLDS   AUSTIN TX

2014

MAYHEM IN MANATAS
© 2014 by Roberta Rogow
ISBN 978-1-61271-255-0
Cover art and design © William Neagle

"Zumaya Otherworlds" and the griffon colophon are trademarks of Zumaya Publications LLC, Austin TX.

Look for us online at http://www.zumayapublications.com

Library of Congress Cataloging-in-Publication Data

Rogow, Roberta, 1942-
 Mayhem in Manatas : the Saga of Halvar the Hireling 2 / Roberta Rogow.
  pages cm. -- (The Saga of Halvar the Hireling ; 2)
 ISBN 978-1-61271-255-0 (print/trade pbk. : alk. paper) -- ISBN 978-1-61271-256-7 (electronic/multiple format) -- ISBN 978-1-61271-257-4 (electronic/epub)
1. Alternative histories (Fiction) 2. Mystery fiction. I. Title.
PS3568.O492M39 2014
813'.54--dc23
                    2014021389

TO MY MOTHER

SHIRLEY WINSTON
1917 – 2013

A woman ahead of her time, my inspiration,
critic and sometime collaborator.

ACKNOWLEDGMENTS

Lynne Holdom and Rachel Kadushin
helped formulate the Universe of Manatas.

Liz Burton took a chance and published the
Saga of Halvar the Hireling.

My thanks to all who made this book
possible.

Part 1

Death
on the
Docks

Chapter 1

HALVAR DIDN'T MEAN TO KILL TWO PEOPLE BEFORE BREAK-
fast.

He tried to think what he could have done to prevent the slaugh-
ter. He had been in Manatas a week. The first three days were spent
in nonstop action, the next three in the cell assigned to him in the
Rabat dealing with the aftermath of multiple attacks. He'd been blud-
geoned, stabbed, shot, drugged, and garroted. He'd been poisoned
by odd food eaten at odder hours.

Now he stood before the enraged ruler of Manatas Town like a
schoolboy being berated by the head of the Madrassa. He shifted
from foot to foot, his shoulders constricted in a coat that had been
remade from the standard uniform issued to the Town Guard, with
extra inserts at the bottom and seams to suit his tall frame.

As the personal Hireling of Don Felipe, the Calif of Al-Andalus,
in whose name the sultan ran the outpost called Manatas Town,
he deserved no less; but he hated not having his own common gear.

He mourned the leather jacket that had been sliced to ribbons
by assassins. At least he had retained his own cap, the leather-lined
item with its plain ribbon band whose hidden boiled-leather lining had saved his life and his wits more times than he chose to count.
He had added a leather vest that served as perfunctory armor under the light coat.

He wished he could have strapped his belt and dagger over the
coat instead of having to button the coat over the belt and dagger,

3

but he'd left one of the toggles open so he could get his hand onto the dagger if he had to fight.

He glanced at the young man sharing the force of Sultan's Petrus's wrath.

How does he do it? Halvar wondered, taking in Tenente Ruiz's dapper appearance.

The tenente's green coat, although taken from the general stores provided for the Town Guard, fit him as if it had been made for him, not a wrinkle marring his sleek form. The braid on his sleeves that marked his elevation in rank from mere guardsman to tenente fairly gleamed in the morning sunlight that filtered through window of the tower room where Sultan Petrus held court. Even the regulation bludgeon that swung from his belt had been polished, and the ivory inlay on the butt of the pistoia thrust into his belt seemed to wink every time he moved.

Under the tall tarboosh worn by the Guards, Ruiz's regular features were stony, only the quiver of the line of mustache on his upper lip and a twitch at the corner of his neatly trimmed beard revealing his anger.

Petrus stumped back and forth across the floor of his personal apartment in the Rabat, the fortress that had been built at the southernmost tip of the island to guard Manatas from invaders from the sea. One foot booted in expensive leather, the other replaced by a silver-embellished ivory peg, the old soldier fairly exploded with wrath, waving his arms and sending the sleeves of his silk caftan flapping. His elaborately folded turban wobbled on his head, its plume bobbing as he wagged his head at Halvar.

"Only seven days here, Don Alvaro, and the death toll is mounting! How do you do it? Is there some daemon, some djinn that sits upon your shoulder and carries its bane with it so that you bring destruction with you?" the sultan fairly spar at the tall Dane.

Halvar tugged at the yellow mustache that swept from his upper lip down to his chin.

"I had no choice," he protested. "The killing of the frater in the Feria was not my doing, and Tenente Gomez, who actually did the deed, tried to kill me, so I had to defend myself. As for the young Mahak, Otter Tail, that was Gomez again. Am I to be blamed because you trusted a man who was untrustworthy?"

"And what about the Franchen?" Sultan Petrus shot back. "Not one, not two, but *three* in one morning! And one of them a woman!"

"They were trying to disrupt our money system," Halvar explained. "They were responsible for dyeing white wumpum purple to get more goods for false coin. And they killed one of your own wife's servants who discovered what they were doing and left her naked body to be swept away in the East Channel. It was only because the killer misjudged the tides that she was found by the Local women who gather clams there. And I wasn't the one who killed Jacques Tavernier, that was Ruiz, here. He's the one with the pistoia."

Tenente Ruiz stiffened even more under the sultan's scrutiny. He had been hurriedly appointed to Gomez's position when the former tenente of the Town Guard was forced into the Great River to be swept upstream where he might (or might not) have been captured by the Mahak.

Now he put on an ingratiating smile and said, "I really had no choice. The innkeeper Jacques Tavernier and his wife Lizette were engaged in criminal activity. You might say I saved you the trouble of a hanging."

"I wanted to take Jacques alive," Halvar interjected in protest. "I didn't want him shot."

"That was unfortunate," Ruiz admitted. "I did not shoot to kill, but you know how unreliable those handguns are. I meant only to frighten the man."

The sultan stamped his ivory peg-leg, a souvenir of the Italia Campaign, in fury.

"What kind of Hireling are you, Don Alvaro?" he demanded. "You come here, unbidden and unwanted, and in a week you've managed to upset everyone and everything here."

"I serve Don Felipe, Calif of Al-Andalus, may he have long life," Halvar stated flatly. "I can't help it if crazed women try to kill me with pokers, or if their servants try to strangle me with garrotes. I defended myself, Excellent Sultan. You would do the same."

"No doubt," the sultan huffed.

"And I did want them alive, to tell me whose idea it was in the first place." Halvar continued to press his position. "I don't think either Tavernier or that wife of his had the wit to think of it on their own. As for their servers, the only people I know of who use the garrote are the thieves of Parigi, and I'm sure you will agree, Excellent Sultan, that Manatas is well rid of such vile persons."

"Again, this is true." Petrus collapsed into his padded chair, a large item made in the Oropan fashion to accommodate his inability to fold himself down to the level of most Andalusian cushions.

5

Halvar glanced at the fourth person in the room. The youth stood in the light shining through a small window that revealed the bay and the ships that brought the goods that were bought and sold at the Feria.

"May I add, Excellent Sultan, that your son Selim was held by Tavernier and his wife, and that now he is restored to you, as you requested?"

Sultan Petrus pulled at his beard.

"I told you to find him, and you did. That's true, too."

"Excellent Sultan, I obeyed your order," Halvar stated. "So, with your permission, I will do what I was sent here to do by our esteemed calif, Don Felipe, may he reign long. I will go back to that Fratery at Green Village, and I will persuade Leon di Vicenza that he must return to Al-Andalus with me, before it is too late and the Franchen overrun all of Al-Andalus, with their guns blazing fire and their men tearing through every village, raping and plundering, and their mad fraters splashing water on everyone, claiming them for the Redeemer whether they believe or not."

He looked far beyond the windows, seeing scenes that still burned in his memory.

"You may go back to Green Village," Ruiz said, with a knowing smirk, "but I don't think you'll have much luck prying Leon out of the Fratery. The Kristos have him, and they won't let him go that easily. Of course, knowing Leon, he's probably got some scheme in mind for getting away from them."

Halvar's blue eyes narrowed over his beak of a nose. "I thought you didn't know Leon," he said.

"I don't, but you couldn't miss him, could you?" Ruiz said with a shrug. "The way he strutted around in his garish garb with Selim trotting beside him like a puppy. Oh, yes, Don Alvaro, Leon di Vicenza made himself well known in Manatas from the moment he came here with the Excellent Sultan."

"He's needed in Al-Andalus," Halvar repeated stubbornly. "It's what I was told. It's why I was sent here. Those are my orders."

"I thought you were supposed to oversee the revenues from the Feria," Ruiz said slyly.

"That, too," Halvar admitted. *And to make sure those revenues get back to Al-Andalus*, he added to himself.

The sultan grunted again. "If you must, then go back to that houri in Green Village and find out from her what is going on there," he ordered. "There are too many Bretains in that den of thieves and vagabonds for my liking."

"But beware of vipers in Paradise," Ruiz warned.

Halvar grinned at the two of them.

"I'll bear it in mind."

The Afrikan who served as the sultan's doorkeeper poked his head in and announced, "There is someone here to speak with Don Alvaro."

The new arrival was a scrawny young man in the long striped shirt and loose trousers favored by the shopkeepers in the souk and on the waterfront. His long hair was tied back with a ribbon under the broad-brimmed hat favored by the Franchen. Behind him was one of the Town Guards, a burly fellow with a bulbous nose over a round beard, his face scarred by smallpox.

"Tenente!" the guard announced. "There has been trouble at the waterfront!"

"When isn't there trouble on the waterfront?" grumbled the sultan.

"I am worried about Manolo, the pawnbroker," the shopkeeper blurted "He hasn't opened his door in two days."

Halvar frowned at Ruiz. "I thought you said he never closed."

"He doesn't, as far as I know."

The young man went on.

"Manolo is my father. He named me Yokanan, but in the True Faith, I am called Jehan. He lived behind the shop and almost never closed, except for one day every year when he would do no business but locked himself away. The following day he always opened. Two days ago, during the big storm, was that one day when he closed.

"The boys who clean the shop, Gavril and Gamal, they went yesterday, and it was closed, tight. I thought perhaps my father mistook the day, because of the storm, so I did not worry, but I went today, and the shop is still closed. I tried to open the door, and it is barred from the inside."

"Locked?" Halvar's eyebrows went up.

"We have a chain and a lock on the front door, but that is only used when both of us are away from the shop and the boys are not there. There is a bar across the door on the inside so that it can be defended. The outside lock was not fastened, only the inside bar."

"And what has this to do with me?" Halvar asked. "Tenente Ruiz is in charge of the Town Guard, let him do the investigating. I have other business to attend to. I can't waste my time chasing murderers and counterfeiters and Franchen spies. My orders are to get Leon back to Al-Andalus, and that is what I am going to do!"

"But you saw my father Manolo just before he locked the store," Jehan protested. "Please, Don Alvaro, come to the waterfront."

"Don't you trust the Town Guard to do their work properly?"

Jehan shrugged. "Tenente Gomez was known to take money from us shopkeepers—to keep the riffraff away, he said. If you didn't pay, Scavengers would come and sit in front of the shops and harass the buyers. Or there would be thefts, or worse. And his men weren't much better."

"I could use your help, Don Alvaro," Ruiz said with another of his wry grins. "Why not go to the waterfront with me and solve this little problem for friend Jehan? After you take care of that, you can chase Leon and have another spat with your redheaded houri Dani Glick."

"Better go and see what this fellow wants," the sultan agreed. "I'll have more to say to you later."

Halvar surrendered. "Very well. I wanted to have a word with Manolo anyway. He has to know more about that wumpum plot than he told us. Leon's not going anywhere, and the Feria's on for another week at least."

"Then let's get to it," Ruiz said, bowing to the sultan.

Young Selim moved to join them.

"Where do you think you're going?" Sultan Petrus demanded.

"Don Alvaro told me he needed someone to write for him," Selim said. "I'm going to be his secretary."

"The best help you can give is to stay out of our way," Ruiz growled. "You've already caused enough trouble. Stay put in the Rabat, and let the rest of us do our work."

Halvar grinned under his mustache.

"Let the lad come with us. He may be of use yet. Bring paper and pen and ink with you," he added as Selim bounded forward, glad to be away from his father's heavy-handed care.

The youngster snatched up some loose sheets of paper on the table in the middle of the room and tapped the pen case that hung at his belt where someone else might keep a dagger.

"I'm ready!" he proclaimed and followed Halvar down the steps to the stone-paved courtyard of the Rabat.

A squad of four Guards awaited them with one of the ever-present donkey carts that were the principal form of transportation in Manatas Town.

"Better bring Dr. Moise," Halvar decided. "If what this fellow suspects is true, we'll need him."

Ruiz yelled, 'Hoy, Doctor Moise! We may have another patient for you at the waterfront."

The tall Afrikan physician emerged from his quarters and joined the group as they clambered into the official donkey cart. Halvar clung to the sides of the frail vehicle as it rattled along the streets and down the hill to the waterfront and wondered whether the possible death of an old pawnbroker was anything more than an accident, or a robbery gone wrong. He'd already uncovered one plot against the Calif. Was there another one?

Chapter 2

THE PROCESSION WOUND OUT OF THE COURTYARD OF the Rabat down the cobbled street to the East Channel. There, a paved plaza had been laid out and wooden pilings set up for the barges, dhows, and other watercraft to tie up and unload their cargoes of foodstuffs and trade goods.

Passengers from the islands across the channel were deposited at one end of the wharf while fishermen dumped baskets of flopping fish at the other. Local women in leather skirts and colorful woolen shirts vied with Afrikan women in dyed kuton wraps and towering headdresses for the best bargains in fish and vegetables. They would carry their wares in baskets into Manatas Town to be sold to Andalusian women confined to their homes by the Laws and rulings of Islim and the Prophet.

The air was full of the scents of salt water, rotting fish, and smoke from braziers where small fish and cakes of maiz were being grilled to satisfy the appetites of the men who loaded and offloaded the cargoes and those who were on the docks to purchase them. The cries of the vendors mingled with the shrill yawps of seagulls swooping down to snatch fish from the boats or offal thrown into the channel.

Ruiz and his squad of green-coated Town Guards swaggered ahead of the donkey cart and its passengers—Halvar, Selim, and Dr. Moise. They pushed through the crowd of curious onlookers to the shack where the pawnbroker Manolo did his business.

Just as Jehan had said, the door was closed. There was no sound from within.

Halvar had last time been here at night. In the daylight, he saw the painted sign with three coins, the universal Oropan symbol for pawnbroker. A small window was set into the wall next to the door with a mirror attached, so the pawnbroker could see who was about to enter.

The shack was constructed of rough planks set upright between heavy beams. The door hung between two of those beams, a solid slab of wood with a large wrought-iron brace on one side. An iron chain was threaded through one side of the brace, but the lock on the other end hung uselessly to the ground.

Halvar frowned at the door.

"No hinges?"

"It opens from the inside," Jehan explained. "There's a bar inside that can be pushed against the door to keep it shut."

"A careful man," Halvar murmured to Ruiz.

"Or a frightened one," Ruiz replied in the same tone.

"Let's see what this door is made of."

Halvar lunged at the door, with no result but a bruised shoulder.

"It's solid oak," Jehan stated. "When we came here, Manolo insisted that this house should be built so he could bar the door from the inside. That way, no one could break in."

"What about the back? There can't only be one way in and out of here."

Jehan led the group around the shack, nodding to a Local woman who sat beside one of the ubiquitous braziers grilling ears of maiz. She looked up from her work long enough to nod back to him.

"My wife, Morning Star," he said. "She sits here all day. She keeps watch for Manolo, so the back door is never locked."

They edged along the narrow alley to the back of the shack. Jehan pointed to the crudely made door.

"I tried that one, too," he said. "I could not budge it. Manolo must have set the inside bar on this door, too."

Halvar could see no outside handle or knob on the blank face of this door, either.

"How do you get in?"

"You push," Jehan said, demonstrating. "But, as you can tell, the door is barred."

Halvar frowned at the blank panel in front of him. There were no windows in these plank walls, no opening for air or light.

"Must have been hot in there in summer," he mused.

"The door was opened to allow a breeze," Jehan explained. "With Morning Star in the alley, Manolo felt safe enough. At night, of course, it was barred."

"Who took care of the shop at night?" Halvar asked. "The old man had to sleep sometime. And he told us he went to the public latrine behind the taberna."

"Sometimes I worked at night," Jehan admitted. "Or Gavril or Gamal would stay in the shop to take care of any business that might come. Manolo slept in the room behind the shop."

"All these precautions. Was the pawnbroker expecting trouble?" Ruiz asked.

Jehan shrugged. "There are those who believe we keep great amounts of gold and silver here, which we do not. And there are sailors who have pledged their goods who want them back but do not have the wherewithal to redeem them."

"Did Manolo have any particular enemies?" Halvar asked as he ran his fingers over the top of the back door. There was a slight gap between the panel and the lintel. His fingers found a tiny groove in the top edge of the door.

"None that I know of," Jehan said.

"Then why bar himself in like this?" Halvar demanded. "And only one day a year?"

Jehan licked his lips, looking uncomfortable.

"I am not sure why he would not open. It was never the same day each year, but always one day in the fall. He would close the shop, bar the doors, and keep to himself. The very next day, he would open early, and all would be as usual.

"That is why I am worried, Don Alvaro, Tenente Ruiz. He's not open. He doesn't answer. I'm very much worried about him. He could have had a seizure of the heart."

Dr. Moise stepped forward.

"Did Manolo suffer from ill health?"

"He was feisty enough when we spoke with him four days ago, just before the storm," Ruiz said.

"He was old," Jehan argued. "Old people get seizures."

"Not all of them," Halvar countered. He tapped on the wall of the shack next to the door. "You, guard!" He motioned to the burly man who led the squad. "What's your name, laddie?"

"Flores." The stout man in the green coat and high-crowned tarboosh flushed under his bristling black beard, waiting for the in-

13

evitable comment contrasting his poetic name with his crude appearance.

Halvar didn't oblige him.

"Help me push this plank out of the way."

Together, the two men leaned against the board that held up the sagging roof of the pawnbroker's shack. It gave way under the pressure of their bodies, and the squad of guards followed Halvar and Ruiz into the pawnbroker's establishment.

Even though one plank of the back wall had given way, the rough door still held firmly between two stout wooden pillars, fastened to the beams that held the walls of the shack in place. It had been barred using a beam that rested between crude iron brackets, a barrier against possible intruders. A leather strap served as a hinge to allow the beam to be moved up and down.

The back room was, as Jehan had said, Manolo's living quarters. A simple plank bed stood in one corner, covered with a straw mattress and a shabby but serviceable woolen blanket. There was a table and stool set against another wall with the remains of a fowl and a bowl of cooked vegetables on it, along with a goblet that smelled of stale wine. A round loaf of white bread sat on a separate plate beside a small dish of honey, already covered with flies.

Pegs rammed into the wall held Manolo's scant wardrobe: a long black coat, a short blue jacket of the kind worn by seamen, two pairs of woolen breeches, and a heavy fur garment that that might have been used as a wrapper or a blanket.

A lantern hung from the ceiling beams that held the walls in place. A small brazier in one corner would have been a source of heat in winter, but there was no sign it had been used recently. A twig broom leaned in one corner next to a large palm frond, the only green thing in the otherwise drab room.

Halvar had become aware of a penetrating odor, one that he had smelled all too often in his days of fighting across Oropa. He knew what had happened to the pawnbroker.

"Nothing to steal here," Ruiz commented as he scanned the meager furnishings.

"We haven't tried the floor. He could have hidden something under the boards." Halvar reminded him. He stamped, experimentally, but there was no sound of a hollow space.

"There is a cellar where we store roots and cider for the winter," Jehan said. "I suppose if Manolo had any treasure, that's where he would keep it, but, as I said, we do not deal in such things. Only small items—trinkets and clothing, such things as sailors and students want to sell or borrow money on."

"Here's Manolo's meal, and his clothes, but where's the pawnbroker? I have a very bad feeling about this." Halvar looked toward the entrance to the shop.

"He's here!"

Guardsman Flores had already gone through another door to the main room of the shop. He stepped aside to let Ruiz and Halvar see the body of the old pawnbroker lying on the floor behind his counter, his sightless eyes staring at the beams overhead.

Chapter 3

DR. MOISE KNELT BESIDE THE BODY OF THE PAWNBROKER as Jehan let out a wail.

"Oh, my poor father! Dead in his sins, without the Redeemer's pardon!"

Halvar let the bereaved son mourn while he looked around the shack. Shelves had been set up against the walls and filled with miscellaneous objects. Oddly shaped Afrikan carvings jostled delicate ivory statuettes, carried all the way from India or Cathay, representing strange gods and demons. Wool, kuton, and silk jackets, coats and shirts hung on pegs over a row of footwear that included Local macassins trimmed with glass beads, hemp-soled sandals favored by Andalusians, and boots with high wooden heels worn by Franchen in imitation of their notoriously short ruler Lovis. A box on the counter held a jumble of trinkets: rings, necklaces, bracelets and brooches made of metal, ivory and wood, some studded with glittering stones that might have been glass or real gems.

The shelves behind the counter held larger items. Brass urns with weird designs chased on their sides, clay pots with weirder designs painted across their rounded bellies, statues of gods with many arms and the heads of beasts were ranged at eye level, beyond the grasp of careless hands.

Halvar frowned down at a small box with an elaborate lock set on the counter for all to see.

"Moneybox," Ruiz said. "He had silver here, to make his purchases and give out as loans."

"Not taken," Halvar commented. "A thief would have gone for that right away. And those gewgaws, some of them might make some wumpum or silver in the souk or at the Feria." A thought struck him. "What about wumpum?"

"He carried strings on his belt," Jehan said.

"Flores?" Ruiz motioned for his minion to check the body.

"It's here," the guardsman replied, after a brief look.

"Not a robbery gone wrong, then," Halvar concluded. "Let's see about this door."

The door indeed opened inward, on hinges whose workmanship matched that of the handle and braces on the front.

"We had Malik the Smith come to put the door up," Jehan boasted.

"He did a good job of it," Halvar said. " Selim, come over here and show me how well Leon taught you. I need an image of this door showing how the bar has been shoved through these iron braces. No latch on this door, Ruiz." He pointed to the bar. "That would take a little strength, don't you think? To push that beam through those iron braces?"

"Manolo was stronger than he looked," Jehan said. "And the bar was usually left on the door, across the braces, so that all he had to do was shove it across the gap when he chose to barricade it."

"Not like the back door," Halvar said. "That one lifts."

"Clever." Ruiz went back into the pawnbroker's sleeping quarters to observe the mechanism then returned. "I don't know about the latch, but whoever made this door wasn't much of a carpenter. There's a gap between the top of the door and the lintel. Must have been cold in the winter, with the wind blowing through."

"Someone could thread a cord around the bar, run it over the top of the door, go out and drop it down." Halvar said. He recalled the feeling of the minute groove in the top of the door.

"But why bother to go through all that for a robbery that didn't come off?" Ruiz wondered.

Before he could get an answer, the voice of the muezzin echoed across the waterfront plaza. Dr. Moise left off his examination to turn toward the east and prostrate himself to acknowledge the Prophet's words and Ilha's dominance, as did the guards. Jehan and Ruiz knelt, made the sign of the crux, and recited the Patri Nostri. Halvar neither knelt nor bowed but clutched the amulet that could have been either the Crux or Thor's Hammer and murmured his own midday prayer.

"May the Redeemer and his Mother Mara and the god Thor help me."

That done, Dr. Moise stood up and pronounced, "This man is dead."

"I can see that," Ruiz said. "How did he die?"

"I am not sure," Dr. Moise said.

"A seizure of the—" Jehan started, but Dr. Moise cut him off.

"Perhaps, but I won't know until I get him back to the dead-house."

"For autopsy?" Jehan was aghast. "You would destroy his body and deny him eternal life?"

"There are signs that this was by no means a natural death. I must make a more thorough examination, and I can't do it here."

"What makes you think this wasn't an attack of the heart?" Halvar asked.

"For one thing, he is face up. Usually, if someone has a seizure, they fall forward. Then there is the very odd angle of the head."

"He could have fallen against the counter," Jehan insisted.

"I saw no bruising on his face or forehead," Dr. Moise countered, "but there is an odd mark here, on his neck. Also, when a body has been in place for any length of time, the blood pools downward. There are signs that this body has been moved. I want to look more closely at that before I make a final pronouncement."

Ruiz cut through the argument. "When did he die?"

"At least a full day ago, possibly two," Dr. Moise told him. "His limbs have gone through the rigor and are loose again."

"We talked to him four days ago," Halvar reminded Ruiz. "Just before we went to the Mermaid Taberna. He was alive then and showed no sign of illness that I could see."

"Are you a trained physician?" Dr. Moise sneered.

"I'm not, but you are. So, I ask you, Doctor, how did he die? If not by the hand of Ilha, then how else?"

"I can't be sure until I examine him further." Dr. Moise motioned to the waiting guards. "Take him to the Rabat. I will be able to tell you more later today."

Ruiz shoved the heavy plank away from the front door to let the squad carry the body of the dead pawnbroker to the waiting cart.

"Don Alvaro!" Selim called out from his post by the front door. "I think you'd better get out here!"

Halvar stepped into the sunlight to find a large crowd had gathered to watch the proceedings. There seemed to be at least two parties, each led by an enraged cleric, both hostile, and neither one ready to let the body of Manolo the Pawnbroker go to the Rabat.

Chapter 4

THE FIRST GROUP WAS HEADED BY A ROTUND ANDALU-
sian with a luxuriant brown beard, clad in the striped robes and
green turban worn by imams who had been trained in the ulema
of Stamboul. Behind him were the Afrikan dockworkers and
market-women, with a scattering of Andalusian sailors adding
their voices to the hubbub.

Across from them stood a tall, gaunt frater in the black robe
and hooded cowl favored by those Kristos who practiced the
Roumi Rite, his thin-lipped mouth and hairless chin tight with
disapproval. His followers included several Local women in their
distinctive wrapped skirts and bead-trimmed blouses and a squad
of Franchen sailors and their captains in tight trousers and broad-
brimmed hats.

Between the two groups, Ruiz had placed his squad of guards
and the wagon with its sorry burden.

"What's going on here? Who are these people" Halvar demanded.

"Imam Haroun, of the Waterfront Muskat, and Prester Nicodemus from the Kristo chapel." Ruiz nodded towards the two enraged clerics. "It's the first time I've ever seen the two of them
agreed on anything," he added, with one of his sly grins.

"Prester?" Halvar wondered at the new title. All Kristo clerics
he had known were called frater, indicating a Brotherhood of the
Redeemer.

"You will not take this man to be anatomized!" Nicodemus declared. "It violates the words of the Redeemer!"

"The Prophet says the same," the imam said, glaring at his rival.

"Whatever the Prophet said was false, and heretical," Nicodemus countered. "But the Redeemer said that the body will be transformed at the End of Days. How can it be resurrected if it is cut into pieces?"

"It won't be cut into pieces," Dr. Moise assured him. "But I must find out how this man died."

"It was a seizure of the heart," Jehan insisted.

"Not with his head at that angle," Halvar stated. "Frater, let us pass."

"It is the will of Episcopus Innocente, who is our Holy Pater, that those who follow the True Faith and conduct the services of the Roumi Rite shall be called prester—that is to say, Elder—to distinguish themselves from the heretical unbelievers of the Bretain Rite. You may call me Prester Nicodemus." The tall Kristo nodded graciously at Halvar.

"I don't care what you call yourself," Halvar retorted. "You're blocking the way, you and your people. We don't want to hurt you, but we've got to get this man back to the Rabat. Jehan can have him back as soon as we've decided how he died."

"A seizure of the heart!" Jehan repeated.

"Prester Nicodemus, hah!" the imam snorted. "You think to upset the followers of the Prophet, may his name be blessed, by your antics. The Episcopus of Rouma may put a crown on Lovis the Franchen's head and call him Imperator, but Ilha, the All-merciful, may his name be praised, will take him to Sheol! For his men seize those who are sworn to the Prophet, may his name be blessed, and put the water upon them, and call them to the Redeemer's service, but their hearts are with Ilha, the All-merciful, may his name be praised!"

There was a mutter of agreement from the Afrikans behind the imam. The Franchen and Locals behind Prester Nicodemus growled their resentment.

Halvar groaned inwardly as he saw the two religious men egging their followers on and tried to assume a soothing tone.

"Reverend Imam Haroun, Prester Nicodemus, I ask you in the names of both the Redeemer and the Prophet, allow this cart to pass. A man has been killed—"

22

"How do you know?" Jehan burst out. "We found him alone, in his shop, with all the doors barred. It must be a natural death, and he must be buried at once. It is true that he once was Yehudit, and faced the fire for it, but we took the water back in Oropa before we took ship, when I was a lad." He turned to Prester Nicodemus. "Am I not your decanus, your faithful layman, the head of your congregation? Does my wife not serve you your meals? Why do you let these men take my father's body to be cut apart?"

Halvar inserted himself between Jehan and the cart.

"Your father will be restored to you for burial by tomorrow," he assured the distraught shopkeeper. "But it is the calif's will that anyone whose death is in question should be examined before burial, to determine if the death was from natural causes and, if from a natural cause, whether there is a disease involved."

"Disease?" Someone in the crowd yelled.

"Plague! A shrill voice answered.

That seemed to be the signal for a riot. Before he knew it, Halvar was in the middle of a fighting mob shouting religious slogans and slinging fists as well as stones.

Where is Ruiz? Why don't his men fight back? This is his job, not mine! It's only a matter of time before knives are drawn!

He was shoved back and forth as he tried to reach under his long coat for his dagger. He used elbows to shove his way through the crowd to get his back to the wall of the pawnshop, but there was someone behind him, pressing against him. He turned to face this attacker and felt a stinging pain across his lower back where the edge of his leather under-vest met the top of his breeches.

"Thor's Hammer!" he roared.

At the same time, an explosion erupted behind him. The sudden noise seemed to shock the rioters into sudden immobility. Halvar jerked his head around to find the source of the nose. Ruiz thrust his pistoia back into his belt, a smug smile decorating his handsome face.

"In the name of the Calif Don Felipe, stop this fighting! By the laws of Al-Andalus, the *convivencia* holds!" Halvar roared at the crowd.

"The Sharia rules!" the tubby imam roared back.

"The Laws of the Redeemer are worth more than the sayings of an idolater!" Prester Nicodemus yelled even louder.

"The laws of Al-Andalus and the customs of Al-Andalus surpass both of them." Halvar lowered his voice to a more normal volume. "By the edicts of the Calif Don Carlus, and his fathers before him, and the word of Calif Don Felipe, there is to be no disruption of the peace on matters of conscience in Al-Andalus or in any lands ruled by Al-Andalus! No Jihad! No Crusade!"

He repeated the words loudly in Arabi and then again in Erse for the benefit of anyone who did not understand Arabi.

"Islim rules, but the followers of the Redeemer may worship as they will, and the Yehudit are allowed to settle where they will, so long as they observe the calif's laws, pay their tolls, and do not disturb the general peace. Prester Nicodemus, if you continue to disturb the Calif's Peace, you and your followers will be subject to the calif's displeasure."

"And who are you to tell me what I can and cannot do?" Prester Nicodemus sneered.

Halvar raised his head and glared across the plaza at the crowd.

"I am Halvar Danske, the Calif's Hireling, and his personal representative in Manatas. I carry the calif's own seal, and what I do is by his orders. Right now, I order all of you to go about your business and allow us to do the same!"

There was an ugly muttering from the crowd. Ruiz stepped forward, one hand on the cudgel at his belt. The Guards behind him unhooked the cudgels from their belts and held them ready to enforce the calif's will on anyone who dared defy it.

"The mullah will hear of this," the imam said as he retreated to the muskat at the entrance to the plaza.

"This is not over," threatened Prester Nicodemus, with a nod to Jehan.

Halvar was suddenly aware of a sharp pain in his side. He pressed his hand to his back and realized that it was wet and, when he looked at it, red.

"You're bleeding," Ruiz observed.

"Someone in that crowd had a knife." Halvar sagged against the door of the pawnshop.

"Get me back inside, and tell Dr. Moise he's got a live patient as well as a dead one." To himself he added, *I've only been out of bed for a day, and someone's tried to kill me again. I must be doing something right!*

Chapter 5

RUIZ FROWNED AS HE HELPED HALVAR BACK INTO THE pawnshop.

"You must be under the curse of a djinn," he decided. "No matter where you go, someone tries to kill you."

"It's a gift I'd prefer to hand on to someone else," Halvar said.

Ruiz and Dr. Moise got him out of the tight-sleeved coat and unlaced the leather vest beneath, revealing a slash where a blade had skidded off his belt to slice through his shirt under the coat.

"A thin, sharp instrument," was the doctor's opinion as he inspected the slash. "It was meant to penetrate to the inner organs, causing bleeding. Your leather belt deflected the blow. I have seen men walk about for an hour or more before succumbing to such an attack"

"A professional assassin's trick," Halvar agreed. "Better bind it up before I bleed to death."

"Not likely," Dr. Moise grunted. "A shallow cut, for which Ilha, the All-merciful may be praised. You, Jehan! Have you any cloths we can use for a bandage?"

"I thought all doctors carried their tools with them," Halvar gibed.

"I wasn't expecting a live patient," Dr. Moise retorted.

Jehan produced a roll of kuton material. Dr. Moise tore a strip off and wound it around Halvar's torso.

"Another coat gone," Halvar groused. "The shirt I can still wear, the vest I can wear, but I need another coat or jacket." He looked around at the contents of the shop. "Jehan! Is there something I can wear here? Surely, there was a big fellow who needed money, who was willing to sell the coat off his back to get it."

Jehan scanned the garments on the wall.

"There's this leather jacket," he observed. "It came from a Dane, caught here without wumpum." He took down a well-worn garment cut in the Danic style, short, with padded shoulders and horn buttons to close the front. It looked so much like the one Halvar had owned when he first came to Manatas that he had to examine it closely before he decided it was not the one he was told had been sliced apart in an attack his second night on the island.

He eased himself into it, shrugged his shoulders, and announced, "It'll do. How much?"

"A gift, if you please," Jehan insisted. "I have no idea how much it is worth, or what my father paid for it. It must have came in on the night of the big storm, after the, um, disturbance, after I had left for the day. I don't remember its being here before than."

He stopped, embarrassed by the mere suggestion of the deaths of Jacques Tavernier and his wife Lizette.

Halvar looked for something to sit on; Ruiz found a stool behind the counter and eased him onto it. He looked around the shop again, taking a mental inventory of the odds and ends.

"There's something missing," he announced.

"How can you tell?" Ruiz said with a sneer, looking around at the conglomeration of items piled on shelves, hanging from hooks, and stacked on the floor.

"There were books." Halvar pointed to the shelf farthest from the counter. "A pile of them, right there. They aren't there now. Where are they, Jehan? What happened to those books?"

"Books?" Ruiz echoed.

"Books," Halvar repeated. "I wouldn't think many folk here would be in the market for those. Yet Manolo had them here. He must have bought them, paid for them, or else he lent money on them. Where did they come from?"

"We have scholars here in Manatas," Jehan said defensively. "There are students who come to the madrassa from the Afrikan settlements in the Southern Territories. The Bretains in West Caster and the other Bretain lands who can't get to the great madrassas in Parigi and Oxenford come here to Manatas Town to learn our philosophy and study from our doctors.

"They stay in lodgings, but sometimes they overstay and run out of money, and have to pawn their books to pay for tuition, until their parents send them more silver. And some of them even gamble!" Jehan shook his head at the folly of young men on the loose in a town like Manatas. "They think because they have studied mathematics that they can beat the odds!"

"There are no odds," Halvar said. "Like Old Sergeant Olav told me, don't bother to gamble—the house always wins." He returned to the problem at hand. "It would appear that our thief, if such there is, wasn't after gold or silver or any of the jewels in this shop, but those books are missing."

"So, this murderer was also a thief who stole books?" Ruiz sounded dubious. "What for? Who reads them? Why bother with them? What kind of money could he get for them?"

"If those books were Leon's notebooks, they could hold secrets men might well murder for," Halvar said. "Remember—Tavernier said he'd sold some of those notebooks to make up for what Leon owed him on rent.

"Leon wrote down everything he heard, and he made images of everything he saw or thought he could make. Leon's ideas about mechanisms might be worth something to some clever Bretain in Green Village." He took another breath, and regretted it. Through clenched teeth, he asked Jehan, "Where did Manolo sell the books he bought?"

Jehan frowned in thought. "Behind the madrassa, in the Souk, there's a vendor called Mendel the Bookseller. He buys and sells books, and rebinds old ones, too. Manolo used to take books to him. They were friends, of a sort. No other Yehudit would deal with my father."

"Benyamin ibn Mendel, the bookseller's son, is one of my friends," Selim said.

Everyone turned to stare at the youngster, whose presence had been forgotten in the riot.

"He was one of Leon di Vicenza's followers, the Seekers of Truth."

"I'd better have a word with Mendel the Bookseller and see if anyone has offered to sell him Leon's notebooks," Halvar decided.

"What about the rest of Leon's things?" Selim asked. "We should get them, too. He wanted his paints and his inks."

"We can stop at the taberna and pick them up," Halvar said, heaving off the stool.

"Why bother? Emir Achmet the Scavenger probably had his people out as soon as the Taverniers were gone," Ruiz said with a dismissive shrug.

"And you didn't think to post a guard!" Halvar turned on the man, aghast at such a blatant lack of competence.

"I posted a guard—of course I did! I had one of my men standing by the front door of the place to discourage sightseers, but I had a few other things on my mind," Ruiz retorted defensively. "Getting you back to the Rabat, for one, and dealing with that gale, for another. I sent two more men to the taberna once the storm was over, but by that time, someone was already there, ready to take the place over. A Dane, no less. He had a signed and sealed paper written in Arabi and Rune giving him the rights to the property. It's his, by law, and for all I know, he's there now."

"A Dane?" Halvar fingered the jacket. "He may well have been the last person to see Manolo alive!"

"Except for his murderer," Selim put in.

"So, Hireling, what do we do now?" Ruiz asked.

"We go see this Dane and find out what he has to say about Manolo. Then, I think I will have a word with this Mendel, about books."

Chapter 6

HALVAR AND RUIZ MADE THEIR WAY THROUGH THE crowd, Selim at their heels, across the plaza to the two-story building that dominated the skyline of the Manatas waterfront. The new owner of the taverna stood in the doorway of his establishment, one hand propped against the doorjamb, the other clutching a stout staff. He was as tall and fair as Halvar, perhaps ten years older, with the same blue eyes and jutting nose without the magnificent growth that adorned Halvar's upper lip.

He wore no jacket or coat, but he had a sleeveless blue kuton vest buttoned over his linen shirt, and long canvas trousers that matched the ones worn by the seamen standing in a group in front of him, A peg with a silver band around the end poked out of his left trouser leg; his right foot was covered by a straw sandal, of the kind used by Andalusian fishermen on board their ships. A few strands of hair escaped from under a cap that might have been the twin of the one on Halvar's head.

He was addressing the four Franchen sailors.

"I'm not open yet. Tonight, I'll be open for business soon as the soup is ready. Nothing but mokka right now."

"Old Jacques had a cook," the leader of the crew, a burly man with a red mustache, stated. "She wasn't a bad cook, either."

"She's dead," the Dane in the doorway said. "I hear some bearshirt went mad and started killing Franchen."

Halvar interrupted the discussion

"It's true enough. Lizette and Jacques Tavernier are dead, and so is their server Henri, and I'm the one responsible, but there was a good reason for it. Now, Dane, who are you, and what are you doing here?"

"They call me Hannes Zilberstam, and I own this place," the Dane retorted. "And who are you?" He regarded Halvar with narrowed eyes. "You're wearing my old jacket!"

"I am," Halvar said. "I got it at the pawnbroker's shop. I'm Halvar Danske, the Calif's Hireling"

"No! Really? They said a Dane had risen up in Al-Andalus, but I thought that was just a tale."

"No tale, any more than your being here. What's this about you owning this place?

"It's mine!"

"Prove it!" Ruiz demanded.

Hannes produced a folded piece of paper from under his vest.

"Here!" he said. "It's all written out, in that curly swirly Arabi and good solid Rune. And sealed, with the mark of the pawnbroker across the way. Just ask him."

"We would, except that he's dead, too," Halvar said.

Hannes's red face paled.

"H–How?" he quavered. "He was hale enough when I saw him."

"Just when was that?" Halvar asked.

"Let's go inside," Ruiz suggested, glancing at the crowd starting to gather around them, ready to hear news or erupt into violence. "This is going to take some time, and we don't need another riot."

Hannes led Ruiz and Halvar into the dark interior of the Mermaid Taberna. All signs of the carnage of the previous few days had been removed. The tables that had been scattered randomly were now neatly set up around the perimeter of the main room, with benches where chairs had been. A fire blazed in the fireplace, and a small pot of water sat on the hob, ready to be poured over ground mokka-beans to make the fragrant brew favored by Andalusians and Afrikans over the malted beverages enjoyed by northern barbarians like Franchen, Bretains, and Danes. A larger pot swung from the iron bracket, giving off savory odors that spoke to Halvar of the hearty soups and stews of his homeland.

Hannes bustled across the room, indicating the one table with chairs made in the Oropan style.

"I'll make mokka," he said, and proceeded to go through the ritual of measuring a cup of the roasted beans, grinding them down with mortar and pestle, placing them into a sieve, inserting the sieve into the brass pot, dipping up boiling water, and pouring it over them.

While the innkeeper was occupied with his cooking, Halvar beckoned Selim over.

"Get upstairs," he ordered. "Take a look around Leon's rooms, and if there's anything left, bring it downstairs."

Ruiz muttered, "I wouldn't put it past those Scavengers to find a way to get even that great bed out of the rooms!"

Hannes had finished his preparations. He placed a little hour-glass next to the brass pot, set out three earthenware cups, and turned back to Ruiz and Halvar.

"Three minutes, by the glass," he stated. "No more!"

It seemed like an eternity until the brew was done. Hannes poured cups for Halvar, Ruiz and himself and set them down on the table.

"Something for the All-Father," he murmured, pouring a few drops before sipping.

Halvar gritted his teeth until Hannes was ready to talk.

"Now, Landsman," he said in Danic, "tell me your tale. Just how did you come to Manatas, and how did you come to own this taberna?"

Hannes glanced at Ruiz.

"Better speak in Arabi," he said. "I don't want this fellow to think we Danes are conspiring against him."

Both his Danic and his Arabi had the singsong lilt of Scania. Halvar suspected this old sailor was one of those who plied the northern seas, sometimes picking up fish, sometimes looking for larger prey.

"In Danic or in Arabi, Hannes Zilberstam, but make it brief. I have no time for long sailors' yarns," Halvar snapped.

Hannes nodded. "As you will. I came on the last dhow that made it through the narrow passage between the Round Island and the Long Island just before that big storm hit. The waves fairly carried us onto the docks!"

Ruiz nodded agreement. "That's so, Don Alvaro. One last dhow came in before it got so rough not even those great Franchen ships could have gotten through. It carried the last letters sent from Al-Andalus before the Franchen took over."

"What were you doing on that dhow?" Halvar asked. "Passenger or crew?"

31

"Crew," Hannes said. "I've been here and there since I was a lad, from the Dane-March to Scania and Bretain. It was a great fish cost me my leg. I love the sea life, but no one wants a one-legged man on board. I was able to get a spot on that dhow as a cook, so I took ship, and worked my way across the Storm Sea. Once we got here, I was paid off and told to find another berth.

"So. I look about me, I see it's a fine town, but how to live, where to go, what to do? I see the sign with the three coins, that's the pawn-broker. I think, I can sell my spare jacket, and get some of the local money to hold me until I can find another ship, or buy into a shop."

Hannes stopped for breath, and took another sip of his mokka.

"Was the pawnshop open or closed?" Halvar asked.

"Door was closed but not barred," Hannes replied. "I could see someone inside through that little window. So I banged on the door, and the pawnbroker opened up for me."

"He dragged the bar from the door?" Ruiz frowned.

"I don't know about that. All I know is, there was this other fel-low there, and he was arguing with the pawnbroker about something. I says, I have a jacket to sell. The pawnbroker looks at it and sneers, says it's not worth a string of white wumpum, which I don't know what it is, but the other fellow looks me over and asks what I need money for so late at night.

"So, I says that I'm just ashore, that I have silver but no local money, that I need a place for the night, and that I thought to sell the jacket and get a room until the storm blows over."

Halvar sipped his own mokka and raised his eyebrows. What-ever else Hannes did, he knew how to brew mokka!

"This fellow with the pawnbroker, what did he look like?"

"Tall as me, skinny, wore a Franchen hat pulled down over his face. The shop was dark, only lit with one lantern, so I didn't see much, but I saw what he was selling."

"And what was this valuable merchandise?" Ruiz sneered.

"I'm coming to it! This bloke says he's got something for sale, he's got to get off this island, and he needs the silver. Then he shows the pawnbroker a book."

"A book!" Halvar echoed.

"Leather-bound," Hannes said with a decisive nod. "I don't go for books, don't read them. I can write my name in Rune, but that's all. As for Arabi, who can tell what those curlicues mean?"

Halvar grimaced his agreement. Arabi was hard enough for him to speak; reading and writing it was impossible.

"So," Hannes went on, "this book-selling bloke looks me over and says, 'You need a place to stay. I need to get rid of one. I'm the only one left of us four who put our money into the Mermaid Taberna, and I've got to get away from that mad Dane who's killing off Franchen. You give me your silver, and I'll give you the taberna.'"

"That sounds like something out of *The Thousand and One Nights*," scoffed Ruiz. "The magician who gave away new lamps for old!"

"That may be, but it's true!" Hannes insisted. "I says to myself, The Three Old Women are looking after you, Hannes Zilberstam. I can brew mokka, I can cook soup, how hard can it be to run a taberna?"

"You'd be surprised," Halvar muttered. Louder, he said, "So, you took him up on the offer?"

"Why not?" Hannes looked from Halvar to Ruiz. "But I'm no fool. I says, give me a paper with a seal, witnessed by this pawnbroker, just in case someone comes along to question what I'm doing there."

"You never thought this fellow just might be selling something he didn't own?" Halvar hinted.

"It sort of crossed my mind," Hannes admitted. "But the pawnbroker swore he knew the man, said he'd draw up the document, in Arabi and in Rune, and here it is."

Hannes placed the paper on the table. Ruiz scanned it carefully and examined the wax seal at the end of the brief statement.

"This says that one Robert Mortmain, resident of Kibbick, surrenders to Hannes Zilberstam, seaman and cook, full use of the property known as the Mermaid Taberna for the sum of ten silver pennies of Bretain," he said. "And the seal is the one used by the official notaries of Manatas, issued by Sultan Petrus in accordance with the laws of Al-Andalus."

"And the signature of the pawnbroker?" Halvar asked, squinting at the elaborate writing on the document.

"Manolo," Ruiz said, laying the paper down. "Manolo signed this paper on the night of the storm. It's dated three days ago."

Halvar took all this in.

"Then what, Hannes Zilberstam?"

"Then, I ran like Loki the Mischief-maker was after me to get to my property before the wind got too bad," Hannes said. "The rain had already started, the wind was up, it was all I could do to get across the plaza without being blown into the river. I got in, I got a fire going, I found some vegetables and a meat-bone to make soup, and here I am!" He smiled happily at Ruiz and Halvar. "Now, are you going to tell me I was taken for a fool?"

"No," Halvar said slowly. "What I can tell you is that this man, Robert, was one of four Franchen of Kibbick who were involved in a nasty scheme to falsify the strings of shells used by the Locals as currency. I'm the mad Dane who went on the bear-shirt spree, but I can swear by any of the gods you like that it was not my intention to kill Franchen in particular. I don't know the laws and ordinances of property in Manatas, you'll have to check with Tenente Ruiz about that, but as far as I know, you're in charge here."

Ruiz frowned at the document as he handed it back to Hannes. "It's legal, I suppose," he admitted.

"Then I'll let you gents be on your way," Hannes said, heaving off the bench. "I've got to keep this soup on the simmer."

"I don't suppose you've been upstairs," Halvar asked tactfully, glancing at the peg protruding from Hannes's trousers.

Hannes shrugged. "I'm not one for climbing," he admitted. "I found a space under the stairs with a plank bed and a straw pallet, and I've been sleeping there. It's not exactly a bed of roses, but it's better than a lot of places I've been. No bugs in the straw, and close to the public latrine."

There was a cry from the top of the stairs, where Selim stood on the landing.

"It's all gone!" he wailed dramatically.

"What's gone?" Halvar asked.

"All of Leon's clothes, and his paints and inks. Even his books and drawings!" Selim bounded down the stairs. "What happened to them?"

"Jacques sold some of Leon's things when we announced that Leon was dead," Halvar reminded him.

"I suppose I should have been quicker to post a guard," Ruiz admitted, sounding rueful. "The Scavengers must have been in as soon as my men took the bodies back to the Rabat." He turned to Halvar. "I told you, I had to get back to the Rabat, I had to explain to the sultan what had happened, and then the storm hit. I'm sorry, Don Alvaro, but all of Leon's possessions—the clothes, the books, the paints—all must be in the souk by now, scattered in shops. Finding one or two items among all the goods for sale will be impossible."

"Leon's taste in clothes was unmistakable," Halvar retorted. "It shouldn't be too hard to find silk trousers and padded jackets with fancy embroidery. As for the paints and inks, how many shops deal in those things?

"Look behind the madrassa, where the students go. And find that image of the Old Roumi goddess that looks like Dani Glick. I didn't see that at Manolo's, not even hidden under a cloth. Leon di Vicenza is going to want his belongings when he goes back to Al-Andalus."

Ruiz opened his mouth to protest then shut it again. Instead, he turned to Hannes.

"I suppose you are now in possession of this taberna," he said. "Have Imam Haroun from the Waterfront Muskat check your kitchen, make sure all is halal, and obey the rules of Islim, and no one will hinder you. There is no alcohol to be sold in Manatas Town, nor swine's flesh, nor eels or other unclean foods. Keep the Calif's Peace, pay the *dhimmi* toll, and all will be well."

"May the All-Father look kindly on you," Halvar added. "But better pay respects to the Redeemer, too. There's a Bretain Rite fratery just outside of the Town Wall, in a place called Green Village, if you're not happy with the Roumi Rite. Obey the laws of Al-Andalus and prosper, Hannes Zilberstam. And let me know when you're ready to serve herring. I haven't tasted good Danic food since I left for the Italia campaign."

Halvar and Ruiz stepped back into the afternoon sunlight, again with Selim behind them.

"What next, Don Alvaro?" Ruiz asked.

"The Rabat," Halvar decided. "I want to hear what Dr. Moise has to say about our pawnbroker's death. And then, the souk, and a word with Mendel the Bookseller. I've got to find those notebooks of Leon's!"

Chapter 7

THE SUN WAS MIDWAY BETWEEN ZENITH AND HORIZON when Halvar and Ruiz reached the Rabat. Word of the disturbance at the waterfront had already reached Sultan Petrus; his Afrikan servant was waiting for them at the foot of the stairs to the sultan's quarters.

"The Excellent Sultan wishes to speak with the Calif's Hireling," he told them, with a disapproving glare at Halvar's disreputable jacket. "He has also told me to bring Selim to him. News has come from Al-Andalus."

"The Excellent Sultan will have to wait," Halvar said.

"Selim, you'd better get up there," Ruiz told the lad.

Selim drew back with a mulish pout.

"I know what he's going to tell me, and I won't do it. I just won't!"

"You must." The female physician, Eva Hakim, had come up behind them. "I will try to help you, but you know your duty."

Ruiz greeted the Sister of Fatima politely.

"Salaam aleikum, Eva Hakim. How is Lady Ayesha doing after her ordeal? And the new arrival? Is the child healthy?"

"Salaam aleikum, Tenente Ruiz. Lady Ayesha is doing well, as is the infant," Eva Hakim said. "I am watching her closely for childbed fever and milk sickness. The Mahak woman Nokomis found a Local woman who recently lost her own child and has plenty of milk for this one who will act as wet-nurse."

"Everybody's so excited," Selim groused. "It's only a baby!"

Halvar glanced at the youth and smiled to himself.

"It's to be expected," he said. "When a man the age of your father produces a new child, it's a sign of hope for the rest of us."

"It's disgusting!" Selim cried.

"Better get up to the harem and be nice to Lady Ayesha," Halvar told him. He turned to the Afrikan. "Tell the Excellent Sultan we'll be there as soon as we've heard from Dr. Moise."

Eva Hakim guided Selim towards the private quarters of the Rabat while Halvar and Ruiz crossed the courtyard to the shed that served Dr. Moise as dispensary, laboratory, and deadhouse.

Manolo the Pawnbroker had been laid out on the table in the deadhouse. Stripped, with only a brief twist of kuton loincloth to give him dignity, the pawnbroker was sturdier than Halvar had thought. The white hair on his head matched the mat on his chest.

"All right, Doctor," Halvar said. "What have you found out about our friendly pawnbroker?"

"That he was undoubtedly Yehudit," Dr. Moise pronounced. "No matter what his son says, or whether or not he took the water later, he bears the mark."

"Not Islim?" Ruiz raised his eyebrows.

"There is no reason to think he followed the Prophet, may his name be blessed," the doctor said. "A few old wounds have left scars. At one time or another, he was in a fire." He pointed to white marks on the dead man's hands and arms. "And he ate sparingly. Most of this is muscle, not fat." He prodded the stomach.

"You didn't open him up to see what he ate?" Halvar asked, with horrified fascination.

"Considering the objections of his son, I felt it unnecessary. We saw his last meal sitting on the table in the back room—leg of a fowl, wine, vegetables, bread, a dish of fruit, a dish of honey."

Halvar stared down at the body.

"He ate fowl and vegetables and drank wine," he summed it up.

"He had been to the baths," Dr. Moise stated. "There are fresh nicks where he was close-shaved, and there is still oil in his hair."

"A man may have a bath," Halvar observed. "But in the middle of the week?"

"His clothes are interesting, too," Dr. Moise observed. "A fine white linen tunic, tied with a cord. Linen shirt underneath."

"His black coat was hung up in his room," Halvar recalled. "So, he's eating his dinner, which is a fine one for a weekday, when someone calls him away from his half-eaten meal, and he goes to see who was there."

"That must have been this fellow Robert Mortmain," Ruiz said. "He was there when that Dane, Hannes Zilberstam, came along."

"And where was he when we were killing off the other two Franchen?" Halvar asked suddenly. "I was behind the taberna, watching the body of that other server, the one called Henri who tried to garrote me. Then you and your men came along with Jacques and Lizette. Henri was dead, Jacques and Lizette were in their own house. We had the row in the kitchens. Where was this fellow Mortmain when all that was going on?"

Ruiz frowned. "He must have seen my men coming and ducked up the inside stairs into Leon's rooms," he reasoned. "I went inside to fetch the jacket Lizette had left, but I only grabbed the jacket, I didn't go into the bedroom. And none of my men went upstairs after the fight.

"Robert could have hidden in the bedroom and stayed hidden until we all left. I set a guard to see that no one came in through the front door. I forgot about that outside entrance, the stairs to Leon's rooms."

"Can't think of everything," Halvar conceded. "So, Robert hides upstairs and grabs whatever he thinks he can sell. Clothes, paints, inks. And then, the books. Why the books?"

"Why not?" Ruiz said. "They had fine leather bindings. Perhaps Robert thought he could sell the pages with images."

"Especially the ones of Otter Tail? I'd like to see who'd pay for those!" Halvar said with a grin, ignoring Ruiz's sudden blush. "So, there he is at Manolo's, and along comes this Dane, sent by whatever gods decree our fates, with silver in hand."

"With the storm brewing behind him," Dr. Moise reminded them.

"Manolo pays wumpum for the jacket and signs the paper giving Hannes the taberna, and seals it," Halvar went on. "Hannes hands his silver Bretain pennies over to Robert and goes to his new quarters."

"Then why kill Manolo?" Ruiz queried. "What good does it do anyone? And how was he killed? I don't see a mark on him, no blood, no cord around his neck. He wasn't garroted, he wasn't stabbed. Poison in his drink?"

"No poison, no knife, no garrote—but his neck was broken," Dr. Moise reported. Halvar said, "I think I know how it was done. Another trick of the Parigi thieves."

He grabbed Ruiz by the hair with one hand and wrapped the other arm around his neck in a chokehold.

"The victim doesn't cry out, he can't breathe. A strong man can twist the neck so the spine breaks. We've got a problem, Tenente. This Robert Mortmain must be a trained assassin like the other fellow, Henri."

"He would be, with a name like that," Ruiz said gloomily. "Mortmain—that means 'dead hand' in Franchen. Hand-of-Death, in other words."

"It would seem that he's our killer," Halvar said. "Very well, Tenente, I leave this in your hands. You've got the men, you've got the power, this is an island, and not all that big. Go find him!"

"Find him where?" Ruiz protested. "Once he gets to the Feria, he can mingle with the rest of the Franchen. He probably has connections with half the seamen who come in and out of Manatas."

"That's your job, not mine," Halvar said firmly. "What I have to do is get Leon di Vicenza on that dhow to Al-Andalus and get the Feria funds back to Calif Don Felipe so he can fight the army that is destroying his country. Murders, however nasty, are not what I'm here for."

Ruiz took off his tall tarboosh to run a hand over his hair in frustration.

"Do you remember what the server looked like? I don't. Except for that tall girl, Sally, who turned out to be Selim, I didn't look at the servers. Who does?"

"You should look at everyone and everything," Halvar chided him. "That's what Old Sergeant Olaf told me when he trained me as a tracker. 'Everything's important, even what's not there.' This Robert, he's got to be tall to get an arm around Manolo's neck. He'll have a Franchen accent. He'll be looking for a way off Manatas Island. Best have a word with Emir Achmet the Scavenger chief. If Robert is looking for fellow thieves, that's where he'll find them."

"And while I am doing all this, Don Alvaro, what are you going to do?" Ruiz said with a sneer.

"I am going to the souk to find out just what was in those books of Leon's that was so important Manolo was willing to pay good silver for them, and why someone was willing to kill to get them."

Selim was waiting for them outside the deadhouse.

"I thought you were supposed to see your father," Halvar chided him.

"I saw the baby, I told Ayesha how nice it looked, and I'm ready to go back to work," Selim said. "What are we going to do now?"

Halvar raised his eyebrows at the "we."

"What do you remember about the server Robert?"

Selim's eyebrows seemed to meet over his nose as he frowned thoughtfully.

"Not much," he said. "He and Henri kept to themselves. They ran in and out of the kitchen with food for the customers. I was kept in the pantry for most of the time I was there, so I didn't get a very good look at anyone but Lizette, and I saw more of her than I liked." He shuddered.

"Can you draw a likeness for Ruiz and his men to take about, to see if anyone has seen him?"

"I can try, but Leon didn't think much of my skill."

He looked around and found the bench next to the table where the Local woman served mokka and maiz-cakes to the off-duty guards. Then he took out the pen and ink, spread one of his papers on the table, and drew a rough oval outline.

"As far as I could tell, Robert looked like anyone else. He was tall and thin, that's as much as I remember. He always wore a broad-brimmed hat, like all Franchen do, so I can't tell you what color his hair is. He didn't have any big scars on his face, and if he had any anywhere else, I didn't see them."

"What about his speech? Did he sound Franchen?" asked Ruiz.

"He didn't say much when I was around, so I don't know whether he knew Arabi or not," Selim said. "But he was Kristo, that I know, because when the muezzin called out, he knelt with Henri and the Taverniers."

"Not much to go on." Ruiz looked at the scrawl before him.

"Oh, I do remember one thing," Selim said. He scratched a line between the circles he had sketched to indicate eyes. "One of his eyebrows was shorter than the other. Not a scar, exactly, but something like it. I didn't get close enough to see."

Ruiz sighed. "It's something," he said. "I'll get my men out in the souk and see if we can find Leon's clothes in the used clothing shops. I just hope this fellow hasn't got across the wall to the Feria. We'll never find him if he has."

The Feria was Mahak territory, the Town Guards not welcome there.

"Do what you can," Halvar said. "I'll have a word with Mendel the Bookseller. If he didn't get those books, he'll know someone else who might have them."

41

Chapter 8

SELIM TUGGED HALVAR AWAY FROM RUIZ TOWARD THE courtyard gate.

"Let's go!" the lad urged, with a glance up towards where his father lurked.

"Your father wants to talk to you," Halvar reminded him.

"I know what he's going to say," Selim said sulkily. "I don't want to hear it. Let's get out of here, Don Alvaro." He strode out the gate, ignoring the pleas of the donkey-cart drivers. "It's not far, we can walk."

He led Halvar along the Broad Way, the principal street of Manatas. Halvar had passed the Grand Muskat, the largest religious building on Manatas Island, a week before when he had brought what he thought was the body of Leon di Vicenza to the Rabat. Now he paused, as much to catch his breath as to take in its splendor. He was uncomfortably aware he had only been out of his sickbed for a day, and that both Dr. Moise and Frater Iosip had warned him of the dangers of overexertion. Even a tough Dane was supposed to let his body heal!

The Grand Muskat was grand, indeed! The two minarets, each topped with a gilded dome; the facade embellished with painted tiles; and the carved inscriptions praising Ilha and his Prophet—all reminded him of its counterpart in Corduva. But, as with everything else in Manatas, there were differences. The tiles were not the polished surfaces of Al-Andalus but smoothed unglazed brick, crudely painted with garish reds and oranges, made from the minerals found in the mountains north of the island of Manatas. The carved stone was not white marble but a dull brown, locally quarried, and the carvings were not as sharply incised as those in Al-Andalus.

Across the street were the buildings that housed the Madrassa, the most prominent seat of higher learning in Nova Mundum, drawing students from as far away as Kibbick to the north and the great farms of the Afrikans in the south. These were more mundane, very much like the houses of the citizens that crowded the district between the waterfront and the Broad Way—brick villas covered in stucco plaster with narrow slits of windows, topped with tile roofs.

A small placard written in Arabi and Ogham letters was affixed to the door of each building, but it didn't take a sign for Halvar to gather what was going on within. The Library door was open, and he could see the students bent over their books and scrolls. Weird odors wafted from the building where the alchemists studied the arcane arts of mixing metals. A loud argument was underway, heard through the window of the School of Philosophy, as the students defended their theses on the underpinnings of the universe.

Halvar grinned. *Just like Corduva*, he thought, remembering his days as the watchdog who followed the young Don Felipe to classes in literature and philosophy. The professors insisted on speaking in exaggeratedly precise Arabi, for the benefit of the Franchen, Bretains, and Danes who flocked to Corduva for higher education. They may have ignored Halvar, as they would have ignored a large dog, but by the time Don Felipe decided he was finished with school, Halvar had absorbed enough Arabi to converse in it.

Behind the Madrassa were the one-story structures that housed the shops and workshops of the vendors and artisans who made up the ordinary population of Manatas Town. The Feria might draw the buyers and sellers in bulk, but the souk was where the householders got their daily provisions and whatever amenities were available in this outpost of civilization. Clothing of all sorts and quality, eating utensils, tools, and foodstuffs were bought and sold in the souk.

Halvar had only seen the souk by moonlight, as a nearly deserted labyrinth of shuttered windows and dusty streets. By the light of the afternoon sun, he could see that it, not the Feria, was the primary marketplace of Manatas Town. The ramshackle structures jostled one another, each seemingly built with no reference to any other on the street. The shutters had been let down in front of each house, providing a shelf where merchandise could be displayed while the shopkeepers shouted the qualities of their wares. Artisans in brass and silver, middlemen dealing in secondhand clothing, farmers with their produce—all contributed to the din in Arabi, Ivrit, Erse, Franchen, even Danic!

Selim ignored the shouting, shoving, bustling crowd as he led Halvar to their destination. It was mostly male, although some Andalusian women moved through the mob, covered by their burkas, each trailed by a male slave carrying a basket for their purchases, and a few Yehudit women, hair covered with kerchiefs or caps, carrying shopping in net bags. The shopkeepers, though, all were men, and so were their most of their customers.

Local women huddled over braziers, grilling corncakes and meat on skewers, and Afrikan women called out *"Nguba! Fine nguba!"* as they held out tiny rush baskets filled with what looked like roasted beans. The scents of spices and cooking meat mingled with those of humanity as the sun warmed the tightly packed streets.

Through it all, green-coated Town Guards poked their noses into shops and stalls, evoking complaints from outraged vendors insisting their goods were perfectly legal, that they never bought stolen merchandise, and that they and their customers were honest citizens of Manatas.

"Good thing I have you along," Halvar admitted to Selim as he sidestepped a donkey cart laden with bolts of cloth. A cat yowled in an alley as it rummaged through scraps, and a pack of dogs trotted past, followed by loud curses from the Local woman selling meat from a three-cornered framework hitched to one of the patient donkeys.

"We're here." Selim announced. "Mendel the Bookseller."

The bookshop was little more than a shack propped up between one selling used garments and another other offering the rush baskets and net bags that were the common containers for purchased goods in Manatas. A selection of books had been laid out on the shutter; more were piled up on tables just inside the door.

Mendel the Bookseller sat amidst his wares, a rotund man of middle years with a perpetual scowl etching deep creases over his nose, his graying beard streaming across his dark coat, a broad-brimmed hat on his head.

"Salaam aleikum," Selim said politely. "Is Benyamin here?"

"Shalom." Mendel wasn't as polite. "Benyamin's not here. He's off somewhere gallivanting instead of minding his own business, and mine."

"Shalom." Halvar decided to get to the point. "Mendel the Bookseller, by now you must have heard the news-criers. Manolo the Pawnbroker was found dead this morning."

"The news-criers were through here earlier," Mendel admitted. "A bad business. Very bad business."

"It's about business I've come," Halvar said, picking up one of the books.

"Business?" Mendel's frown deepened. "You want to buy books? The Calif's Danic Hireling reads? A miracle!"

Halvar smiled ruefully. "Oh, I don't pretend to be a scholar, Mendel Bookseller," he said. "I can't read Arabi. Too many twists and turns, and it reads the wrong way around for me. I can sign my name in Rune letters, and that's the length and breadth of my schooling. But I can tell what letters are in which language, and I can tell numbers."

"Useful," Mendel said with a scornful sniff.

"Which is why I can tell that this book..." Halvar opened the one he'd picked up. "...is about numbers. Mathematics, they called it when I followed young Don Felipe to his classes at the Madrassa in Corduva. The interesting thing about *this* book is that it's in three languages, besides the numbers. I don't recall seeing anything like this when Don Felipe was at Madrassa in Corduva."

"You don't say." Mendel tried to retrieve the book, but Halvar kept it carefully out of his reach, turning the pages with one finger.

"One side of the page is written in Arabi, the other is in both the square Roumi letters they use in Italia and Franchenland and even parts of the Dane-March, and the round Ogham letters they use in Bretain. It's new, too. No signs of handling, no one's written notes in it."

"New? Of course it's new," Mendel blustered. "I get a shipment every year at the beginning of the term at the Madrassa. The students come with their fathers for the Fall Feria then stay for their classes until the spring. Some of them sell their books to buy new ones. What's so odd about that?"

Halvar rubbed a page between his fingers.

"What's interesting is this paper. It's rough. Most of the paper in Al-Andalus is smooth. What kind of book is this, Mendel Bookseller? New, fresh printing; even the binding's different—cloth over thin wood. So's this one." He picked up a second book and compared it to the first one. "Both exactly alike. And neither one like the mathematical books I saw in Corduva."

Mendel sniffed again. "Haven't you heard, Hireling? There's a thing called a printing press. It makes lots and lots of copies, each one exactly alike. A new thing, to be sure, but common enough in Oropa these days. What does the Calif's Hireling know about books, anyway?"

"When I was guarding Don Felipe, may he rule long, before he came to be calif, we had to pass the Street of Printers to get to his classes in the Madrassa at Corduva. There was one old chap used to work for the fraters who was always complaining about his workers and his suppliers, saying that the quality was lacking, that the inks were wrong, and there was no pride in the product. All the students wanted was a book that would give easy answers to the professors' questions, so all he did was turn out copies of copies of copies.

"He kept complaining about the paper he was given; every time he sold young Don Felipe another book, he said it wasn't as good as the ones he'd copied by hand when he was at the fratery in Bretain."

He turned to the bookseller. "One thing I do know about printing presses is that they are not easily come by. They're big, clumsy things, make a lot of noise, take up a lot of room." He looked around the tiny shack. "Good thing, too, because if anyone could have one then books could be printed anywhere, and the mullahs wouldn't be able to check them for their contents, and the printers wouldn't pay for the license to distribute them."

Mendel looked blandly back at Halvar.

"As you say, Don Alvaro. Printing books, it's a dangerous business sometimes. People will believe anything if they see it in print."

Halvar put down the new book and moved two others off the pile to reveal one bound in soft leather.

"This isn't printed," he pointed out. "It's hand written."

Selim peered over his shoulder.

"That's Leon's notebook" he exclaimed. "I know that writing of his. It's Arabi but written backwards, and in a kind of code of his own."

Halvar turned to face the bookseller.

"Mendel Bookseller, just how do you happen to have a book written by Leon di Vicenza?" he demanded.

47

"He sold it to me," Mendel blustered.

"When did he do that? Because I know where Leon di Vicenza's been for the last week, and it wasn't here in Manatas Town. I also know Leon's notebooks were taken from his rooms four days ago. They were sold to Manolo the Pawnbroker just before the big storm hit—that was three days ago. So tell me, Mendel the Bookseller, when did you buy these books? And who sold them to you?" He loomed menacingly over the bookseller.

"Leave him alone!"

Halvar turned to see Benyamin, Mendel's son, standing in the doorway of the shop; Selim hovered next to him.

"He has nothing to do with this!"

"With what?" Halvar asked.

"With what happened to Manolo," Benyamin blustered. "He wasn't anywhere near the waterfront yesterday. None of us was!"

"None of who?"

"None of us Yehudit," Mendel explained. "It was our Day of Repentance. We do not do business on that day. We go to the study house and pray that we may be forgiven our sins, and that the Great Judge will spare us in the coming year."

Halvar digested this information.

"You close up shop," he repeated. "Don't do business. Like your Shabat?"

Benyamin nodded vigorously. "I can swear to you, Don Alvaro, my father and I were with the rest of the Yehudit of Manatas Town. If you don't believe me, you may ask Rav Shimon Layzar, our great teacher. Even that miserable bigot Mullah Abadul respects Rav Shimon Layzar."

"Then when did you, um, acquire these books?" Halvar laid a hand on the nearest one.

Mendel glanced at his son. "It was early yesterday morning, just after dawn prayers," he said. "We'd lost a whole day's trade with the holy day. A man was waiting for me with the books."

"Did you know what they were?" Selim asked.

"More to the point, did you know *whose* they were?" Halvar added.

"Of course I knew," Mendel said. "I'd sold some of the printed books to Leon di Vicenza in the first place! The students at the Madrassa are always looking for things like the *Almagest*, and the works of Averroes, and he had some of the new poetry that he'd embellished with his own pictures. I could get a good price for that. As

48

for the notebooks, the private journals, I assumed they were for sale because Leon had gone over to the fraters in Green Village."

"You didn't question the seller?" Halvar's voice took on a menacing edge. "Even though you knew it wasn't Leon? You must have suspected the books were stolen."

"I thought...well...perhaps he'd found someone to sell them for him," Mendel protested.

"Who was this man who sold them to you?" Halvar asked, eyes narrowed.

"I couldn't tell who it was," Mendel said. "Only that he was tall, and perhaps thinner than most men. He had a scarf over his chin, and his hat was pulled down over his face, and he wore a long coat, and it was still dark, so I can't be sure of anything more."

"What did he sound like?" Halvar was relentless. "Did he speak Arabi with an accent? Danic, Franchen, Bretain?"

"He spoke Arabi," Mendel admitted, "but very softly. A kind of hoarse whisper—he coughed and said he had been caught in the storm and taken a chill. He said he was selling the books for Manolo the pawnbroker. We've done business before, I thought it was all right." Mendel looked from Halvar to Benyamin. "How was I to know it was stolen merchandise?"

"You must have known," Selim shot out. "You knew Leon would never sell one of his own notebooks, not Leon. He kept everything!"

"I didn't even know what they were until it was light, and I could look at them more closely," the bookseller whined.

"A Yehudit bought merchandise without looking it over? I don't believe that." Halvar sneered. "You must have known what you were buying, Mendel Bookseller. How much did you pay for the lot?"

Mendel shifted uneasily in his seat.

"Two strings of purple wumpum. The seller didn't even haggle."

"That would have made *me* suspicious," Benyamin put in. "Tateh, what have you done?"

"I've done nothing! I got a set of books at a good price. There are people who will pay well for some of the drawings in those notebooks, even if they can't read the text," Mendel argued.

"It's not worth losing a hand over it," Halvar said. "You know the penalty for selling stolen merchandise is the same as if you'd stolen it yourself."

"I didn't know for sure they were stolen," Mendel insisted. "All I knew was they were well-made, that some of the books were bound copies I had sold to begin with and could sell again. And that some of them were hand-written, with images I could cut out and sell separately. The man wanted money, and I gave it to him, and he went away. That was all!"

Benyamin exploded. "Tateh, you're always telling me to be careful of strangers with odd merchandise. How could you succumb to your sin of greed! And right after the Day of Repentance, too!"

"I've done business with Manolo before." Mendel repeated, returning his son's accusing stare with a bland look. "No one else would, but I wasn't going to let a little thing like his taking the water to save his skin get between us. Business is business! If he had something I could sell, and we could settle on a reasonable price, I'd do business with him. As for this fellow who brought the books, before I could ask anything else, he was gone." Mendel gazed at Halvar, pleading for mercy. "What was I to do?"

"Once you knew what you had, you should have brought the book to the Rabat," Halvar said sternly. "You heard the news-criers. You said it yourself—Leon is alive and in the fratery at Green Village. Anything belonging to him should have been sent to the sultan, to be returned to Leon."

"So, nu, you came to me!" Mendel countered. He faced his son. "And where have *you* been? Playing with your fine friends from the Madrassa? The Yeshiva's not good enough, you have to go by the goyanim, to learn how to be like them? Like that birdie Leon?"

Benyamin's round face reddened.

"Tateh, we've been through this before, we don't have to do it again. Yeshiva might have been good enough back in Oropa, but here in Nova Mundum, it's the Madrassa where the real learning is. The Calif's Law is clear—anyone who can pay the fees can study at the Manatas Madrassa. I pay the fees from what you pay me—and it's not all that much, either."

The argument between father and son might have gone on into the evening, but someone called out, "Salaam aleikum, God be with ye, anyone within?" from the door to the shop.

Everyone turned to face the newcomer, a husky young man with a shock of copper-colored hair, dressed in the smock and multi-colored trews worn by the Bretains.

"Padraig!" Selim greeted the ironmonger's son. "What are you doing here? Aren't you supposed to be helping your father at the Feria?"

"I was," Padraig said. "He sent me to the Scavengers' Pit to see if they'd picked up any old tools, and I heard the news-criers calling that Don Alvaro was looking for stolen books. Then one of the Scavengers said he thought there was a book in the trench, only he wasn't going to the Rabat, let them come to him!

"So, I went and looked, and sure enough, there's a book in that trench. So I went to the Rabat, and Tenente Ruiz of the Guard told me Don Alvaro was going to Mendel the Bookseller's stall in the souk. So here I am, and that's my news."

"The Scavenger's Pit, hey?" Halvar recalled the fetid clearing at the western end of the Manatas Wall where he had fought with the late Tenente Gomez and shoved the would-be ruler of Manatas into the Great River. "Well, lad, I can see why you wouldn't want to get too close to that dirty hole, but you should have tried to get the book out, used a shovel or a billhook.."

Padraig hesitated. "Um…there were some Scavengers there, and they would have gone into the pit, but a sekonk was chewing on the book, so of course, nobody was going anywhere near it.

Benyamin, Padraig and Selim giggled. Mendel made a face.

Halvar looked from the young people to the old one and asked, "What is a sekonk?"

Benyamin said, "It's an animal. One of the local kind. They eat bugs and worms, when they're not eating garbage at the Scavenger's Pit."

Halvar thought about this. "How big is this animal?"

"About the size of a small dog or a large cat," Padraig said.

"It is fierce? Does it bite?" Halvar was puzzled at the reluctance of his new allies to confront this beast.

Selim stifled a giggle.

"I don't think so. Mostly, it runs away, but if you get between a mother and her babies, or if you try to take its food, it does have a way of making you sorry."

"Oh?" Halvar didn't understand the joke.

"It makes a smell," Benyamin said.

"A smell?" Halvar echoed. "A brave lad like you. Afraid of a smell?"

"You would be, too, if you smelled it. It's a stink like you've never encountered," Padraig warned him. "Think of the worst midden, the worst tannery, and that's nothing to the stink of a sekonk."

Halvar squared his shoulders and settled his leather cap on his head.

"Boys, I've gone through battlefields where the dead were piled up by fives and sixes. I've been in towns after a siege when they

51

were reduced to eating rats and no one cleaned out the latrines for months. Bring on your sekonk! I've got to get that book!"

Chapter 9

PADRAIG LED THE GROUP OUTSIDE TO HIS TRANSPORT, A cart hitched not to one of the ever-present donkeys but to a shaggy pony. She was the same size as the donkeys but much livelier, kicking her feet and prancing with anxiety to be away from the distracting noises and smells of the souk.

Halvar, Selim and Benyamin joined Padraig in the cart, which tilted alarmingly under their combined weight. It took all of Padraig's skill to steer through the crowded alleys back to the Broad Way, where the pony could show her speed and sprightly paces. From the souk to the Scavenger's Pit took only a few minutes.

Halvar thought over what he had learned as he jolted back and forth along the narrow streets, holding the side of the cart with one hand and tugging at his mustache with the other. Manolo had been killed three days ago, just before this Yehudit Day of Repentance. At that time, Robert Mortmain, the Franchen server, had taken the books from Leon's rooms and sold them to the pawnbroker then handed over the Mermaid Taberna to Hannes Zilberstam.

Robert was probably a trained assassin, like his compatriot Henri. He was, therefore, the most likely suspect in the murder of Manolo. But if Robert had sold the books to Manolo, why would he steal them again and not just kill the old man and be done with it? How would he know where to sell the books in the souk? Who had taken the books to Mendel, if Robert didn't? And why abstract one of the lot, and having kept it, why discard it again? None of this made any sense!

"We're here." Padraig announced. It was not necessary. Halvar could tell by the reek that combined excrement with rotting vegetation and the salty spray of the Great River that they had arrived at their destination, the designated dumping-ground for the offal produced by the inhabitants of any settlement as large as Manatas Town.

Small huts had been built along the end of the stone wall to house the Scavengers, men and women who scoured the streets of Manatas with baskets, picking up donkey dung and whatever else the residents discarded. Most of what went into the pit was whatever bits of food could not be salvaged by a thrifty cook or gobbled down by the roving cats and dogs. Odd ends of leather discarded by the leatherworkers, scraps of metal from the workers in brass, rags left over from tailors—those were hoarded into a pile, to be sifted through and possibly rendered down into something salable.

Nothing went to waste in Manatas, Halvar realized, not even dung, which was dropped into a separate pit to be used as fertilizer.

He grimaced as he approached the pits. He'd already paid two visits to the Scavengers, and neither had turned out well.

Achmet, the so-called Emir of the Scavengers, greeted them with an extravagant salaam that set the ends of his ragged caftan fluttering.

"Salaam aleikum, Don Alvaro, you honor me once again with your presence. What brings you to this place this time? Please, do not fight anyone else here, it's too distracting for my people. We have more than enough to do picking through all that comes here, to save what we can and dispose of what we can't."

"I brought him," Padraig said. "It's that book. The one the sekonk got hold of. Didn't you hear the news-criers? Manolo the Pawnbroker at the waterfront was found this morning, murdered. Some books were taken from his shop. That was one of them, I'm sure of it."

Achmet squinted over his beard at the young Bretain.

"Books aren't all that common, and they don't get tossed about," he agreed. "Rachev! Osman!" he called out to his two lieutenants. "What fool let a book get thrown into the pit?"

Rachev, the lanky one, scratched his head.

"I didn't see anyone bring in a book," he said. "We would have given it to you right away, Baas. Books is important. They cost money,

54

the students want them. No one throws a book away, Right, Osman?"

Osman, short and squat, nodded agreement.

"Wasn't in nothing that none of our folks brought in," he stated.
"Must have been thrown in by someone passing through."

Halvar glared at the three Scavengers.

"You let anyone pass by here? A war party of Mahaks could take
the whole town, and you Scavengers wouldn't raise the alarm!"

"That's not so!" Achmet protested. "We've got houses here, they
don't let nobody through!"

"I got by," Padraig pointed out.

"Oh, that's different, we know you," Osman said.

"So, if someone came through that you knew, no one would raise
the alarm," Halvar concluded.

Achmet shrugged. "Maybe, if we know who the person is, maybe
we let them pass," he admitted. "There's a few folks from Green
Village come this way as a shortcut to the souk."

"And to avoid paying the calif's tolls," Halvar muttered.

"We don't ask questions," Achmet said with another shrug. "Tenente Gomez and his Town Guards used our path, sure, but we
take care that no one comes through we don't know."

"What about last night," Halvar asked. "Did anyone hear or
see anything unusual?"

Achmet glared at his two lieutenants.

"I thought I saw you two fools outside before daybreak. What
were you about?"

"We had to get out early, Baas," Rachev insisted. "Had to catch
the donkeys. Some fool let the paddock gate open, and the critters
got out. We had Shaitan's own time getting them back."

Halvar said, "Did you find out who opened the donkey paddock?"

"Not yet," Osman said. "We asked, but no one said. Could be
Ibo, the Afrikan who collects the night soil at the waterfront. He's
a halfwit."

"Halfwits usually do exactly what they've been told to do and
nothing else," Halvar observed.

"The news-criers said there was shooting on the waterfront, too,"
Osman said, eying Halvar with respect.

"That wasn't my doing," Halvar protested. "That was Tenente
Ruiz."

"Our new tenente is very handy with that pistoia of his." Achmet smirked.

Halvar looked sharply at the Emir of the Scavengers.

"You didn't see a stranger come through that gap, did you? Tall, thin, probably in Franchen dress? Speaks Arabi with a Franchen accent, is missing part of one eyebrow."

Achmet gave him a bland smile.

"No one of that description has passed through this settlement."

"You wouldn't lie, would you?" Halvar held up a hand to forestall any of Achmet's protestations. "Who else comes here, if not your people?" he asked with a glance at the odoriferous pit.

"There's always someone thinks he can do your job better," Achmet complained. "They dump almost anything. They don't take the time, like we do, to sort things out. We're careful that way. If we spot something that can be used, we get it out of the pit."

"And sell it," Padraig sneered.

"So." Halvar tried to steer the conversation back to the book. "Someone, you don't know who, came here, you don't know why, and threw this book into the pit, you don't know how."

"Someone from Manatas Town," Benyamin pointed out. "Not from outside the walls."

"How do you reason that?" Halvar eyed the Yehudit youth, who took the stance affected by the Yehudit teachers when making their points—feet square, one arm raised to point to the heavens.

Benyamin continued, in a singsong cadence, "The thief had to have come to the pit from the town, because the books were taken from Leon's rooms and sold to the pawnbroker. He must have gotten them from Manolo between the time they were sold…"

"Three days ago," Halvar filled in. "Just about the time your Day of Repentance was starting, and so was the big storm."

Benyamin nodded. "Between then and dawn yesterday, when he came to my father's shop. This book must, therefore, have been left here this morning, before dawn."

"He could have gone to Green Village yesterday and come back," Selim observed.

"He could have, but he didn't leave the book here then, because if he had, the book would have been found by Emir Achmet and his people yesterday," Padraig pointed out. "They would have taken it before the sekonks and araghouns tore it apart. And it wasn't thrown there during the storm, because it would have been drowned in water like everything else."

The trio looked at Halvar like eager students ready to impress their teacher.

"So," Halvar summed up, "the book thief had a full day to examine the book. Why take the time, if he'd already sold the others?"

"Maybe he didn't sell all of them to Mendel, just the ones he didn't need. Maybe there was something special about that particular notebook," Selim concluded.

"Why that one and not the others?" Padraig asked.

"Leon wrote his books in a private code, and in backwards Arabi," Selim said. "So no one could read it but him."

Halvar tugged at his mustache, recalling his encounters with Leon di Vicenza in Al-Andalus

"Leon didn't just write," he reminded the group. "Leon drew images—portraits of people he was with, plants and animals he saw, pictures of devices he'd thought of making that he'd then bring to Malik the Blacksmith. Oh, yes, those notebooks of Leon's had value beyond the leather binding, even if the words were unreadable."

"How much would Leon give to get one of his notebooks back?" Benyamin wondered.

"Doesn't matter now," Padraig said with a knowing nod. "The Beggar Fraters at Green Village own everything in common. Leon wouldn't get to keep his books. Abbas Mikhail is strict about things like that."

"So, why does the book thief come all the way here?" Halvar asked, not expecting an answer.

"To pass the book on to someone else!" Selim exclaimed with a sudden grin.

"Who?" Halvar demanded. "And why? And where are they now?"

Benyamin scratched at his sprouting beard. Padraig frowned.

"It would have to be something to do with what was in that particular notebook," Selim said, thinking it through "Maybe, there was some image, or maybe a plan for a device the thief knew was worth money."

"What image?" Padraig wanted to know. "What device?"

Halvar shrugged. "We won't know until we see the book."

"So, he contacted the buyer and told him to meet him here," Benyamin picked up the argument.

"Contacted how?" Selim wondered. "How would he know who would want to buy whatever was in the book?"

Halvar's smile was not pleasant.

"Because the Emir of the Scavengers is lying through that scabby beard of his when he says he doesn't know where Robert Mortmain is. Ruiz and his men should keep better watch on this nest of thieves.

"Our man waited out the storm right here, in one of these huts, and sent word to his buyer through the Scavengers." His voice rose as he looked around at the collection of sorry shacks and sheds that housed the Scavengers. "If I sent Ruiz and his Town Guard here, they'd find him soon enough. There's not enough silver to hide behind, Robert Mortmain!"

There was no answer from the Scavengers' settlement.

"So," Padraig continued, "there was a meeting between the two, Robert and this other person, the one who was ready to buy what Robert had to sell. Then what?"

Halvar tugged on his mustache.

"Robert would head for Green Village, to mix with the rest of the Franchen who deal in goods at the Feria. Green Village seems to be where folk go when they know they're not welcome in Manatas Town, and it's full of Franchen. If he wants to book passage on a Franchen ship that's leaving after the Feria's over, that's where he'd find one." That settled, he squared his shoulders and settled his cap firmly on his head. "Now, lads, show me this sekonk. I've got to get that book."

Achmet and his Scavengers followed them over to the clearing at the end of the wall where two large holes had been dug out of the clay of the riverbank. The stench emanating from one proclaimed its use as a depository for the contents of latrines and chamber pots; the other held more miscellaneous oddments. Between the pits was a wide trench where the Scavengers deposited their larger finds. A rutted path indicated the route taken by the donkey carts as they brought their burdens to be deposited and picked through for anything salvageable.

Halvar could make out the leaves of plants, the inedible parts of root vegetables and maiz stalks, and the bones of animals that had been slaughtered for cooking. In the middle of the mess, a small animal something like a weasel, with a sharp snout and a bushy tail and covered in black fur adorned with two white stripes on its back, was busily gnawing on what looked like a duplicate of the leather-bound notebook currently resting on Mendel's table. From its squeaks and squeals of delight, it appeared to be enjoying its meal.

"Don Alvaro," Achmet warned, "I beg you, do not alarm that sekonk."

"It's already smelly here," Halvar said. "And I need that book before he destroys it."

"Not even my men will interrupt a sekonk," Achmet stated.

As it became aware of Halvar's intent, the sekonk looked up. It edged away from the book and stamped its front feet.

"That's the first warning," Benyamin said. "Don Alvaro, get out of that trench right now."

Selim and Padraig drew back to the pony cart. The Scavengers huddled together, horrified, as Halvar strode forward to face his foe.

The sekonk raised its tail.

"That's the second warning," Benyamin called. "Most people don't wait for the rest. Get out now!"

Halvar reached out, grabbed the book and turned away, just as the sekonk spun around and demonstrated exactly what the Scavengers and the Seekers of Truth had warned him about.

He staggered back, eyes running, nose filled with a devastating reek that drowned out all the others, but he still held onto the book! He groped his way out of the trench, ignoring the anguished cries of the Scavengers.

"Get him to the bathhouse in Green Village!" Achmet ordered. "And don't come back till he's clean! Books! Who throws away books?"

Padraig gasped and tried not to breathe as he got Halvar into the pony cart.

"Meet you at the common ground, in Green Village," he called out to his friends, who chose to walk well behind the cart.

Halvar had to agree with them. If he could have gotten away from himself, he would have!

Deprived of that option, he flipped the pages of his prize, which were covered with Leon's weird scrawl and interspersed with drawings. He blinked away the effects of the sekonk's attack to clear his vision. He recognized some of the faces sketched on the first few pages of the book—friends of Don Felipe, students at the Madrassa in Corduva. He frowned.

There was a jagged tear at the end of the book where a page had been removed.

He shook the book, sending more sekonk reek into the air. It fell open to the front, where another page had been removed.

59

That's what this is about, Halvar thought. *Whatever's on those pages, it was important. I'll have to have another talk with Leon.*

But first, he admitted, *I'd better have a bath.*

Chapter 10

PADRAIG CLICKED HIS TONGUE AND SHOOK THE REINS. The pony obediently started out. Then, unexpectedly, the animal let out a whinny and bounced backwards, eyes wide open, as she saw something no human eyes should see.

Padraig tried to sooth his beast. "What's the matter, Mollie?"

The pony had her own ideas. She rose up on her hind legs, nearly upsetting the frail cart. Then she bounded forward, eyes rolling in fear, jolting along the narrow path that led from the Pits to Green Village, skirting the grounds of the Feria.

The pony stormed down the path as if demented, Padraig trying to control her; and Halvar gripped the book with one hand and the side of the cart with the other. She only stopped, exhausted, when she reached the common ground in the center of the houses that formed Green Village. She stood, froth spewing from her mouth, panting and snorting.

Halvar tumbled from the cart, still clutching Leon's book. Men and women poured out of their houses, torn from their daily activities by the cart's dramatic arrival.

The largest of the men was Padraig's father, Cormack MacCormack, an ironmonger from West Caster, across the East Channel from Manatas Island, who had taken on the role of leader of Green Village's Bretains. He strode forward to grab his son by the neck of his shirt and haul him out of the cart.

"What do you mean, racing Mollie like that! Look at her! She's knackered!"

"Not my fault!" Padraig stammered. "Something spooked her at the Scavenger's Pit!"

"Blood," Halvar gasped out. "She smelled blood. Horses don't like it. They have to be trained to it. I've seen horses act that way when they come to the battlefield, if they aren't used to the smell."

"Faugh! What have you been doing, Hireling? Playing with a sekonk?" Cormack echoed the exclamations of the rest of his fellow Villagers. They had approached the wagon, only to be driven back by the penetrating stench.

"It had this book," Halvar stated, shaking Leon's notebook. "It belongs to Leon di Vicenza." He held the book towards Cormack, who stepped farther back. "I want him to look at it and tell me what's missing. Someone tore pages out of it. Only he knows what was on those pages."

"What makes you think he'll tell you?" Donal, the Bretain bouncer and self-appointed guardian of Dani Glick, stood in the gateway of the cast-iron fence that surrounded the Gardens of Paradise. It was the largest building in Green Village, and the principal reason for the village's notoriety in Manatas.

"Get out of here, Hireling. There's no place for you in Green Village! You've done enough damage! Crawl back over to Manatas Town and kiss the sultan's arse!"

A week's worth of resentment, exacerbated by the sickening smell that enwrapped him, bubbled up within Halvar. He launched himself at Donal and slapped the man backhanded across the face, using all the force of his frustration and anger. He followed it up with a blow to the Bretain's midsection, and a third punch to his jaw.

The blows fell hard and fast, giving the Bretain no time to retaliate. Donal staggered backward down the path through the shrubbery as Halvar continued to land blow after blow, slap after slap. They reached the building as a final slap sent a stream of blood flowing from Donal's nose.

Halvar slammed the Bretain against the wall, both of them breathing hard

"You owe me a jacket, Donal." he gritted out. "No, you owe me two! One leather jacket, one woolen! Twice you got me down, but no more! You had to fill me with cider and hemp the first time, and the second time you jumped me from behind and got two others to do your dirty work. Now, Donal of Bretain, you've made me angry. Get me my jackets!"

He grabbed Donal's ear and banged his head against the wall.

"Leave him alone!" Dani Glick, too, had been watching from behind the iron fence that marked the boundaries of the Gardens of Paradise. "Halvar! Leave him be!" She might have been talking to a large dog that had cornered an intruder.

Halvar threw Donal down into a patch of spiky bushes.

"I'm not your plaything, Dani Glick," he told her. "I don't take your orders. And I will find out what it is you are so anxious to keep hidden."

"You've see the Gardens of Paradise, I have nothing to hide." Dani Glick was not impressed by either fisticuffs or verbal bluster. "What brings you back to Green Village this time?"

"I have to get this book to Leon," Halvar said, holding it out to her.

She stepped away, her hand over her nose.

"Then do it, although I suggest you get rid of that stink first," Dani retorted. "But I can't help you. Abbas Mikhail doesn't allow women in the fratery. They take the Holy Meal in the chapel outside their walls so females can attend without disturbing the appetites of the fraters within their compound."

Halvar's anger seeped slowly away, leaving him ashamed of his outburst. He glanced at Donal, who had managed to get up on his knees, crawling away from the reek of sekonk.

"The sekonk wasn't my fault. As for Donal, you keep that lout and his boys away from me." He turned to Donal. "What brings me here is a question. Has a stranger come here in the last day or two? Someone with half his right eyebrow missing, probably speaks Arabi with a Franchen accent."

"And what's he to us?" Donal was on his feet, glaring at Halvar with undisguised loathing tone arm against his bleeding nose.

"He's a trained assassin from Parigi," Halvar told him. "Connected with the doings at the Mermaid Taberna, where they were painting white wumpum purple. You may not have heard, but Manolo, the pawnbroker at the waterfront, was found dead this morning. His neck was broken, in the manner of Parigi thieves. This man I'm looking for, Robert Mortmain, may be his killer."

"May be?" Donal echoed.

"Or maybe not. I won't know for certain till I find him. It's likely that he made for Green Village to mix with the Franchen from the Feria. If he did, I want to know about it."

"A stranger, you say?" Cormack frowned at Donal. "In the last two days? There's been none that I know of."

The two men had moved even farther away from Halvar.

Dani, a scented handkerchief now pressed over her nose, struggled between laughter at Halvar's discomfort and revulsion at the sekonk smell. "No one I don't know is staying at the Gardens of Paradise," she said firmly. "I have no business on the waterfront, and whatever happened to those Franchen *chazzerim* at the Mermaid Taberna, they had it coming." Her tone was surprisingly bitter.

"I need answers!" Halvar declared.

"You won't get them until you get rid of that sekonk smell— you need a bath!" Dani told him. "Get out of those clothes—they'll have to be burnt." She looked him over. "Where did you get the coat, anyway? It looks like your old leather one."

"I found it at Manolo's. It's the fourth coat I've lost since I got to this island. At this rate, I should keep a tailor on my payroll just to keep my back covered."

Dani sighed. "I may have something big enough to fit you. Come with me, Halvar, and let's get that stink off you before you send all Manatas into fits."

Halvar tugged his mustache. "I won't wear another of those Local leather shirts," he protested.

"I think we can find one of the Bretain plaids," Dani assured him. "But you really do need a bath. Unless you'd like to spend the next month announcing your presence five minutes before you arrive?"

Halvar gave in. "Bath, then Leon," he agreed, and followed her to the Gardens of Paradise.

Chapter 11

DANI SKIRTED THE MAIN BUILDING AND HEADED FOR A
smaller one that had been erected beside the small stream that
wound through Green Village to the Great River.

"The Gardens of Paradise provide all sorts of pleasures," she
told Halvar. "Including those of cleanliness. The baths await you,
Halvar Danske."

She stepped well away and motioned for him to go ahead of
her. Two tall women, one Afrikan, one Danic, both muscular, both
dressed in brief kuton tunics and loose trousers, grimaced as he
stepped within.

"He's been playing hero with a sekonk," Dani said unnecessar-
ily. "Birgit, fetch some tomatl sauce from the kitchen. Farrah, get
those clothes off him and throw them outside. Then heat up the
big tub—I'll deal with him myself."

The large fair-haired Danic woman disappeared into the kitchens of the Gardens of Paradise. The even larger dark woman approached Halvar with determination.

"Clothes! Off!" she ordered.

Halvar took a step backwards, only to be stopped by the high
wall of a wooden tub set on bricks over a fire-pit.

"I'll undress myself," he said.

He wriggled out of the jacket he had owned for less than a
day. This was definitely getting expensive! He handed it to the Afrikan woman, who held it at arm's length and tossed it out the door,
then hesitated.

"Boots! Off!" She pointed to his feet.

"I can't take a bath with them on," he agreed, removing his foot-gear and stockings.

"Vest, off!"

Halvar unlaced the leather vest that had protected him from a fatal knife-thrust.

"Don't throw that away," he pleaded. "It's not as smelly as the jacket."

Out the door it went; Farrah was implacable. He took note the odor of sekonk immediately became less.

"Belt, off!"

Halvar unbuckled the belt that held his dagger, the only relic of his past life in the Dane-March. The businesslike blade had a plain hilt embellished only with a lump of amber. He held his baggy breeches with one hand as he placed the belt on the bench over his boots.

"That's enough, isn't it?" He edged away from the tall Afrikan woman.

Farrah was not finished with him yet.

"Trousers, off!"

Reluctantly, he removed his breeches, leaving only his shirt and braes.

"Shirt, off!"

The smell all but vanished once that garment had jointed the rest outside. Halvar clutched at his modesty.

"Underpants, off!"

"Oh, no, not these!" he declared. "No sekonk on these!"

"Off!" Farrah insisted.

By this time, Dani had removed most of her own garments and was wearing only a thin kuton chemise.

"Oh, let him have his way," she said as Birgit joined them with pottery jug. "Halvar, get into that." She pointed to a small tub, just large enough for him to stand in. "The only way to remove the scent of sekonk is with the juice of tomatl. Stand there, and let us do what we have to."

The three women surrounded him. Birgit poured the red juice over his shoulders while Farrah scrubbed his chest. Dani watched the procedure.

Halvar patiently endured three scrubbings and a rinse before Dani was ready to let him into the tub for a final dousing. He eyed the large tub cautiously. The only way in seemed to be a ladder, propped up against the wooden barrel. Dani scampered up and plopped into the waiting water with practiced ease. Halvar took a deep breath and regretted it. If that is what he still smelled like to himself, perhaps it *would* be a good idea to bathe.

He felt the ladder wobble under his weight and carefully edged up and over the rim into the tub. The water was hot but not uncomfortably so, and he settled down with a sigh.

Dani frowned at a trickle of red that stained the water in the tub.

"You're bleeding!"

"Someone knifed me this morning at the waterfront." He held up an arm. "This is going to dye me orange," he muttered.

"The sekonk didn't get your cap," Dani said. "Why do you insist on wearing that awful thing?"

"It keeps me warm and hides what's not there." He pulled off his cap, revealing how far back his hairline had receded.

Dani sighed. "Halvar, dear Halvar, we've had twenty years to wonder what might have happened if..."

"If your father and mine hadn't interrupted us?" Halvar grinned under his mustache. "If the Free Company of Danes hadn't needed new recruits? If the Yehudit hadn't been on the move, and you weren't already promised to Mauritz?"

"I wasn't promised to Mauritz until after our encounter," Dani said. She caressed his chest with one hand.

"But I was ready for adventure," Halvar told her. He felt stiffening down below. This wasn't part of his plan!

"We lost so much time," Dani crooned, moving around to face him, the thin cloth of her chemise clinging to her still-firm breasts.

She straddled his legs. Her breasts pressed against him as her hands worked their way down his body. He pressed back against the rough slats of the tub. He could have taken her, but something in her sudden insistence made him glance over the rim of the tub.

Birgit was fumbling in the folds of his discarded breeches.

What was she up to? Simple robbery wasn't Dani's style. Then he thought of his sliced jacket, of when she had fuddled him with drink and hemp, and now this distraction.

They won't find what they're looking for in those trousers. They're looking in the wrong place!

"That's enough!" he said aloud, heaving out of the water. "I wondered how far you'd go, Dani Glick, to get me out of my clothing. Now I know." He splashed to the ladder, flung a leg over the side, and slid down to face the Valkyrie and the Afrikan goddess. "Get me fresh, clean clothes. Now!"

Dani provided specifics.

"Farrah, get him the trousers that Danic sea captain left behind, and the Bretain plaid hunting shirt the fellow from New Plimoth forgot when he didn't pay his bill." She climbed out of the tub, to be enveloped in a kuton robe by Birgit. "You…Dane!"

"I don't like getting raped any more than you did," Halvar said. "And I think I like you better when you're not trying to seduce me, Dani Glick."

Farrah returned minutes later with a pair of wide trousers and a garish red-and-black checked woolen shirt sewn in the same style as the Algonkin *wamus*, even to the fringes on the yoke. He grimaced at the garments but put them on over his soaking underclothes. They would have to do until Yussuf could make him yet another coat.

He turned to face the three women.

"And now, Dani Glick, I am going to find out what Leon wrote in his book that was worth a man's life. After that, I will find out just what it is you are so anxious for me not to find at the Gardens of Paradise."

Chapter 12

ONCE MORE DECKED OUT IN CLOTHES THAT WERE NOT his own, Halvar left the bathhouse for the fratery at the northern end of the straggling path through Green Village. The gate in the log palisade that surrounded the compound was shut. Behind it, he could hear the faint sound of the fraters chanting their evening prayers as the sky flooded with brilliant red and gold and the sun set beyond the Great River.

He banged impatiently on the wicket and reflexively clutched his amulet and recited his evening prayer: "May the Redeemer and his Mother Mara and the God Thor protect me this night." Thus fortified, he waited until the irascible gatekeeper opened the wicket just wide enough to allow Halvar a glimpse of the fratery's courtyard.

"What d'ye want now, Dane?" The porter was not impressed with either Halvar's height or his authority.

"I want to speak with Leon di Vicenza, who has taken the name of Frater Leonidas."

"He's in the Great Silence. We don't talk to nobody after sundown." The porter started to swing the door shut. Halvar inserted the toe of his boot between the opening and the palisade to prevent it.

"This is important. A man's life may depend on it!"

"I'll get Abbas Mikhail."

Halvar prepared to wait, feeling the rumble in his stomach that reminded him his last meal had been interrupted by the murder investigation. The thought of a dish of hearty Danic stew from the pot of Hannes Zilberstam sustained him until he heard the slap of hard leather sandals on the stones of the courtyard that announced the arrival of the two fraters.

Again he requested a visit with Leon.

"You disturb our brother unduly," Abbas Mikhail objected. "Every time you come, he is distracted from his prayers."

"He'd be distracted anyway," Halvar said. "He's easily distracted. Right now, I need him to look at this book and tell me what it contained." He shook the book, sending waves of sekonk odor through the air.

The two fraters recoiled.

"I will send Frater Leonidas to you," Abbas Mikhail said. "Just promise that you will remove that smell."

Halvar studied the pages of the book in the twilight while Abbas Mikhail sent the porter off to fetch Leon then departed. The Arabi writing seemed to writhe across the page, but the sketches that punctuated the writing were clear enough. He was looking at the scenery around Corduva. An image of a face adorned with a sweeping mustache seemed to jump from the page.

So, that is what Leon saw when he looked at me! Halvar thought as he surveyed his younger self.

He recognized two other faces—students at the Madrassa—and a close detail of one of the arches of the Old Roumi watercourse that had not been torn down when the Legions left. It still brought water into the city the Old Roumi had built when Al-Andalus was called Hispania.

Two pages, three pages, then a break. He would not have known a page was missing were it not for the thin line of paper left in crack of the binding. What had been on that page?

He tried to recall what had happened on that sun-drenched day recorded in Leon's notebook, the first time he had accompanied his charge outside the city walls. There had been a lot of joking in the slangy Arabi he couldn't quite follow and some horseplay, which Leon, as the person in charge of the group, allowed to go unchecked. They had bathed in a stream, they had wrestled, they had listened to Leon read some Old Greco poem.

Then they had headed back to Corduva, only to be met at Don Felipe's student lodgings by a squad of the calif's personal guards, who marched Leon away while Felipe gazed after him in bewilderment.

Halvar also recalled the aftermath of that afternoon by the river. Young Felipe and Lady Zulaika screaming at each other, the old calif scolding both of them while he, the watchdog, stood silently at the door of the chamber keeping the rest of the world away.

That was the past, Halvar told himself. *This is now.*

Between the missing page at the front and the one at the back were images of sails, fish, and half-naked sailors. Sultan Petrus glowered up from one page, his features distorted but recognizable, and a sulky-looking girl with heavy eyebrows peered out from under her bangs on another, braids framing her face. Where had he seen those eyebrows before?

Halvar was jolted out of his rumination by Leon's shrill cry.

"My books!"

The porter let Halvar into the courtyard, then stood holding a lantern on a pole to provide enough light for Leon to see what had been brought to him. Behind Leon and the porter, Halvar noticed Abbas Mikhail hovering in nearby shadows, keeping his distance from the aroma of sekonk,

One whiff was enough for Leon.

"What have you done with my notebook, you clumsy Danic lout?"

"Not me," Halvar protested. "Jacques Tavernier sold some of your books to Manolo the Pawnbroker, and it looks like his servant, Robert, took the rest. Some got sold to Mendel the Bookseller in the souk. This one got thrown into the Scavenger's Pit, and a sekonk got it."

"I can smell that," Leon retorted. "Why bring it to me?"

"Because I have to know what was on the pages that got torn out," Halvar said, handing the book to him.

The reluctant frater held it gingerly with two fingers at arms' length.

"What makes you think I'd tell you?"

"Because I'm asking nicely," Halvar said. "By the images that are left, I can tell this is one of your notebooks from Al-Andalus. You were writing in it and drawing images when I went with you and young Don Felipe and his friends outside Corduva."

Leon nodded as he opened the book, still holding it as far from his nose as possible.

"Of course! I regularly took my students to view the Old Roumi ruins. The Barbarians who took over from the Old Roumi knocked down most of the arches, but this one was still standing." He smiled to himself. "They were such lovely boys."

71

"Especially Don Felipe," Halvar said meaningfully.

"He was young, but very clever," Leon admitted.

"And he was devoted to you. He was really upset when he found out you were going away, all the way across the sea to Manatas."

"That wasn't my idea, you know. That was those three harpies, Lady Zulaika and her fellow crones Lady Maryam and my sister, Eva Hakim."

"Cronies, not crones. Lady Zulaika is not much older than I am, and Eva Hakim is a handsome woman."

"Really, Halvar? Cracking jokes in Arabi?" Leon sneered. "I know why Lady Zulaika was so anxious to get me across the ocean. She doesn't want anyone to come between her and her son. Her cousin, Lady Maryam, wanted her husband to have a high post, but one that would get him away from Al-Andalus and her management of that estate in the mountains. As for my sister, she never understood my way of life."

"She got you out of Al-Andalus before you could be jailed, or worse," Halvar pointed out. "And Don Felipe met you on the docks before you got onto the riverboat to the dhow that would take you across the Storm Sea. He even gave you a parting gift."

"Indeed, he did." Leon shot a look at Abbas Mikhail then said, "But I have repented of all that."

Halvar said nothing, just raised skeptical eyebrows.

Leon continued to thumb through his old notebook.

"I wrote this when I was first exiled," he sighed. "This is the notebook I had with me on the voyage to Nova Mundum. Do you know there are fish that jump out of the water to escape their enemies?" He pointed to one sketch. "And that there is a current of warm water in the middle of the cold ocean? I felt it myself."

Halvar wasn't interested in the temperature of the ocean.

"What was on the pages that have been torn out?"

Leon looked up from his examination.

"You know, I do believe these pages were torn by two different hands," he said. "This one, in the front, the image I made in Al-Andalus, that one's been carefully removed, perhaps with a knife, or some other sharp tool. See? Its edges are even. But this one, at the end of the book, it's been torn out by hand, very quickly. The edges are ragged."

"I think I know what was on the first page," Halvar said. "You have images of all the other lads on the facing page, and one of me, but where's Don Felipe?"

Leon nodded approvingly. "Very clever, Halvar Danske. I drew an image of young Felipe and some others of his friends as they went into the stream and wrestled." He glanced back at Abbas Mikhail. "I was studying the musculature, you see, and the way they lay on the bank of the stream. Nothing more!"

Halvar tried to picture the scene.

"I remember how warm it was, so the youngsters took off their clothes and bathed, and I stood guard beside the river. They cracked jokes about me that I didn't quite understand, being new to Al-Andalus and not knowing much Arabi, let alone student slang. One thing I recall, you showed them the picture, and they laughed and signed their names to it."

Leon smiled at the happy memory. "So they did! Don Felipe and two Bretains, MacArtur and Og-Tyrell, and an Afrikan—I think his name was Feroz." His expression changed to a peevish pout. "Then I was arrested and taken before Lady Zulaika, who seemed to think she was bestowing a great favor on me by telling me I had a new position, tutoring the child of the Sultan of Manatas Town, and that I had a week to pack my things, cancel my lectures, settle my accounts and get to the riverboat.

"And there was Eva, looking as if it were the most wonderful thing that could ever happen to me, and behind her that other harpy, the sultan's chief wife Maryam."

Halvar broke into Leon's reminiscences.

"That last page," he gritted out. "The one that was torn out. What was on that one?"

Leon's face went blank.

"I don't recall exactly what was on that page," he said. "I must have written something just after I arrived here in Manatas. There were no more pages, and I was starting a new life, so I started a new book, to record my impressions of the place."

Halvar nodded again. "I can let you have this notebook," he said. "Maybe, if you let it air out, you can get the smell off it. Meanwhile, I wish you well in your new home, Frater Leonidas."

He turned to leave.

Leon caught him by the sleeve of the garish red shirt.

"You mean you're not going to try to persuade me to leave with you? What game are you playing, Hireling? I know you. You never give up! You stick to your quarry like fish-glue! You can't tell me you're going to leave me here in Manatas."

Halvar shrugged. "You just said it yourself. You've renounced your evil ways, turned to the Redeemer and his Mother Mara. Of course, you know that if you follow your usual bent, you'll be facing the fire as well as the water."

Leon's eyes narrowed in suspicion.

"Meaning what?"

"You've heard the tales from the students from Franchenland and Bretain. The Bretains are broad-minded, but even they don't like man-lovers. The Franchen burn them alive. Al-Andalus is the only place where a man like you can follow the dictates of his heart and flesh, Leon di Vicenza. You can stay safe here in your fratery, while Al-Andalus crumbles and the Franchen take over, driving everyone and everything you love into exile, or worse, as long as you don't act on your desires." Halvar ended with a dramatic sigh.

Leon stiffened with defiance.

"You think you can shame me into coming back with you to Al-Andalus?

"I can't take you bodily from this fratery," Halvar admitted. "But Don Felipe needs you. He needs your wit, he needs your ideas. And I don't understand why you want to stay here. The letter you wrote him made it clear you wanted to go back to Al-Andalus. Why the change?"

Leon leaned forward, his voice low so Abbas Mikhail couldn't hear.

"I won't be penned up in this fratery for much longer. There is much, much more to Nova Mundum than this little island, and I am going to see all of it! I didn't understand before, but when I met Otter Tail, I realized how much there was to do and see. Nova Mundum really is a new world, one where I'm not just an apothecary's son who has a few tricks up his sleeves."

"No matter where you go, I will follow you." Halvar promised. "That is, *if* you get off this island."

"When!" Leon insisted as the porter opened the gate and Abbas Mikhail stepped forward to claim his prize penitent.

The gate closed behind him. Halvar's grin faded. The lanterns on the Green Village common had been lit. The Gardens of Paradise glowed with candles and oil lamps. Beyond Green Village, he could see the glimmer of the lanterns that showed the way through the Feria to Manatas Town.

He trudged back to the commons where he found the three young Seekers of Truth waiting for him.

74

Chapter 13

BENYAMIN, PADRAIG AND SELIM HUDDLED TOGETHER near the donkey cart. Halvar thought he heard a giggle, but there were other things on his mind besides wayward teenagers. Whatever mischief they'd been up to was no concern of his.

They faced him with expressions of bland innocence

"What do we do now?" Selim asked.

"*You* go back to the Rabat," Halvar said. "Your father's waiting to have that little talk with you that you've been trying to get away from. Padraig MacCormack, you keep your eyes open for that man, Robert Mortmain. Benyamin, you'd better get back to your father's shop and go through all the books he got from Manolo."

"And what are you going to do?" Selim glared at Halvar resentfully.

"I am going to have a decent Danic meal. Maybe no one will try to knife me, poison me, or knock me on the head before I finish it."

"What is it that makes you so popular, Halvar Danske?" Dani Glick called from her post at the gate of the Gardens of Paradise. "No matter where you go, someone tries to kill you. You don't even allow yourself the pleasure of a hot bath."

Halvar strolled over to her.

"It must be my winning ways," he said. "There *is* something I wanted to know, Dani Glick. Every Yehudit I run across is certain that no other Yehudit would do anything else but go to the study house on this Day of Repentance. What is there about that day that makes it so special?"

Dani's smile faded.

"Why do you want to know?" she asked suspiciously.

"Because it may have a bearing on the murder of Manolo the Pawnbroker."

Dani spat.

"Manolo the Apostate! He took the water, not because he believed but to save his skin. There were those who chose to die rather than give in to Lovis and his Questioners and his presters, forcing the Roumi Rite on every village they took. None of the Yehudit in Manatas Town would speak directly to him, and none of us here in Green Village would trust him."

Halvar knew of at least one Yehudit who had befriended Manolo but kept that to himself. Instead, he said, "You have Yehudit here, in Green Village?"

"We have a few. Not as many as in the town but enough to make up a quorum, if you include women. They don't in Manatas Town, but here in Green Village, we do. We couldn't pray together if we didn't," she added.

"And one of them is you, Dani Glick?" Halvar said with a knowing smile.

"Once in a while, I will go to the study house," Dani admitted. "To say the memorial verses for Mauritz. I can tell you that every one of the Yehudit of Green Village was there in the study house on the day of the storm, saying the prayers and asking for forgiveness for our sins. Even me. We weren't in Manatas Town killing the pawnbroker, no matter what we thought of him."

Halvar tugged at his mustache.

"Suppose I told you that, every year, this apostate you revile closed his shop, would not do any business, and would not speak to anyone until the next day. The day before the storm, he had a bath and cut his hair, put on a white tunic, and ate a fine meal that he never finished. What would that tell you?"

Dani's face paled under her cosmetics.

"That perhaps I was wrong about him, and for that I am sorry. And that he would be in very great danger if those of the Roumi Rite were the only Kristos in Manatas.

"They are always sniffing around the Conversi—the Yehudit and Islim who have taken the water—just in case they are backsliding into their old ways. It only takes a small sign, like taking a bath on the wrong day or not lighting a fire or closing a shop."

"All of which are...?"

76

"Signs that your soul is still Yehudit," Dani said firmly. "That means the fire, if the Questioners decide so."

"The water, or the fire," Halvar summed up. "Not a pleasant prospect, either way."

"There are a few folk here in Green Village who will not go into Manatas Town because they might be caught by some Franchen and put on a ship back to Franchenland to be Questioned. At least the Bretain Rite fraters do not question a person's private beliefs. All you have to do is appear at the Holy Meal once a year, and that is enough for them."

"What about you, Dani? Do you go to the Holy Meal once a year?"

"That's for the ones who claim to be Kristo. I never claimed to be anything but what I am."

"And the others?"

"We have a prayer—you might call it a way of accounting for oaths and promises made under duress. We say it just before the Day of Repentance. It absolves us of such oaths and clears our consciences."

"Useful." Halvar looked over to Selim, who had been waiting patiently for him with Padraig and Benyamin. "Dani Glick, if you see this man Robert Mortmain, send word to the Rabat. Don't try to hold him yourself. He's a trained assassin out of Parigi and very dangerous."

"If I see any assassins, I'll certainly let you know...after Donal and his men have finished with them. Meanwhile, enjoy your evening, Halvar Danske. And don't play with any more sekonks!"

With that, she waved and turned back to the inviting lights and tempting odors that wafted from the Gardens of Paradise.

Halvar rejoined his young followers.

"Back to Manatas Town," he ordered.

"What about Robert Mortmain?" Selim asked.

"I'll find him. But first, I have to get the one who killed the pawnbroker."

"I thought..." Selim began.

"There's more to this than a simple robbery gone bad," Halvar said. "Let's see what Ruiz and his men found in the souk."

Once more, he started out across the common to the footpath that led to the Scavenger's Pit. He was stopped by Donal.

"Fru Glick says you're to have this back." He handed Halvar a leather jacket that had been patched together with mismatched scraps, giving it a zany, ragtag appearance.

"My old jacket." Halvar seized it with glee. "You didn't find what you were looking for, did you?"

"It wasn't in the lining," Donal said.

Halvar thought he heard an odd clanking sound. He glanced toward the uppermost story of the three-story building that stood at the center of the formal gardens, head tilted and eyes narrowed. There was something there, he was sure of it, but now wasn't the time to go looking for it.

"Thank you for the return of my jacket," he told Donal. "Are you planning to escort me back to Manatas Town?"

"There are still sekonks out there," Donal reminded him. "And bears are fattening for their winter rest. And there's a pack of wolves up-the-hills; we've heard them howling. Be careful, Hireling. Manatas can be very dangerous at night."

"I've survived so far. It's the lad who needs protecting. It seems he's the only one knows exactly what this Robert Mortmain looks like."

"If a man with one eyebrow shows up, I'll hold onto him," Donal promised. "I'm no friend to Parigi assassins."

With that assurance, Halvar turned to his band of followers.

"I'm staying here," Padraig told him. "My father is already angry with me about the pony. No point in making things worse by going back into Manatas Town with the rest of you. Besides, I have things to do here in Green Village." He grinned at Selim and Benyamin.

They're up to something, Halvar thought, *some youngsters' mischief.*

He shrugged and plodded back down the path in the direction of Manatas Town. Youthful indiscretions didn't bother him. He had a murderer to find.

Chapter 14

HALVAR AND HIS TWO REMAINING ASSISTANTS PICKED
their way carefully along the path to the Scavengers' Pit. The rising
moon shone fitfully through the branches of the birch trees on either side of the dirt path, and small animals rustled and chirped.
Halvar caught a glimpse of something that might have been an ex-
ceptionally large rat bumbling through the woods.

"Opassom," Selim informed him. "It's nothing like the sekonk,
except that it eats the garbage at the Scavengers' Pit."

"It doesn't smell, but it will bite," Benyamin warned. "And it's
terefah, although I'm told the Locals eat them."

"They eat anything they can catch," Selim said with a scornful
sniff.

Halvar let the youngsters chatter while he considered what he
had learned at Green Village. He was beginning to understand what
had happened in that small, dark shop on the waterfront, but he
still didn't understand why.

The Scavengers' Pit was lit with torches that cast dark shad-
ows into the woods and flashed on the ripples in the Great River.
Achmet was waiting to greet the returning hero, with Osman and
Rachev behind him.

"Salaam aleikum, Don Alvaro. I am glad to see that you have removed some of the aroma from your person." The Emir of the Scavengers bowed extravagantly. "Young Master Selim, I have had word
from your father, the most excellent Sultan. He has sent his personal guards, not the Town Guard, to escort you back to the Rabat."

79

Two men in the dark-red coats of the Sultan's Own Guards stepped out of the shadows, hands on their curved swords.

"He didn't have to do that," Selim complained. "I was coming back."

"Better go with them," Halvar told him. "Whatever your father has to say, listen. He *is* your father, after all."

Selim's sulky frown turned into a full-blown pout.

"Besides, I want you safe in the Rabat until we get this Robert Mortmain safely into a dungeon."

"You need me with you," Selim argued.

Ruiz stepped into the circle of torchlight with his own squad of guards.

"Selim ibn Petrus, you are ordered back to the Rabat."

"Go!" Halvar glared at Selim.

The youngster scuffed his feet in the dirt.

"I thought I could trust you, but you're just as bad as all the rest of them. No one understands me."

"Except for Leon?" Halvar shook his head. "I understand you better than you think, young Selim. Get back to the Rabat, and I'll have a word with your father in the morning. Nothing's going to be settled until then."

Selim cast a tearful glance at Benyamin and allowed himself to be marched off between two of the Town Guards, with the Sultan's Guards and Ruiz following him.

"What was that all about?" Benyamin asked. He gazed after Selim with a worried frown. "Can I help?"

"Nothing you can do about Selim, Benyamin ibn Mendel," Halvar said. He turned to Achmet. "So, Emir, do you have any news for me about our mysterious book-thrower?"

Achmet shoved Osman forward.

"This piece of dung thinks he saw something yesterday morning," he growled.

Rachev joined his comrade-in-thievery.

"He don't like to talk much," Rachev explained. "It was early, not yet daybreak. He woke me up—"

"I heard a noise," Osman whispered.

"You was snoring!" Rachev jeered.

"I was not! It was a noise, like thunder, only not thunder because it wasn't raining. I put my head out the door to see if it was still raining, because the roof leaks, and after the big storm, there was water on the floor."

"If you'd fix the roof it wouldn't leak," Rachev complained.

"I've only got the one hand." Osman waved the stump accusingly.

"This noise." Halvar interrupted what was apparently an ongoing argument. "It wasn't thunder?"

"It was a ghoul!" Osman exclaimed. "I saw it. It was tall, and it had no head!"

"No head?" Halvar echoed.

Osman nodded vigorously. Rachev frowned.

"You mustn't take him serious, Baas. He gets unhappy, and he drinks alcohol. The Prophet, may his name be blessed, is right about that. Better to use hemp."

"I wasn't drinking the night of the big storm," Osman protested. "I know what I saw! It must have been the ghoul that let loose the donkeys."

"What would a ghoul want with donkeys?" Rachev asked scornfully.

"What, indeed," Halvar mused.

"So, now that we have told you what we know, what is our reward?" Osman held out his good hand.

Halvar felt in his trousers for the string of wumpum beads he had taken with him to the waterfront. He was astonished to find they were still there. Whatever else they were, the two Amazons in the bathhouse were not petty thieves. He counted out five white beads for each of the ragged informants.

"That's all?" Rachev was disappointed at Halvar's lack of generosity.

"It's all I have. I didn't think I'd need more when I left the Rabat this morning."

"If you're forgetful, why should we suffer?" Osman added his five beads to the ones on the string that hung from the cord around his tattered robe.

"I'll remember to bring purple next time," Halvar promised the Scavengers.

Achmet accompanied him to the edge of the clearing, where the brick-paved road toward Manatas Town began.

"A ghoul! What will they think of next? I am sorry to disturb you with such ramblings, Don Alvaro, but Rachev and Osman are usually truthful."

"Thieves? Truthful?" Halvar shook his head. "But something happened early yesterday morning, Emir Achmet. I don't know what this ghoul has to do with the book that no one admits to tossing into your pit, but those two certainly saw and heard something, even if they aren't sure what it was." He looked ahead to where a donkey cart waited.

. "Keep your eyes open, Emir Achmet. Robert Mortmain is still at large, and he's a very dangerous person. Don't try to take him yourself. I want him alive!"

With that, Halvar settled his cap firmly on his head and headed for the town. Benyamin joined him for the ride back to Manatas Town.

"You can drop me off at the souk," the young man said when the donkey driver looked at them for directions.

"And then take me to the Rabat," Halvar ordered. He only hoped he'd find some more answers to the questions that had bubbled up in his mind.

Chapter 15

THE MOON, IN ITS THIRD QUARTER, WAS HIGH WHEN HAL-
var reached the Rabat. The two Town Guard on duty casually waved
him through the gate.

Ruiz was waiting for him, tapping his feet on the stones of the
courtyard. One sniff, and his nose wrinkled in disgust.

"The Scavengers said you'd been fool enough to meddle with
a sekonk. I see they were right."

"You mean I smell," Halvar said with a rueful grin. "I had to
bathe in tomatl, and it doesn't take all the stink off. I went to Green
Village and had some words with Leon about a book."

Ruiz's face stiffened. "A book?"

"One of his notebooks found its way into the Scavenger's Pit,"
Halvar said. "That's what the sekonk had."

"You got it."

"I certainly did!" Halvar's grin turned into a chuckle. "But there
were some pages missing."

"I don't suppose Leon recalled what was on them?" There was
an anxious tone in the man's voice that caught Halvar's attention.

"Leon recalls what he wants to recall and forgets the rest until
it's more convenient for him to remember it," Halvar said. "In fact,
one of the images on the first pages was of me. The book was one
of the ones he kept when he was in Al-Andalus."

"Nothing to do with Manatas, then." Was that a note or relief
in Ruiz's voice?

"Only on the last few pages. Half of the book was taken up by his notes and images of Al-Andalus, the rest was about his voyage here. Interesting, if you like pictures of half-naked sailor-boys and fish." Halvar didn't care for either "Mendel the Bookseller had some of the other notebooks. I told him to send them here. What did you and your men find in the souk? Have you got Leon's clothes and the rest of his gear?"

"My men have been through the souk," Ruiz reported. "We found some garments that might have been Leon's, but the vendors insisted they had been bought legally from the Scavengers."

"Who stole them from the taberna before you remembered to post a guard," Halvar reminded him. "Leon will have to go on wearing the fraters' robes for a while longer."

Ruiz smirked. "He won't like it, but he made his choice. It's Green Village Fratery or the dungeon here in the Rabat."

"He seems to think he'll get off this island somehow," Halvar said.

"He may think it, but unless he can fly like a birdie, he won't." Ruiz glanced upward at the sultan's quarters. "My men have also been looking for this assassin, Robert Mortmain," he said. "No sign of him in the souk."

"I've got my feelers out for him in Green Village. He can't leave the island any more than Leon can."

Ruiz thought it over. "There are ways. He could steal one of the Local's canoes and try to get across the East Channel into West Caster. He could even try to get to Mahak country."

"Not if he's connected to the Huron," Halvar pointed out. "Mahak and Huron are enemies. That's been made clear to me by our friend Firebrand."

"No friend of mine!" Ruiz sniffed. "But you're right about the Mahak and the Huron. If this Robert Mortmain is from Kibbick, he's more likely to have friends among the Huron than the Mahak, and there's a goodly distance between here and Huron lands, most of it mountains, and all of it patrolled by Mahak bands. If Robert wants to get back to Kibbick, he'll have to do it by sea."

"That means the waterfront," Halvar decided. "I want another word with our Danic innkeeper, Hannes Zilberstam. He promised me a good Danic stew. What do you say, Ruiz? Shall I treat you to a better meal than the last one?"

"If you are paying, I'll eat it," Ruiz said. "But Hannes had better obey the laws of Halal. No swine flesh, no eels."

Their culinary discussion was interrupted by two new arrivals. Dr. Moise ducked out of his quarters, and a party of Yehudit in long black coats and fur-trimmed hats were admitted through the gates of the Rabat.

"Salaam, Dr. Moise," Halvar called out. "Anything more about our late pawnbroker?"

"I was not allowed to cut, but I can tell you that whoever killed Manolo the Pawnbroker was wasting his time. The man would have been dead anyway, possibly within the year."

"What?" Halvar's eyebrows went up.

"I could feel a growth, possibly a canker, in his, um, lower male parts." Dr. Moise lowered his voice and glanced toward the entrance to the sultan's quarters, as if to make sure his voice would not carry upwards to where it might be heard by the females in the harem.

"You're sure of this?" Halvar demanded.

"Manolo was dying."

This from the man at the center of the Yehudit contingent, an aged specimen who barely came to Halvar's chest. The voice was firm, slightly rasping, even though the man was held up by the strong arm of Benyamin ibn Mendel.

"This is Rav Shimon Layzar," Benyamin announced. "He came to my father's shop when he heard the news of Manolo. He wants to speak to Don Alvaro."

"Here I am," Halvar said. "Do you want to go somewhere to sit down, Grandfather?"

"I can stand well enough," Rav Shimon Layzar said. "What I want is the body of Manolo the Pawnbroker, for proper burial."

"No!"

A third group burst into the courtyard, this one led by Jehan, with Prester Nicodemus close behind him.

"You shall not do this! My father took the water, he was Roumi Rite Kristo! He shall not be buried with unbelievers and heretics! I have come to take his remains back to the chapel, to be buried with the Kristos of the Roumi Rite, away from the heretics of the Bretain Rite and the Islim and Yehudit who deny the Redeemer's message!"

"Manolo came to me before the Day of Beginnings," Rav Shimon Layzar said. "He was worried about his health. He wanted to know whether the Eternal would receive an apostate into the World To Come. I told him that the Eternal is a forgiver of sins, even apostasy, if the penitent is sincere."

"But he took the water," Jehan insisted. "That makes him Kristo. Is that not so, Prester?"

Prester Nicodemus frowned down at the little Yehudit, daring him to deny Jehan's impassioned plea.

Rav Shimon Layzar was not intimidated.

"Manolo was born Yehudit, and so he died," he stated. "He will be buried as he wished to be buried, with his people."

"He will be buried with the Kristos!" Jehan yelled. "He must not spend eternity in the fire!"

Halvar had had enough of this.

"Manolo will stay where he is until I catch the one who put him into his grave, wherever that grave may eventually be." He glanced at Ruiz, who had stepped away from the religious dispute. "Until then, Prester, Rav, get back to your own places and leave the disposition of the law to those who have the authority here. Sultan Petrus has decided to hold a Grand Divan. This matter will be decided then."

And the sultan had better do it, he thought, *because I don't want to be around if this boils over into the kind of fighting I saw in Italia.*

The Roumi Kristos and the Yehudit grumbled at each other as guards strode forward, hands on the cudgels at their belts. Then, Prester Nicodemus and Jehan went eastward toward the waterfront, and Rav Shimon Layzar led his group west, back to the souk and the Yehudit quarter on the west side of the island.

Ruiz watched them leave. Then he turned to Halvar with his usual smirk.

"So much for the *convivencia*! Well, Hireling, shall we try the new cuisine at the Mermaid Taberna?"

Chapter 16

BY NOW HALVAR FELT CONFIDENT ENOUGH TO NAVIGATE the narrow alleys that led down to the waterfront, even though the moonlight was faint and the flickering lanterns next to the doors of the houses they passed cast shadows across the street. The narrow, barred windows of the houses were shuttered against the chilly wind that blew from the bay.

Halvar shivered in his borrowed woolen shirt. He would have to replace his old leather jacket with something more suitable to the brisk weather in Manatas if he was going to stay after the Feria. He had become used to the mild temperatures of Al-Andalus, where he rarely needed more than a jacket, even in winter.

I'm not going to spend the winter here, he told himself. *I'm going to get Leon on that boat, and I'm going back to Al-Andalus, where I know what's what and who to trust and who not to trust. And the plants don't burn, and the animals don't spray stink!*

The Mermaid Taberna was back in business. The sign swung in the freshening breeze, creaking eerily, and beneath it men in sailors' trousers and coarsely woven shirts lined up, bowls in hand, as Hannes doled out a thick soupy stew from his cauldron.

"Stay in line!" he ordered as one daring fellow tried to shove ahead. "Otherwise, no soup for you!"

"What about me, Hannes Zilberstam?" Halvar asked, in Danic.

Hannes whirled about, ladle in hand.

"Landsman!"

"I see you've got your shop set up," Ruiz commented.

A lanky Halfling lad ran up and down the line taking wumpum beads in exchange for the wooden bowls. Another Halfling doled out thick slices of bread to sop up the soup. Once served, the customers took their bowls inside, where they found seats at the tables, which had been lined up in orderly rows.

"I have," Hannes said with a wave of the ladle. "And I've had your Imam Hassan into my kitchen. Nothing but goose meat in this soup. No swine, no eels. Plenty of carrots, some of the broad beans the Locals grow, some maiz. It's good, solid food, not maiz-cake. Even the bread is good wheaten flour." He snorted his opinion of the Locals' diet.

"When you have a chance, I want to go over what you told me about Manolo," Halvar said, accepting a bowl of soup.

"Nothing more to tell. I saw what I saw, I did what I did."

"I want to hear it again," Halvar insisted.

He moved forward, ignoring the complaints behind him, accepting an earthenware mug that contained a murky drink that wasn't mokka. He squeezed into a space at the table nearest the door, easing onto a bench, and spooned up his soup with the bread. Ruiz dipped his bread into the semi-liquid stew and nibbled gingerly, not sure of this exotic dish.

"A taste of your homeland, Hireling?" Ruiz clearly didn't care for Danic cookery.

Halvar grunted his enjoyment of something that didn't burn his tongue on the way down to his stomach.

"We like our food hearty and plain."

"What can that Dane tell you that he hasn't already?"

"I don't know what it is, but I have the feeling I've missed something."

Halvar finished his soup and sipped the liquid in his mug.

"What's this stuff?"

Ruiz tasted it. "It's made from roots," he decided. "The Locals harvest them and dry them out, then make a drink out of them. Not bad, and not alcohol." He finished his mug.

Halvar decided this was one local drink he'd leave to the Locals.

"Hannes!" he called

Hannes stumped over to their table, balancing himself with his staff and by hanging on to the backs of chairs and bracing against tables. "What is it, Hireling?"

"Sit down. Tell me again what happened the night of the storm. When did the dhow put it? Was it before or after nightfall?"

Halvar pushed the bowls aside to lean closer to his informant, who collapsed onto the nearest seat.

Hannes frowned. "It must have been just before nightfall, because the captain wanted to make port in daylight, or what there was left of it. The clouds were closing in, you see, and the wind was picking up. He wanted to sell what was left of his cargo. Not that I cared—just palm fronds and citrons. Who wants citrons?"

"Tell me exactly what you did," Halvar said. "No matter how petty, no matter how ordinary. The dhow tied up. Who tied it?"

Hannes shrugged. "Some Halflings, I suppose. I was below, getting my galley stowed away and packing my bag. The captain called us all on deck, said he'd sold off the cargo, and doled out our pay. Mine was ten silver pennies from Bretain."

"Quite a sum," Halvar commented. "And in silver, too? Bretain pennies?"

"I got picked up at the South Port in Bretain. The ship had been blown off its course into Bretain waters. The captain was Franchen, the crew was Andalusian, and the cargo was Afrikan. He'd lost a few men on the voyage and needed a cook, and he wanted to make sail as soon as he could, so he took me on, cripple or not."

"So, you got across the Storm Sea to Manatas,"

"I did .In any case, by the time I got up on deck the captain was impatient to get his letters delivered. He'd got his cargo off—I could see the folk with the palm branches leaving the waterfront. I couldn't tell who they were, their backs were to me, but some of them were wearing dark coats and broad-brimmed hats. Could be Franchen, could be Yehudit.

"All I wanted was to get off that ship, find lodgings, and get a meal I hadn't cooked myself. I took my pennies and got onto the docks. I looked about, but the sailors were all gone, and there wasn't anyone to show me the way."

"The sailors' lodging-places are up the hill, behind the warehouses, on Maiden Lane," Ruiz said. "Why didn't you go there?"

"The rest of the crew wouldn't wait for a crippled man," Hannes complained. "Not even the captain. He left me to fend for myself."

"What about the taberna?" Halvar asked.

"This place?" Hannes shrugged. "It was all dark. As far as I could tell, it was closed."

"So, you went to the pawnbroker," Halvar said.

"I did. I figured that if anyone knew of a place to stay, he would. And if anyone could give me local currency for my silver it was him. If he wouldn't, I could sell my old jacket. Which I did."

"For wumpum," Halvar said. "What about the other man in the shop? What can you tell me about him?"

Hannes frowned. "I wasn't looking at him especially. He was Franchen, I could tell that much. He spoke Arabi with the Franchen twang—they all talk through their noses. He wore one of those broad-brimmed Franchen hats, pulled low over his face."

"And that didn't make you suspicious?" Ruiz sneered. "You handed over your silver pennies to a complete stranger, for a building that might not even belong to him?"

"The pawnbroker vouched for him," Hannes protested.

"And you believed the old man?" Ruiz was persistent.

"He wasn't that old," Hannes said. "Younger than me."

"Not old?" Halvar's eyebrows went up. "What did he look like?"

"Like a pawnbroker!" Hannes exclaimed. "Big nose, little eyes, stringy hair tied up behind. Broad-brimmed hat, like the other fellow."

"What color coat did he wear?" Halvar's voice took on an edge. "Light? Dark? Blue? Green?"

"It was dark, I couldn't tell what color." Hannes looked from Halvar to Ruiz. "He was the pawnbroker, wasn't he? I do own this place? I wouldn't like to think I'd paid for something and got nothing."

"You got what you paid for," Ruiz assured him.

"The man you saw behind the counter was a pawnbroker," Halvar said slowly. "But it wasn't Manolo. Manolo was already dead by the time you arrived." He turned to Ruiz. "Tenente, go back to the Rabat, and come back as soon as you can with a squad. I want to take Manolo's murderer alive to the Rabat so the sultan can pronounce sentence at the Grand Divan.

"The laws must be obeyed, even here in Manatas, or we descend into the same state as the savages of Scotia, who have no law but revenge and blood-feud."

"Then you know who killed Manolo."

"I do. And I know why. But I need a confession, and witnesses, which you and your men will provide. And leave that pistoia of yours back at the Rabat!" Halvar ordered. "There will be no more surprises like that!"

Ruiz stood up stiffly.

"You do not give me orders, Hireling," he said. "But I will do as you ask. I only hope you are right."

Chapter 17

HALVAR CONSIDERED HIS POSITION CAREFULLY AS HE FIN-
ished his stew and root-drink. He had come to Manatas with spe-
cific orders, but every time he had tried to execute those orders, he
had been blocked. He felt as if he'd been deliberately sent on a fools'
errand, an elaborate joke, like the ones played on the Spring Festival back home in the Dane-March, when folks celebrated the release
of the grip of the Frost Giants by dancing, singing, and general rev-
elry.

He pointedly ignored Hannes's glare as he took up space that
could have been used by another customer. The Mermaid Taberna
might be under new management, but the clientele was still male,
and the entertainment nil. This was a place for serious discussion,
for business, not for pleasure. There was a hum of soft speech in
which no one word could be distinguished from the general buzz,
with notes of Franchen, Erse and Danic mixed with the Arabi that
was the common language of Manatas.

Hannes stumped to Halvar's table.

"Your friend is back," he announced grumpily. "And he's brought
the rest of his company. If you're going to arrest someone, do it
quietly. I just got the blood off the floor."

"We're going to arrest someone, but not here," Halvar assured
him. "Come with me. I'll need you as witness."

"I can't leave now!" Hannes protested. "There are still customers to be fed!"

"Your lads can take care of them." Halvar gripped Hannes's arm to steady him. "Get your stick, or whatever you use. We're going to pay a visit to the pawnbroker's shop."

Hannes had little choice. He picked up his staff, yelled "Keep serving soup!" to the Halflings, and let Halvar drag him across the plaza.

The pawnbroker's door was open. A lantern swung in the wind above the door; another lit the interior. Jehan stood behind the counter. The smell of frying maiz-cake and fish wafted from the door to the room behind the shop. Clearly, he had wasted no time in setting up house with his Local woman.

"What is this?" Jehan looked from Halvar to Ruiz. "What do you want?"

"Taking care of the old man's business, are you?" Ruiz sneered. "And him still unburied!"

"That is not my fault," Jehan shot back. "I will not have my father buried with heretics and unbelievers."

"That's not why we're here," Halvar said. "I'm arresting you on a charge of falsifying an official document."

"What?" Ruiz yelped. "You haul my squad all the way here for *that*?"

Halvar pulled Hannes forward.

"Hannes Zilberstam, do you see the pawnbroker who signed and sealed the document that gives you possession of the Mermaid Taberna?"

Hannes pointed to Jehan.

"He's right there! Now, is that all? Because I've got a taberna to run!"

"You come to the Grand Divan in two days, and tell that to the court." Halvar let Hannes go and turned back to Jehan. "So," he said casually. "Did you kill your father yourself, or did you watch Robert do it?"

Jehan sputtered indignantly. From the door to the inner room, the Local woman watched, her broad face unreadable in the flickering lamplight.

"I can understand why," Halvar went on. "Here you are, a rising man among the Roumi Rite Kristos. You're not a prester yourself, but you're the next best thing—a decanus, a leader of the congregation.

"According to the Taverniers, the Franchen are taking over most of Al-Andalus. It's only a matter of time before they come here from

Kibbick. If they do, it won't just be Manolo who will be in danger, it will be you! The Questioners look into every connection, every family member, to find heresy, and if they do, it's the fire for the heretic, and the heretic's fortune for the Questioners."

Ruiz nodded to Flores, who edged closer to Jehan.

"I don't understand what moves folk to kill for the sake of their faith. It doesn't matter to me if a man prays to Ilha or the Redeemer or Manitou, or whatever the Locals revere."

"It should matter!" Jehan burst out. "My father would have burned in the fires of Sheol!"

"Would he?" Halvar shrugged. "I don't know where we go when we leave this Earth. No one's ever come back to tell us, even though the fraters say the Redeemer did. I don't believe in ghosts, either. No, Jehan, you killed Manolo for the very good reason that you wanted to save yourself from the Questioners' fires."

"He didn't," the woman said. "It was the other one, the Franchen."

Jehan tried to stop her. "Morning Star..."

"I was in the sleeping room, waiting for my man to finish with his father so we could get back to our own place before the storm. I saw it all. If you take my man, you must take me."

"I suppose it was you who stuck me," Halvar guessed. "Not helpful to your husband's cause."

"You would have taken him from me," Morning Star said.

"We'll do it anyway," Ruiz said. "Sharia doesn't allow women to testify in court."

"Come with us to the Rabat and make your man comfortable," Halvar told her. "Jehan ibn Manolo, you are accused of murder. You will be taken to the Rabat to face the Sultan and the Grand Divan in two days' time. Have you anyone to be your advocate?"

"Prester Nicodemus will speak for me," Jehan said, raising his head defiantly. "He will make you understand. What is the life of this world against the agonies of eternity? I was saving my father's soul!"

"By breaking his neck?"

"You heard the doctor," Ruiz reminded him. "Manolo was suffering from a growth, a canker, that would have killed him anyway."

"But he would have died as Yehudit!" Jehan cried out. "He would have renounced the True Faith and gone back to his unbelief! I could not let that happen. He died as a Roumi Kristo."

"No, he didn't," Halvar said. "He had talked with Rav Shimon Layzar, he had a white garment on, and he'd made preparations to observe the Day of Repentance. You must face facts, Jehan. Your father may have taken the water, but he was born Yehudit, and Yehudit is how he died.

"Take him to the Rabat, Ruiz, and make sure he doesn't die on the way. I want all Manatas to know that the laws of Al-Andalus override all else."

Chapter 18

ONCE AT THE RABAT, HALVAR FOLLOWED RUIZ AND FLO-
res to the cells on the ground floor of the central tower, where he sat
the miserable Jehan on the single stool that was the only furnishing
in a room in the middle of the row. A torch had been jammed into
a sconce near the door. Flores touched his own torch to it so the
cell was lit enough to see by, although the flickering flame sent eerie
shadows dancing along the walls.

Ruiz held a lantern in the doorway.

"What now, Hireling?"

"Get Selim in here," Halvar ordered. "I want a record of what is
said."

"At this hour?" Ruiz was aghast. "The boy is surely in his bed by
now."

"Wake him up," Halvar insisted " Flores, go get him. Selim's the
only one I trust to make a true statement of what's said. I want a document that will stand up in front of the Grand Divan. No mistakes,
no killings. No private justice. The laws of Al-Andalus will be o-
beyed!"

Flores went off, muttering, while Halvar and Ruiz stood by the
door to the cell, watching their prisoner.

Jehan sat on the stool, rocking back and forth mumbling in Old
Roumi, with his wife on the floor next to him. Halvar leaned against
the wall, his face unreadable in the flickering torchlight.

Selim arrived, dressed in a loose kaftan, breathlessly clutching
his pen-case and papers.

"You've caught the killer!" He stared at the two in the center of the room. "Him?"

"He didn't do it himself," Halvar said. "Take your pen, Selim, and write all this down."

Selim looked for some place to put his paper and pen then squatted on the floor, where he could lay out his materials.

"I'm ready," he announced.

Halvar grabbed Jehan by the front of his shirt.

"Jehan ibn Manolo, listen to me. Stop that praying for a minute. You may yet save your worthless neck from the rope. I'm going to tell you what I think happened, and you tell me if I'm right."

Jehan looked up at the stolid figure looming over him.

"Have you some special sight, Don Alvaro? Were you there?"

"No, but you were," Halvar said. "You've been telling me a pack of lies, Jehan. You said you didn't know why Manolo spent one day a year alone with his shop shut. I think you knew perfectly well it was the Yehudit Day of Repentance."

"I didn't know," Jehan insisted. "I have nothing to do with the Yehudit. Nothing! I took the water when I was a child, I've never been Yehudit!"

"Your father must have been in the fire when he changed," Halvar said. "He had burns on his hands. Did he pull you out of the fire, Jehan? "

"The fire!" Jehan's face was a mask of terror, as if he saw something he had long forgotten.

"That was long ago, and we took the water. I am a good Roumi Kristo! Ask Prester Nicodemus, he will tell you, I am decanus of the congregation!" He dropped back to the stool and rocked back and forth.

"You wouldn't be if it got out that Manolo was still practicing his Yehudit rituals," Halvar said. "So, you had to kill him, before the Franchen came down from Kibbick to take Manatas from Al-Andalus and bring in the Questioners."

"What has that to do with anything?" Ruiz asked from the doorway.

Halvar tugged at his mustache. "The Taverniers had those letters from the Franchen in Kibbick. They were supposed to foment unrest here in Manatas so it would be easier for the Franchen to take over while the folk here fought amongst themselves. That's the Franchen way.

"The Taverniers and their servants were Roumi Rite Kristos. They came to the chapel for the Holy Meal. You knew them, you heard what they said, and you thought they were right, that Imperator Lovis would send ships to take Manatas at any time, as soon as he finished his work in Al-Andalus."

"And he will!" Jehan said defiantly. "He will make this island clean again! He will scour the land of heretics and unbelievers, Islim and Yehudit!"

"What about the Locals?" Halvar mused.

"The Huron have already accepted the Redeemer and are loyal to the Imperator," Jehan stated. "They have promised their aid. They will destroy the Mahak and Algonkin and establish the Redeemer's rule under Imperator Lovis."

"No arguing with fanatics," Ruiz declared. "This man is clearly insane. No matter what happens in Al-Andalus, Lovis can't reach us here."

"He can try," Halvar said grimly. "Jehan, I'll try one more time. Did you yourself kill your father, or did you just distract him while Robert Mortmain did it? And why now? Did you know your father was dying?"

"He told me, just before he shut up his shop," Jehan said. "I'd seen him coming back from the souk. He used to go there to sit with Mendel the Bookseller, to talk about books and other things. He said he'd seen Rav Shimon Layzar and made his peace with him. He even bought a palm frond and a citron, to make the petition for a good harvest.

"I told him that he was courting disaster, that I had heard Imperator Lovis had taken most of Al-Andalus, that there was going to be a fleet sent from Kibbick before the winter storms set in, and that he was putting himself and me in danger of the fire."

"Just when did you hear all this?" Ruiz stepped closer to the wretched man. "Jacques Tavernier and his wife were killed four days ago, two days before the storm."

"The letters that came with the ship that dropped Hannes on the docks," Halvar answered for Jehan. "The captain took them to the Mermaid Taberna, not knowing the Taverniers weren't there anymore. Robert Mortmain got them, read them, grabbed whatever he could, including Leon's books, and got to the pawnbroker's shop with the news. He found you and your father fighting."

"The Franchen stopped the fighting." Morning Star said with a satisfied grunt.

"And you had a dead father on your hands," Halvar said. "Then along came Hannes, with his silver pennies, and Robert sold him the taberna. You signed your father's name and used his seal."

"I had to get rid of the old sailor," Jehan protested.

"Your father's body was behind the counter," Halvar continued. "You left it there. Then you and Robert shut up the shop, put the bar across the front door. He ran the cord of his garrote around the bar on the back door, the two of you left, and he dropped the bar down."

Jehan stared at him, amazed.

"How did you know?"

"I felt the nick where the cord bit into the top of the door." Halvar pulled Jehan off the stool. "Where did you send Robert Mortmain? He didn't stay in the Mermaid Taberna during the storm."

"I told him to go to the Scavengers," Jehan gasped. " My father sometimes would do business with them. From time to time, they came to us with things they had picked up."

"Stolen!" Ruiz sneered.

Jehan shrugged. "My father did not always ask the right questions. I would not take merchandise if I thought it had been stolen."

"But you knew Emir Achmet and his people," Halvar said. "So you told Robert to go to the Scavengers."

"They'll hide anyone for silver," Jehan said. "Go to the Scavengers if you want to find Robert Mortmain. He left the pawnshop, and I went to my own house, and then the storm came. It is an omen of war! Lovis will come, like the storm, and sweep all before him!"

Halvar had heard enough. He threw Jehan onto the floor in disgust.

"Then you came running to the Rabat with your tale of woe. You asked for me, in particular, because I'm new here, I didn't know Manolo at all, and you thought I'd take your word for what had happened to him."

Jehan picked himself up and settled back onto the stool.

"I was told the calif had sent a Dane to oversee the Feria. All the Danes I've ever met were large, stupid men who never looked beyond their noses. I thought you were the same."

"You were wrong," Halvar turned to Selim. "Do you have all that down, laddie?"

"As much as I could write," the boy said, corking his vial of ink. "What happens to him now?"

Jehan, was rocking back and forth on his stool, while Morning Star tried to comfort him.

"Not the fire, not the fire," he moaned.

"He stays here, in the Rabat," Halvar decided.

"And the woman?" Ruiz cocked an eyebrow in Morning Star's direction.

Halvar shrugged. "She's a witness."

"She saw nothing, she heard nothing, she knows nothing. Let her go!" Jehan cried out.

"Morning Star, go to Prester Nicodemus. Tell him what has happened. He has to speak for me at the Grand Divan."

Morning Star rose with dignity.

"I go to Prester Nicodemus," she stated.

"Not to Sachem Mahmoud?" Halvar asked. "Isn't he your leader?"

"Sachem Mahmoud is Islim. I have taken the water, I am Kristo! I answer to Prester Nicodemus and the Episcopus Innocente."

Ruiz tried to stop her, but Halvar said, "Go on, woman. By the laws of Al-Andalus, even the guilty deserve to have an advocate, someone to speak for them. Go, tell Prester Nicodemus what happened, and pray for your man."

Morning Star regarded Halvar intently.

"The Redeemer's blessing be upon you," she said, and left, followed by one of the guards.

"See she goes straight to the waterfront," Ruiz ordered. "You two, you stay and make sure this lunatic doesn't try to escape."

He joined Halvar and Selim in the corridor as the door shut behind them.

"What next, Hireling? It's too dark to see anything, and I have no liking for the smell of the Scavengers' Pit, with or without sekonk added to it.

Halvar yawned mightily.

"I'd better report to the sultan," he said. "And then I'm for my bed. Tomorrow, we'll get Robert Mortmain."

Chapter 19

HALVAR AND SELIM RETURNED TO THE COURTYARD, where the lanterns were sputtering, burning themselves out. They stood silently as Ruiz joined the rest of the Town Guards in their barracks.

Selim spoke first. "That man killed his father over religion. That's awful!"

"He's mad," Halvar agreed. "And he didn't do it himself, just let someone do it for him. It's Robert Mortmain we want. "

"But where is he?"

"A good question. Here's another. Why, if he knows you can identify him, are you still alive?"

"When I was in the taberna, I was Sally," Selim protested. "He doesn't know who I am."

"Let's hope he doesn't hear the news-criers announcing the sultan's young son has been found." Halvar glanced upward. "Now, young Selim, it's time for you to face your father. You've been avoiding him all day."

"I know what he's going to tell me, and I won't do it." The boy pouted.

"How can you know what he's going to say until he says it?"

"He had letters from home."

"He had letters from Al-Andalus, sure, but what makes you think they were about you?" Halvar headed for the stairs that led to the Sultan's private quarters. "You may think they had to be, but there's more in this world than you, laddie. There's a war going on across the ocean. That's what those letters are about."

They found Sultan Petrus enthroned in his Oropan chair, his ivory leg propped up on a footstool. He was draped in a striped kuton kaftan, a small knitted cap on his head instead of his usual elaborate turban. A copper pot of mokka sat on the little table next to his chair, where a packet of folded papers drew Selim's attention.

The sultan glared irritably at Halvar. Either he was about to go to bed or he had been called out of it. Either way, he was in no mood for pleasantries or politeness.

"High time you reported to me, Hireling!" he snapped, ignoring Halvar's salaam. "What is this about me holding a Grand Divan?"

"It's customary, at the end of the Fall Feria, isn't it?" Halvar reminded him. "And there are matters to be decided."

"It takes time to organize these things," Sultan Petrus grumped. "And there's nothing that needs our attention, anyway. The Franchen are dead, the counterfeiting has stopped. Gomez is gone, the frater has been avenged. What else is there?" Sultan Petrus spotted Selim. "And you! Where have you been? I want to talk to you!"

"There's the matter of Jehan ibn Manolo," Halvar pointed out.

"Ruiz just told me about that. You've done a good day's work. Quelled a riot, found a murderer, and fought a sekonk." Sultan Petrus chortled happily. "You should go to bed, rest. It's finished, done with. This Jehan will hang for the murder, that's that. The cadi will find him guilty, no need for a Grand Divan."

"It's not over," Halvar said. "There's this assassin, Robert Mortmain. He's either with the Scavengers or at Green Village. If he's at the Scavengers' Pit, Emir Achmet will sell him for enough silver. If he's in Green Village, Donal will turn him over to us. Either way, I'll have him."

"Then what?"

"Then, you can pass judgment on him. As sultan, it is your duty to act for the calif, may he have long reign.

Sultan Petrus grunted, "Humph" He tapped the papers on the table in front of him.

"If these reports are correct, your calif's reign is going to be very short, indeed. According to the captain of the last ship in before the storm, Don Felipe's been trapped in the fortress at Jebel Tarik with his mother, Lady Zulaika. No one's sure whether he's still there or

104

if he's escaped across the channel to Afrika. If he can rouse the Afrikans to join him, he could still save Al-Andalus for the Prophet. If he can't get help, he's dead meat."

"Until I hear he's dead, I am his Hireling," Halvar said stubbornly. "I do what I've been paid to do."

Sultan Petrus grunted again. "This Jehan ibn Manolo. What made you fix on him?"

Halvar tugged at his mustache.

"At first I didn't," he admitted. "But there were things that didn't sit right. When he came in that first time, he spoke of his father as if he was already gone. How could he have known that? And there were two men in the shop when Hannes Zilberstam came in. One was Mortmain. I thought the other was Manolo, but then Hannes said the pawnbroker was young, Then I knew that Jehan was involved in his father's death.

"I didn't think he'd done it himself. He's not strong enough, nor tall enough. But he is Roumi Rite Kristo, like the Taverniers and their servants, so he'd know Robert well enough to let him into the shop.

"Manolo had bought some of Leon's books from Tavernier, so it was only natural for Robert to try to sell the rest to Jehan. Jehan knew about the bookseller in the souk, so he could act as the middleman."

"But what was so important about the book?" Selim interrupted.

"Not the book itself, but one image in it." Halvar's lips twisted under his mustache. "What would happen if folk saw an image of Don Felipe in the arms of another man? And a signed image, at that, so there could be no mistaking who it was."

"No!" Selim gasped.

"Only once, and that was in play," Halvar assured him. "But it would look as if it was more intimate than it actually was. If someone were to copy that image, make more of them with a printing press, get it back to Lovis, and perhaps spread it about, it would destroy any hope Don Felipe has of getting aid from any of the Afrikans, the Ashanti or the Dahomey or the Ghana. They take as dim a view of man-lovers as the Franchen, and they're a good deal stricter about their adherence to the Prophet's teachings than the Sufis of Al-Andalus."

"And that's what this Mortmain is planning?" Sultan Petrus thought it over. "He's going to take this scandalous image back to Franchenland, where it can be copied and distributed?"

"Or he'll take it to Kibbick, which is the same thing," Halvar amended. "Wherever he is, he's not going anywhere at night. I'll find him tomorrow morning, and you can pass judgment on him at the Grand Divan."

"Leave us, Hireling. I want to have a word in private with Selim."

Halvar salaamed, shot a warning look at Selim and left the boy to his father's lecture. He grinned to himself at the cries of adolescent rage that came through the closed door. Whatever the sultan had in mind for his son, Selim wanted no part of it.

Halvar yawned again. Had it really been only a day since he'd faced the sultan's wrath? He unhooked the dying lantern from the sconce to find his way back to his own tiny cell in the Rabat.

He had done his duty. He had found the killer. He had planted the seeds of doubt in the mind of Leon di Vicenza.

He eyed the hard plank bed, the little table next to it, and his own sea-chest, the only furnishings in the room. The twinges in his shoulder and lower back reminded him he had been wounded and was only a few days out of sickbed.

The thought of the wide, comfortable bed in Leon's room at the Mermaid Taberna crossed his mind. Now, that was a bed! There was something else about that bed, something that he'd missed…

He'd think about that tomorrow…or was it already today?

Doesn't anyone in Manatas ever sleep? he thought just before he succumbed to fatigue.

Part 2

The Body
in the
Brickyard

Chapter 20

WHAT I HAVE TO DO, HALVAR THOUGHT AS HE EYED HIS scanty wardrobe the following morning, *is get back to the Feria and see what those rascally Franchen merchants are up to.*

But what was he going to wear to do it in?

There was one more jacket left from the wardrobe he had packed in Al-Andalus, a black coat tastefully trimmed in silver braid with silver buttons on the sleeves. He wasn't going to risk that being sliced, smeared with garbage or dung, or sprayed by a sekonk. It had cost far too many of his hard-earned coins, and he would need it for the Grand Divan.

He grimaced as he picked up the wool hunting shirt he had been given to replace the leather jacket sprayed by the sekonk. His original leather jacket had been returned, the slits mended with such a fantastic collection of mismatched scraps the garment was more fit for the Spring Festival of Fools than for daily wear.

To replace the jacket he'd been given a coat from the store used by the Town Guards, but that had been so tight the seams had split the first time he tried to fight in it. He had found another at the shop of Yussif the Tailor, but that one had been ruined in a fight with the maddened Lizette Tavernier. Another coat provided by Te-nente Ruiz had been ripped in the riot at the waterfront the day before.

At this rate, Halvar thought, *I should put Yussuf the Tailor on my payroll, and just have him turn out jackets and coats for me to ruin!*

On the day after the big storm Yussuf had, in fact, presented him with another coat of the tailor's own design, one with a skirt that covered his legs to his knees and with a high collar to protect the neck. Halvar regarded this garment with distaste, but it was the only choice left to him.

"You Andalusians! You wear too much."

Firebrand, the Mahak warrior, stood in the doorway of Halvar's grim little cell. It was obvious the Local had no such problems. He wore only a breech-clout, a single leather thong around his waist, his macassins, and a sleeveless vest decorated with dyed porcupine quills. His skull had been shaved except for one strip of hair that ran from his forehead to the nape of his neck. His only other decoration was the eagle feather inserted into the scalplock.

Halvar glared sourly at the Mahak but remembered his manners, even if the other man didn't.

"What cheer?" he greeted him politely.

"Good cheer, in that you are back on your feet. I heard you were taken ill."

"I was. I'm better now. As to our habits of dress, in Oropa and Al-Andalus, it's not polite to show your arse in public."

Halvar dragged his baggy woolen breeches over his braies and pulled them tight with the cord that ran through the waist hem. He buckled on his leather belt, adjusting the simple sheath that held his dagger, a businesslike weapon with a plain handle, its only ornament a lump of amber at the top. He shrugged himself into Yussuf's offering, testing its seams by stretching his arms back and forth.

It will do, he decided, and topped off his outfit with his round cap, a deceptively soft item trimmed with a plain band, that concealed a boiled-leather lining, hard as steel and much more comfortable He smoothed the mustache that swept from his prominent nose to his chin, decided that he could put off a visit to the barber for another day, and faced his visitor.

"What are you doing here, Firebrand? I thought you don't like Manatas Town."

Firebrand grinned nastily. "I come from my sachem, Gray Goosefeather. We have another body for you to take back to your own burying-place."

Halvar absorbed this news as the two of them strode out into the courtyard of the Rabat and squinted at the sudden light of the rising sun that seemed to bounce off the stone walls of the fortress.

106

It would be another fine day, although a chill breeze gave a hint of the winter to come.

"Another body? Who is it this time, another female?" The last time he'd been summoned by the Mahak to retrieve an Andalusian corpse, the trail had led to the sultan's own household, and the result had not been pleasant.

"Not female," Firebrand assured him. "Definitely not female."

"Where?" Halvar accepted a mug of steaming mokka from the Local woman who had set up a stand just inside the gate of the Rabat. He took a cautious sip, his lip twisting at the bitterness of the chicory she'd used to stretch the expensive mokka beans.

"Up-the-hills," Firebrand said, jerking his chin northward. "Where the Afrikans make the bricks to build all these square houses."

"Why send you, and why me? Can't you Mahak deal with your own murders? Tenente Ruiz is in charge of the Town Guard, why not him?"

"This is not a Mahak killing," Firebrand said. "This man is Oropan. My sachem doesn't trust the Manatas Town Guard, won't have them past the wall. He thinks you are better suited to find murderers among your people than I, and that I can learn from you how to find them. So, here I am."

The courtyard was starting to fill with people, some with business for the sultan, some who lived in the Rabat. A delegation of merchants from the Feria waited by the door to the sultan's tower. There was a mutter of apprehension when the sachems of the Mahak and Algonkins made their way through the gates, accompanied by their honor guards of young men. A squad of Town Guards marched from their barracks with Tenente Ruiz behind them.

The tall young guardsman had taken some care with his appearance. He was freshly shaved except for the small beard at his chin. His long-skirted green coat fit smoothly across his shoulders without binding, his tall tarboosh was well-brushed, and his boots were shined. He carried a regulation bludgeon at his belt on his right side and a pistoia thrust through that belt on his left side. He passed Halvar and Firebrand in time to overhear the last statement.

"What is this about a killing?" Tenente Ruiz turned to Halvar. "I am just on my way to question the prisoner Jehan about his dealings with Robert Mortmain."

Halvar was about to answer when another voice was heard across the courtyard.

"I am here, Don Alvaro!" Selim, the sultan's teenage son, fairly danced across the stone flags of the courtyard, dressed in a loose silk jacket whose sleeves fluttered in the morning breeze, worn over linen trousers that were tucked into the tops of his soft leather shoes with their upturned toes, in the latest Andalusian style. Under his small turban pinned with a flashing ruby, his round face expressed his delight in joining the adults.

He was an odd-looking youngster, with eyebrows that met over his snub nose and the beginnings of a mustache on his upper lip, a few dark hairs that seemed to flicker in the morning sunlight. He carried a small leather-bound book in one hand; his pen-case with its vials of ink and quills hung from his belt.

"So you are, but what do you think you're doing?" Halvar took another sip of mokka.

"I'm coming with you," Selim announced gaily. He smiled brightly at Firebrand, who did not appreciate the gesture of friendship.

"Who told you you could leave the Rabat?" Ruiz snapped. "You are the only one who knows what the assassin Mortmain looks like, so you should stay here, where you will be safe."

Selim made a rude noise. "I'll be with Don Alvaro, won't I?"

"What does your father have to say about this?" Halvar handed the mug back to the Local woman.

Selim wrinkled his nose in disgust.

"He's too busy doting on Lady Ayesha and the new baby to pay any attention to me. I can't stay here, I'll go mad if I do. Let me come with you, Don Alvaro. You said it yourself—you need someone with you who can read and write, to make notes."

"How do you know where I'm going?"

"It doesn't matter, just as long as it's not here."

"I thought you were going to look for Mortmain among the Scavengers," protested Ruiz.

"I may have to help this Mahak first. He wants me to look at another body." Halvar said. "We'll pass through the Feria on our way up-the-hills, as I understand it?"

Firebrand nodded.

"Then I can ask a few questions there and make sure he hasn't been seen." Halvar tugged at his mustache, then gave his orders. "Tenente, you can have another go at Jehan, but be gentle. I want him alive to testify at the Grand Divan.

"And have your men check the souk again for Leon di Vicenza's clothing and other belongings. Those thieving Scavengers must have sold them by now. Selim, if there's an Oropan or Andalusian dead at the brickyard, he'll have to be brought back here. Get a donkey cart and meet us there. Bring Dr. Moise."

"Our own shaman, Sees-in-the-clouds, is there," Firebrand objected. "He knows what to do in the case of a violent death."

Halvar snorted his opinion of Local medicine men.

"This calls for a doctor, not a spirit-seeker. If this Oropan died by violence…"

"He did!" Firebrand assured him.

"You know this how?"

Before the Mahak could answer, the voice of the muezzin rang out, announcing the first of the daily prayers—"Ilha is mighty! May all praise his name!" Ruiz knelt to say the Patri Nostri. Selim prostrated himself, as did most of the guards and Mahmoud, the Algonkin Sachem. Halvar did neither, but clutched the amulet that could have been a crux or Thor's hammer, and murmured his morning prayer: "May the Redeemer and his Mother Mara and the god Thor help me this day."

Firebrand watched the proceedings, unimpressed by Andalusian, Algonkin or Danic piety.

"Now, Firebrand, tell me how you know this Oropan died by violence," Halvar said when everyone had completed his devotions.

"He is lying there with a great hole in his chest," the Mahak stated. "His heart has been taken out of his body. Now, Hireling, you will come with me and bring him back here where he belongs, before his spirit has a chance to do any damage to my people."

Ruiz headed toward the cells as Selim trotted to the stable where the donkeys assigned to the Rabat were munching their hay.

Halvar settled his cap firmly on his head.

"All right, Firebrand. Show me this body."

Chapter 21

FIREBRAND SET THE PACE, A LONG LOPING STRIDE HALVAR tried to match, mentally cursing the coat that hampered his efforts as he followed his Mahak escort along the Broad Way.

The main road of Manatas was thinly populated this early in the morning. Worshipers at the Grand Muskat mingled with the students at the Madrassa at the mokka-houses that nestled between the large residences in which lived merchants and those who served them. Signboards had inscriptions in both Arabi and Erse letters, often accompanied by a crude picture to help the illiterate find the correct merchant. A bale indicated a dealer in kuton, a sheaf of wheat meant a grain-dealer, scales showed that the people within would explain the laws of Sharia to those unfamiliar with them.

Halvar's legs started to ache, and he felt telltale twinges in his back and shoulder, reminders of his wounds. He had not done so much walking since he had left Al-Andalus nearly two months ago. Six weeks on the dhow, four days on his back, and he was puffing away like an old man!

Firebrand didn't break stride, didn't even sweat. Halvar wished he could tell the infuriating Local to stop for one moment, but that would be a sign of weakness.

He grimly kept moving, past the houses surrounded by fences, past a section of grass where geese fed, to the Manatas Town Wall, where they were stopped by the Town Guard, and Halvar could take advantage of the halt to catch his breath.

He recognized Flores, the spectacularly ugly Guard who usually accompanied Ruiz on his rounds.

"Not with the tenente? Put you on Wall duty?" he commented as Flores waved him through.

"Tenente Ruiz wants to find the Franchen assassin Mortmain," Flores/explained. "My orders are to question everyone going into Manatas to ask if they've seen anyone like him."

"Makes sense."

"If you say so. But this Mortmain, if he's the terror you say he is, he won't be showing himself at the Feria, will he?" Flores looked at the line that snaked along the wall. "Orders are orders, but Tenente Ruiz isn't the man Tenente Gomez was, and he don't know half his business."

"You were Gomez's man."

"Gomez, he was a hard man, but Ruiz?" Flores shrugged. "He was Gomez's pen-pusher, he counted the coats and clubs at the Rabat. The only reason the sultan put him in charge was because he was handy when Gomez..."

"When I pushed Gomez into the river," Halvar finished for him. "Well, Guardsman Flores, no one's seen Robert Mortmain since the night of the big storm, but keep your eyes open. He's got to be on this island somewhere."

A Local woman burdened with a leather sack and a small bundle of firewood called out, "Are you going to stand there all day, Big Man? We have to get through!"

Halvar stood aside, and the Local woman pushed through the crowd, on her way to set up a corncake brazier wherever she could find a space. A man in a Bretain smock and trews shooed a gaggle of geese ahead of him, bound for the souk, where they would wind up on someone's dinner plate.

There was a sudden blare of a trumpet and a burst of drumming as three people took up a position next to the line that seemed to stretch clear to the Feria grounds. A young man in Bretain trews and kuton hunting-shirt darted up and down the line, handing something to those awaiting their turn at the gate while a young woman in gauzy trousers and kuton shirt jingled a tambourine. A man in striped trousers, checked coat and broad-brimmed hat trimmed with a sheaf of gobbler feathers flourished a trumpet and declaimed, "Listen, good people, as I, Willem of Cos, tell you of an adventure that befell just yesterday!" He blew another blast, drawing the attention of everyone within earshot, inside and outside the wall.

112

Halvar recognized the player who had told comic tales on his first disastrous visit to the Gardens of Paradise.

"What's this all about?"

Flores shrugged. 'Buskers, entertainers from the Gardens of Paradise. They're sure to turn up wherever they can find someone to listen to their tales and songs. They're harmless."

Willem mounted a small stand set up by his two aides. He blew another blast on his trumpet to attract more attention then began his recitation, in the style of the marketplace storytellers of Al-Andalus:

> Oh, hear my story, listeners all,
> Beware the evils that befall
> Those who disturb the dread sekonk
> A creature dangerous, though small.
>
> A sekonk found a tasty treat,
> A scrap of leather, good to eat,
> Around the pages of a book
> Tossed in Scavengers' Pit to reek.
>
> A stranger to Manatas came
> I do not know the stranger's name.
> He saw the book and the sekonk,
> And said, "This book I hereby claim."

Halvar realized where this ballad was going, but there was nothing he could do to stop it.

Willem continued:

> The Scavengers gave warning clear:
> "That's a sekonk, go not near."
> The stranger said, "I want that book,
> Of sekonk I have no fear."
>
> The sekonk stamped its two front feet,
> The first alarm, which all must heed.
> The stranger reached to grab to book,
> He would not let the sekonk feed.

A chuckle ran through the crowd. The people who held the papers with the words to the ballad started staring Halvar. He bit his lip under his mustache. It was one thing to have been sprayed by the sekonk, quite another to have his misadventure spread across Manatas!

Willem suddenly realized he had at least one member of the audience who might not appreciate his performance. He paled, gasped, then decided that if there was going to be retribution, at least he would finish his performance before punishment fell.

He took another breath, and went on:

> Then the sekonk raised its tail,
> A signal that makes strong men quail.
> The stranger said, "The book is mine,
> Against all odds, I will prevail!"
>
> The sekonk turned, and you know well
> What followed. I don't have to tell!
> The stranger cried, "I have the book!
> But what has made that awful smell?"
>
> And so the stranger got his prize,
> But I am sure, he is more wise,
> As all can tell, because the smell
> Precedes him well before your eyes.

Willem bowed, to much applause.

"Good people, if my song has pleased you, show your appreciation by purchasing a copy, written by those who witnessed the event. Only one white, for your delight!"

The girl with the tambourine collected wumpum while the lad passed more song-sheets to the crowd.

Flores beckoned the youth forward. For one bead of white wumpum, he received a sheet of paper. He glanced at it and let out a snort of laughter.

"Something interesting, Guard Flores?" Halvar held his hand out.

He had seen such things in Corduva. The students at the Madrassa would write lampoons, jokes about their classes or the teachers. They would take them to one of the printers who usually reproduced books for students to make copies, then passed them about the Madrassa, to be chortled over by their fellow students. When a noted criminal was to be executed, one of the balladeers would write a poem about his exploits, to be hawked at the execution-ground,

"Let me see."

Flores's round face turned purple with embarrassment under his scruffy black beard. His bulbous nose twitched as he handed it to Halvar. Firebrand looked over his shoulder as Halvar examined the song sheet.

"Very clever."

The paper was printed in both Arabi and Erse, embellished with a cartoon—the outline of a big fellow with a sweeping mustache and a tall cap facing a small animal with its tail raised. Wavy lines indicated a foul odor emanating from the animal. From the glances sent his way, he was now and forever identified to all Manatas as the Man Who'd Defied the Sekonk. Even if the owner couldn't read the verses, the picture told it all.

He looked closely at the ballad sheet and rubbed his fingers over it. This was the same kind of paper that had been used in the mathematics text at Mendel Bookseller's stall, and the letters looked like the ones used in that same book, both the Arabi and Erse.

The implication hit him like a blow. This must have been printed in Green Village, since, so far as he knew, there was no printing press in Manatas Town. He examined the illustration again. He'd seen something very like it recently, but whose hand had drawn it?

"Thor's Hammer!"

Firebrand stared at him as if he'd gone insane.

"What's wrong?'

"Those brats!"

"You know who did this?"

"Seekers of Truth? Hah!"

Firebrand frowned at the paper.

"This is like calling you a fool to your face. You should kill the ones who did it."

"Not worth it. As Old Sergeant Olaf told me, 'It's a poor man can't laugh at himself.' I'll grin, and bear it." Halvar handed Flores one of the white beads from the string at his belt. "I'll keep this for myself." He folded the paper and put it into the pocket of his breeches. "Now, let's have a look at this body of yours."

Chapter 22

THE FERIA WAS BACK IN BUSINESS AFTER A BRIEF HIATUS
when the big storm had torn the place apart. It had dumped tor-
rents of rain that turned the unpaved ground to a sea of mud, and
had torn the sheds and stalls with gusts of wind that also knocked
branches off larger trees and bent smaller ones to the ground. The
merchants who had come from the Southern Territories to sell their
kuton, tabac and indigo and the manufactory owners who had come
to buy them had had to wait until the ground dried to resume their
activities.

But resume them they had.

Halvar plodded after Firebrand, who'd had to moderate his
stride to accommodate the crowd. Afrikan planters in long tunics
and striped robes, Franchen in tight trousers, Bretains in colorful
shirts and trews, and Locals in a mixture of their own and Oropan
garb filled the clearing between the Manatas Town Wall and the edge
of the forest that covered most of Manatas Island. The vendors
stood behind rough tables of planks set on trestles, set under hast-
ily built canopies or inside small sheds that could be knocked
down at the end of the Feria.

Each row was designated for a particular type of merchandise,
echoing the customs of Oropa and Al-Andalus. One row of stalls
offered the brightly colored cloth favored by the Locals, woven in
mills powered by the many streams of West Caster and the Bretain
settlements north of Manatas. Another held furs, some already

tanned, some stretched on boards. There were stalls where iron tools were on display—knives ground to a keen edge and hammers guaranteed not to fly off the handle. Barrels held cured tabac leaves and salted meats and fish, preserved for the winter. Bundles of dried herbs were peddled by Local women moving between the rows, carrying their wares in tightly woven baskets. Every vendor praised his or her own goods and denigrated all others at the top of his or her lungs in Arabi, Erse, Franchen or Munsi, the trade language spoken by both Mahak and Algonkin Locals.

The smell of roasting meat made Halvar remember that his last meal had been a bowl of soup the previous night at the Mermaid Taberna, some twelve hours ago. He desperately wanted one of the Bretain sausages being grilled by a Local woman alongside the eternal maiz-cake, but Firebrand was in no mood to stop for breakfast.

"One moment, Firebrand. I haven't broken my fast with anything but mokka."

"You eat too much," Firebrand sneered. "It makes you slow. We must hurry. The sun is risen, we must get the body away from the brick-pits. It smells bad."

"Just how long has this body been lying there?" Halvar complained as he handed the Local woman a white wumpum bead and received a sausage wrapped in maiz-cake on a sliver of birch bark and a folded-birch bark cup filled with sweet cider.

"Since yesterday. The Afrikans who make the bricks found it then and went to the Bretains at Green Village for help. They sent for my sachem, he sent me to you."

"What do these Afrikans have to say about it?" Halvar consumed his breakfast while Firebrand fidgeted.

"Nothing. They are all fools. Have you finished, Hireling?"

Halvar handed the birch bark cup back to the sausage vendor, took another breath, and nodded.

"How much longer?"

"Not far."

They had reached the northern boundary of the Feria. Here, the brick-paved road ended, and the Broad Way turned into a narrow trail through the woods used by countless generations of Locals. It wound northward around huge boulders and red-leaved shrubbery. Halvar recognized burn-weed and prudently kept to the path. He wanted no part of the dangerous plant that could leave ugly reminders of its fearsome blisters

He could see the roof of the Gardens of Paradise to his left, and the Great River just beyond winking in the morning sun. On his right were the woods and the wigwams of the Algonkin. Clearings had been cut within the stands of maple and oak trees, and Local women walked among stalks of maiz, picking the ripe beans that curled around the stalks and cutting the round orange pumpkins that sprawled between them off their vines. A large dog trotted after them, a three-cornered travois strapped to his back to hold the baskets for the harvested foodstuffs.

Harvest time, Halvar thought with a sigh of nostalgia.

It was the same in the autumn everywhere, in Al-Andalus and in the Dane-March, and here in Manatas. When the leaves turned, the farmers gathered in their crops. In Manatas, the crops might be different, but farmers were farmers the world over.

They passed the beaver pond where Halvar had been shot. There, the path forked, one side heading east towards the Mahak encampment, the other west towards the river.

"This way," Firebrand ordered, heading west.

Halvar followed him down a steep incline to a clearing, where a row of conical huts had been built. Beyond them were three dome-shaped ovens, smoke curling from holes in the tops, stacks of split wood next to each one. Halvar inhaled the familiar odor of burning wood then sniffed again. He had smelled that before, but not in Manatas. It was hard to forget the stink of burning flesh in a town destroyed by an invading army.

Men and women in filthy rags were busily digging yellow clay from the riverbank, piling it onto boards where other workers could shape it into the bricks that would be fired in the ovens then set out to dry. The bricks were then carried back to the river, where they were ferried downstream to Manatas Town, where they would be used to build yet more houses.

A stout Afrikan in the long kuton tunic and twisted headdress favored by Afrikans from Egypt stepped forward, waving a willow switch to clear a path among the workers.

"Salaam aleikum," he greeted them. "I am Farouk. I am the headman here. Are you here for this body? Someone must take it away. I do not want it here."

"Salaam aleikum." Halvar returned the Afrikan's greeting. "I am Don Alvaro Danske, Hireling of Don Felipe, Calif of Al-Andalus, here at the orders of Sultan Petrus of Manatas and the sachems of

119

the Mahak and Algonkins. Where is this body, and why do you think it is the concern of Al-Andalus or Manatas?"

"Here." Farouk pointed to the ovens. "We found him here, two days ago. He is not one of us, and the folk at Green Village say he is not one of them. Therefore, he must belong to Manatas." He punctuated his reasoning with another wave of his switch.

"Two days!" Halvar was aghast. "And you left him here all that time!"

Farouk glanced at Firebrand then turned back to Halvar.

"We did not come to the ovens on the day of the storm," he explained. "The fires went out, and the wood was too wet, and the clay too loose, so we do not work at the ovens but make wooden frames for the bricks.

"The day after the storm, I send one of my people to check the ovens. The wood is wet, so he comes back to me. Then comes a woman, she says she has heard something in the night, she fears bad juju. So, I come here to show her this is foolish, that Chesu the Redeemer and his Mother Mara protect us, and I find this."

He led them to the end of the row of ovens. Halvar took one look and gulped.

He had seen corpses after a battle, bloated with gases and ravaged by animals, but this one was worse than anything he had seen before. The head was there, its eyes pecked out by crows. The arms were there, splayed out in linen sleeves, the fingers of the hands chewed away by small animals. The legs, clad in Franchen striped trousers, were there, ending in bare feet. The smell was, if anything, worse than the sekonk.

Halvar struggled to contain the rising taste of bile and swallowed hard to retain the sausage and cider he had consumed at the Feria. There was a gaping hole where the chest should have been, covered by buzzing flies and crawling with maggots.

A Mahak stood over the body. He wore leggings and a sleeveless vest, decorated like Firebrand's with porcupine quills, and carried a rattle made of a turtle's shell. Around his neck were strings of shell beads, and his head was covered with a length of cloth wound into a turban.

"What cheer!" Firebrand greeted the other Local.

"No cheer," the man said. "There is evil here." He shook the turtle rattle in the direction of the corpse to keep the evil spirits at bay.

"This is Sees-in-Clouds," Firebrand introduced him. "He is our shaman. He sees things that others do not."

120

"I see what is there, and what is not there," Sees-in-Clouds declared with a shake of his rattle.

"What do you see here?" Halvar indicated the body.

"I see a man who was not killed here."

Halvar swallowed hard and took another look.

"You're right," he admitted. "There's not enough blood. His heart was cut out but he was not killed here."

"Why take away his heart?" Firebrand asked.

Behind Farouk, a lanky Afrikan youth gasped, "Bad juju! Someone takes the heart to make bad juju!"

He made the sign of the crux and clutched a small leather bag that hung on a string around his neck.

"If you mean black magic, there's no such thing!" Halvar snorted. "Whoever did this had a good reason."

"He is insane," Firebrand said. "Insane people have no reasons."

"Oh, they do. They just don't make sense to anyone else but them."

Halvar looked up at the sound of donkey hoofs on the path above them. Selim scrambled down the steep path, leaving the cart and its driver behind.

"Dr. Moise won't come," he gasped. "He said he's got better things to do than run around Manatas looking at your dead bodies. He has living ones to attend to. I've got Frater Iosip from Green Village with me, though. I had to pass through there to get here. I thought you'd want a doctor, to certify that the man was dead, for the Grand Divan. He said he'd seen enough dead folk in Oropa to have a good idea as to what killed them, so he got his abbas's permission to see this poor fellow, and to see if he knows who it is."

A stout frater in a brown woolen robe joined the group.

"This lad told me about finding the body of an Oropan here."

"I have seen him," Sees-in-Clouds said. "He has gone to where the evil spirits go."

"I'd like a look myself." The frater squatted beside the body, his face a mask of disgust. "The bugs and flies have already laid their eggs, and the maggots are at work. I'd say he's been here two days, at the very least."

"I told you that!" Sees-in-Clouds snapped. "Do you call me a liar?"

Firebrand stiffened. "No one calls a Mahak a liar!"

Frater Iosip glared at the two Locals.

121

"I was called away from my prayers to look at this body, and I have. Now, I will return, since it is clear these two savages do not want me here."

Halvar stepped in to make peace between the contentious factions.

"I don't care who looks at this man, I want to know who he is, and what he's doing here. Brick-maker, what can you tell me?"

"We know nothing of this man, or how he came here," Farouk insisted. "We do not know who he is. We only want him gone!"

Frater Iosip shook his head. "I cannot put a name to him. I don't think I've seen him at our chapel."

Selim moved forward to get a look. Halvar tried to stop him.

"This is no sight for you, lad."

"But you might want me to make an image of him," Selim protested.

"I've seen what I have to see. You don't have to see it."

Selim, however, pushed forward then gasped, "Oh, merciful Ilha! That's Robert!"

Then, he sagged to earth in a dead faint.

Chapter 23

THE YOUNGSTER BEHIND FAROUK SPRANG FORWARD TO catch Selim before he landed in the pile of ashes that had been raked out of the oven. Halvar picked the youth up, carried him away from the buzzing flies and propped him up on a stack of bricks at the far end of the row of ovens.

"Breathe in and out, laddie," he soothed. "Let your stomach settle." He tried to loosen the cord of the shirt under the boy's silk jacket.

Selim opened his eyes then pulled out of Halvar's grasp.

"I'll be all right," he muttered, clutching his shirt closer to his chest. "It was just...awful!"

"Like I said, no sight for a lad of your years," Halvar assured him. "Are you sure that was Robert Mortmain?"

Selim nodded. "Oh yes, it's him. I could see the scar on his face." He tried to stand. Halvar pushed him back down onto the improvised seat.

"I'll look about," he told the boy. "You get your pen and paper and write what I say."

Selim unhooked the pen-case from his belt. He took a small knife from the case, sharpened a reed stylus, and uncorked a vial of ink. He opened his book, balancing it on his knees, ready to take dictation.

Halvar stalked around the brick-ovens muttering in Danic, while Frater Iosip and Sees-in-Clouds conferred over the body. The Afrikan youth resumed his task of shoveling the remains of previous fires out of the ovens and patting them into a neat pile with his long-handled shovel. Halvar squinted at the ashes.

Frater Iosip and the shaman joined Selim and Halvar while Firebrand stood guard over the body. Frater Iosip looked the lad over.

"Are you all right, boy?"

Selim smiled weakly. "I just wasn't ready to see such a sight," he said. "I'm ashamed to be such a baby."

"Not at all." Frater Iosip consoled him with a pat on the shoulder. He turned to Halvar. "This Mahak and I are agreed on a few things. For one, this man was not killed here. You may rest easy on that score," he told Farouk. The Afrikan grunted assent then turned to the young helper, who had stopped work long enough to hear the news.

Farouk applied the willow switch to the boy's legs.

"Get back to work!" He turned to Halvar. "This boy is not worth what I paid for him. He does not do his work. Look at this!" He pointed to the pile of ashes. "We must give these to the Mahak, it is what they ask of us for using this land."

Halvar studied the pile of ashes. "This stuff?"

Firebrand explained, "The women need ashes to soak maiz, but they do not like to burn the trees. This way, these people burn the wood, we get the ashes, all are pleased."

"Hmmph." Halvar poked at the ashes with his foot. "I thought the ovens weren't fired during the storm. Where did these ashes come from?"

The Afrikan lad shook his head.

"Don't know," he muttered. "I shovel ashes out. Don't ask how ashes got in."

Farouk glared at the boy.

"He is only a slave, he knows nothing."

Halvar frowned at the pile under his toes.

"Who has charge of these fires? When they go out, who lights them?"

"There is a woman who keeps one fire burning, always, in our chapel. Even in the big storm. When the rain came, all the ovens were flooded. We had fire in our houses, and that fire did not go out, so yesterday the ovens were lit, to make ready for today so that we could bake our bricks. Whatever was in this oven, we did not put it there.

Halvar listened to the brick-maker while he strolled around the row of ovens.

"You burn wood," he remarked. "But this doesn't smell like wood, Do you cook in these ovens?"

"Cooking? No, no, we have our own fires for cooking..." Farouk's voice trailed off as he realized what might have been left in that oven. "The heart was burned in our oven?"

"More juju!" the slave-boy exclaimed.

"Magic? I don't think so," Halvar assured them. "The heart was burned...I don't know why. But there has to be a good reason, and magic isn't it."

Firebrand sifted through the ashes and discovered a lump of metal. Halvar picked it up. Before he could examine it more closely, one more item fell onto the pile.

"That looks like paper," Selim said, seizing the object as it fluttered in the breeze.

Halvar took it from him and held the scrap carefully between thumb and forefinger, turning it from one side to the other.

Selim peered at it, and exclaimed, "That's Leon's writing! I'd know it anywhere!"

"The one who was besotted with my cousin Otter Tail?" Firebrand said. "What has he to do with this?"

"There's a page from one of his notebooks that's gone missing," Halvar told him. "I think we may have found it."

"It's burnt," Selim pointed out.

"Not quite burnt," Halvar corrected him. "The fire wasn't hot enough, or maybe this bit of it wasn't close enough to the flames."

Selim turned the paper over and squinted at the image.

"I don't know what this is," he said. "It looks like a piece of a person. A toe, maybe?"

Halvar retrieved the scrap and turned it around.

"A piece of a man, definitely. Not a toe." He grinned to himself then said, "If this is what I think it is, it may explain a lot." He took the ballad out of his breeches pocket, carefully folded it around the scrap, and tucked it back into its hiding place.

"There's a pile of dung up here," the guardsman in charge of the donkey cart called from the path. "There hasn't been any rain since the big storm, so the tracks of a cart are still here, too."

"The killer brought the body here in a donkey cart, tipped the cart over so the body fell down behind the ovens. Then he came down himself to make sure it was hidden, took the heart, which had been wrapped in paper, and put it into the oven to be burned," Halvar said.

"But the paper didn't burn?" Selim asked.

"That's the trouble with fires. They don't always burn the way you want them to. This little scrap may be enough to hang a man." Halvar turned back to Farouk. "Brick-maker, help us get this body up the hill onto our cart. You have done well to send for me before the animals got to this body.

"This was an evil man. He was an assassin, he took part in the murder of the pawnbroker Manolo. I know not how many more murders in Oropa can be laid at his door. He would have reached an evil end in time. He should have been brought to trial, so that his crimes would be punished by lawful authority. Someone decided to play judge before I could get to him, to bring him to Sultan Petrus for the Grand Divan."

"Not me!" Farouk protested.

"Not you, nor any of your people," Halvar assured him.

"Then, who?" Selim scrambled up the steep path, back to the trail that led to Green Village and Manatas Town.

Halvar frowned. "I'm not sure yet. But I will have the murderer before Sultan Petrus at the Grand Divan, and he will face the justice of Al-Andalus."

Together, they made their way back to the cart and followed it back to Green Village.

Chapter 24

THE ENTIRE POPULATION OF GREEN VILLAGE CAME OUT to greet the arrival of the cart from the brickyards, to gawk at its awful burden and chatter about what had brought the man to such a dreadful end. Craftsmen in breeches, trews or trousers, their leather aprons around their middles; housewives in long skirts of wool and linen covered with linen aprons, their hair neatly tucked under white caps; small children in clothes cut down from their elders'. A few dogs trotted over to see what was happening, and the geese in the common hissed their disapproval of having their grazing disturbed, while the sheep continued to munch the grass.

Halvar stood beside the cart and considered what he should do next, while Firebrand assessed the gathering audience with his usual impassive stance. Selim gazed over the crowd from his seat next to the donkey-driver, relishing the attention.

Abbas Mikhail came out of the fratery to greet Frater Iosip.

"I heard there was a hue-and-cry for a Franchen assassin escaped from Manatas Town. I also heard a body was found in the Afrikan brickyard. Is this the man?"

"It is," Frater Iosip stated. "According to Don Alvaro, he was Franchen, and he was Kristo, but Franchen are Roumi Rite"

Halvar didn't see what difference it made in the disposition of the dead man.

"You've a dead-house here? Take him there and examine him carefully."

127

"We have a place at the fratery where the dead are prepared," Frater Iosip admitted. "But I cannot take this…this person there."

"He's dead, isn't he?" Halvar wasn't about to argue fine points of theology.

"We are of Erse Rites," Abbas Mikhail said loftily. "We do not wish to be associated with those of Roumi Rites. They subscribe to heresy."

"Whatever heresy he had, he's past it. He's met whatever awaits him beyond the grave, good or bad. Considering what I know about him, he's either roasting in Sheol or freezing in Niflheim. What I want is someone to examine him as soon as possible."

"To what end?" Frater Iosip asked. "He is dead, there is no doubt about that."

"I want to know what made him dead," Halvar said stubbornly.

"His heart was cut out," Firebrand pointed out.

There was a gasp of horror from the people crowding around the cart, and Halvar heard murmurs of "witchcraft" and "Devil's work."

"I know that," Halvar told Firebrand. "I want to know what else happened to him. He didn't just sit down and let someone butcher him."

Frater Iosip considered this.

"He was Kristo, even if he was a Franchen. He must be taken to the Kristo burying ground."

"But not before someone has a good look at him," Halvar said. "Inside and out."

"I cannot cut into him," Frater Iosip protested.

"Someone else has already done it," Halvar pointed out. "I want you to tell me whether there is any sign of what killed him."

Abbas Mikhail and Frater Iosip exchanged exasperated looks. Then, Abbas Mikhail nodded his assent.

"Frater Iosip, by all means examine this poor body, and let him be buried as a Kristo," he said. "I will not associate with the heretical Prester Nicodemus of Manatas Town, but the Redeemer's blessing is always upon those who honor the dead."

"And I want another word with Frater Leonidas," Halvar added, pressing his advantage.

"If you must," Abbas Mikhail said with a sigh. "You are distracting him from his work. He is decorating our refectory with a most interesting image of the Redeemer and his followers."

"Shalom, Halvar Danske!"

Halvar turned from the cleric to see Dani Glick at her usual post just inside the iron fence that surrounded the Gardens of Paradise, her Bretain bodyguard Donal behind her. She was in her daily dress of a close-fitting dark jacket and full skirt, her hair neatly tucked under a white linen cap edged with lace. Her bland expression gave no sign of their encounter the previous day.

"I see you've found another body for your collection."

"Not my idea," Halvar said, strolling to her. He noticed an addition to the formal garden, a ramshackle structure that looked like a canopy of branches held up by four poles, with leafy branches forming insubstantial walls. "The sultan and the sachems think I'm the only one on this island who can solve murders. Whenever one pops up, they call on me."

"But you're so good at it!" Dani said with a sly grin. Then she turned serious. "Halvar, I think I may have some information for you. Come along."

She beckoned him through the gate and led him to the back door of the main building, where a buxom, fair-haired young woman waited for them.

"Karina, here, has been telling her friends ghost stories that have everyone spooked. Maybe, just once, she's telling the truth."

Halvar studied the girl. She looked like many of the Oropan farmers' wives or daughters with a round face, snub nose, blue eyes, and fair hair braided into a crown on her head, wearing the linen blouse and multicolored skirt favored by Bretain women. Under the shirt, her pert breasts heaved with emotion, unbound by bodice or bands.

"Ghosts? Goblins? Ghouls?" Halvar asked. "Djinn?"

"I don't know which," Karina said in Erse-accented Arabi. "It was two days ago, the morning after the big storm. We didn't have much custom that night—everyone stayed in their own houses, and the merchants were worried about their goods—so Fru Glick let us all go up to our beds early.

"Then, around daybreak, I woke up to go to the necessary, and I heard a noise. I thought it was thunder, that the storm had come back, but there wasn't any rain. I went outside, and then I heard another noise, like wheels on the path. I looked out of the necessary, and I saw a cart, and the Death Angel was driving it. I stayed inside the necessary so he would not find me." Karina clutched at the crux hanging around her neck.

Dani snorted her derision at the girl's superstitious fear.

"If the Death Angel was looking for you, he'd know where to find you, no matter where you were."

"Death Angel? How do you know?" Halvar asked.

"I could see his wings behind him."

He blinked at this description.

Dani Glick would have none of it.

"This is nonsense. How could you see anything? The torches were burnt out." She turned back to Halvar. "What do you think, Danske? Is this girl telling the truth or not?"

"She just might be," Halvar said slowly. "Your girl heard a noise that woke her up early in the morning. Then she saw a cart go past. A pair of thieving Scavengers heard a noise two days ago, and their donkeys went loose. According to one of them, there was a ghoul with no head about."

Karina's blue eyes widened. "Black witchcraft!" she gasped.

"Don't be daft!" Dani snapped.

"That poor fellow's missing his heart," Halvar said, gesturing towards the hideous burden in the cart on the common. "There's got to be a reason for it."

"Lunacy?" Dani shrugged.

"I don't think so," Halvar said. "But until I have a doctor take a good look at our friend Robert Mortmain, I won't know for sure."

"Robert Mortmain? The Franchen you were looking for so eagerly? Is that who it is?" She called out to Donal, "Did you ever hear of this fellow, Mortmain?"

"Franchen, was he? A pack of them came from Kibbick and set up shop at the Mermaid Taberna two years ago. We are Bretains, we don't deal with Franchen." Donal snorted his disdain of upstarts who came to Manatas to take custom away from Green Village and the Gardens of Paradise.

"But there are Franchen here in Green Village," Halvar observed, looking at the varied garb and hearing the mixed chatter of the people in the crowd.

A group of teenaged boys had emerged from the chapel school, jeering at the donkey driver and trading insults with Selim. The sultan's son stayed on the cart, trading insults with the Green Village boys while the girls hung back, avoiding the cart and its horrific burden.

"Some," Dani admitted. "They came to get away from the Questioners, or to be able to practice their trade or their craft without hindrance. Merchants, to be sure, come south to buy tabac for the folk in Kibbick. The scum that haunt the Mermaid Taberna, they can stay on the waterfront."

"The Mermaid Taberna is under new management," Halvar informed her. "A Dane, one Hannes Zilberstam. He serves soup and mokka."

"Good luck to him," Dani said. "But it's nothing to do with me, and I had nothing to do with this Robert Mortmain."

"I don't suppose you had anything to do with this, either?" Halvar pulled the offensive lampoon out of his pocket.

Dani glanced at it. Her lips twitched in a brief grin.

"Have you read the verses?"

"I've heard them. They're clever," Halvar admitted. "What I want to know is, where is the press that printed this paper?"

"Printed?" Dani's eyebrows rose.

"I know when," Halvar went on. "It had to be overnight, because I had my meeting with the sekonk yesterday, and this was on sale this morning in the Feria. And I know who wrote it, because I saw them giggling over it yesterday. Fast work, Dani Glick. But where did you get this paper? It's not like the stuff they use in Al-Andalus. It's rougher, and it's yellower."

"My, my, how observant you are, to know the difference between two grades of paper. One would not have thought it of a coarse Danic soldier."

Halvar said sharply, "I can take a joke, even at my own expense, but I tell you, Dani Glick, I will find that printing press, and when I do, there will be consequences."

"*If* you find it!" Dani shot back. "And let me remind you, Halvar, that this is Green Village. We are not under the rule of the Calif of Al-Andalus. We answer to the sachems of the Mahak and Algonkin, and they don't care one way or the other about what gets printed or who buys it. They don't have writing themselves, although they're starting to understand the need for it. There's talk of a glossary, a word-book, that lists useful phrases in Munsi, Erse and Arabi, for traders up-the-river. Someone has actually made such a list, I do believe."

She stared past him to where Selim and Firebrand guarded the body of Robert Mortmain.

"Useful," Halvar echoed. "And as long as you keep to books about numbers and words in Munsi, there won't be any objection in Manatas. If there are other things, nasty tales of doings at the court in Corduva, or libels against Lady Zulaika, then there may be some trouble."

Dani smiled sweetly. "Oh, I don't think nasty stories about the calif and his dear mother are libels."

"Ahem!"

Halvar turned to the source of the interruption. Frater Iosip had made up his mind about the final destination of the late Robert Mortmain.

"Don Alvaro, I will examine this man at the fratery," he declared. "You may attend."

"Good," Halvar said. "Because I want a word with Frater Leonidas about an image he made a while ago." He strode over to the cart. "Selim, once we get Robert to the fratery dead-house, I want you to take this cart back to the Rabat and wait for me there. I am going to have some more words with our friend Leon, and then I will shake some truth out of those rascals at the Scavengers' Pit. Tell Tenente Ruiz to meet me there."

"I will go to my sachem and tell him what we have learned," Firebrand said. "I will meet you at the Scavenger's Pit. If they do not want to tell you what they know, they will tell me!"

He stalked off into the woods that surrounded the settlement.

"How does he do that?" Halvar wondered aloud as the Mahak seemed to vanish into the shadows. "No matter. I have to talk to Leon. He knows more than he's telling me."

Chapter 25

HALVAR WATCHED THE DONKEY CART HEAD BACK TO-
wards Manatas Town; he only hoped the wayward youth would
do as he was told. He tugged at his mustache as he considered what
he knew of that youngster, then shrugged. He would deal with Selim in due time. Right now, he other maiz-cakes to fry!

The bell of the fratery chapel rang to signal the noon prayer. Halvar clutched his amulet and recited his rubric: while the rest of Green
Village population knelt to recite the Patri Nostri. That done, he followed Frater Iosip and Abbas Mikhail into the palisade that surrounded the fratery compound.

He hesitated, not sure which to tackle first. He felt there was
something he had missed about the dead man, but it would take
Frater Iosip some time to examine the body. Leon was alive and might
even be willing to talk.

Halvar found Leon hard at work in the refectory, where the fraters were eating their noon meal of bread and cheese. The artist had
placed a short plank on two trestles to form a small table, where
he had laid out the pigments Selim had managed to salvage from
his rooms before the big storm. He had made a preliminary drawing of the Redeemer and his followers having their Holy Meal before the Roumi came to take the Redeemer to his death, and stood
on a ladder, using a brush made of a reed to trace the image onto the
wall over the stand where the lector read from the Holy Book while
the fraters were at their meals.

Leon eventually acknowledged Halvar's presence.

"What do you want now, Hireling? I'm busy!"

"I see. Very interesting image."

"Look at it, you ignorant Dane! What do you see?"

"Men at a table. Very lifelike."

"Precisely!" Leon stepped back from his work. "When I am finished, it will look as if we are sitting in the same room with the Redeemer and his followers, eating with them."

Halvar had no time for art.

"I want you to look at this piece of paper."

He thrust the folded ballad and the scrap of notebook at him. Leon unfolded the ballad, scanned it and grinned.

"Clever fellows! And the illustration, too. I didn't know the lad had it in him."

"You didn't draw it?"

"Not my work," Leon said. "But my student, nonetheless. Only a few lines, but the essence was captured. Quite an achievement for one so young."

"Selim?"

"Of course. I don't think he wrote the verses, but he definitely did the picture."

"So I thought." Halvar grinned under his mustache. "I know who wrote it."

"Then why are you bothering me again? I told you, I'm not going back to Al-Andalus, so don't try to persuade me. I have work to do here."

"That's as it may be. I want you to take a look at a piece of paper with your writing on it I found in an oven at the brickyard. I think it may be part of one of those missing pages from your notebook."

That was enough to turn Leon away from his painting.

"My notebooks? The ones that were stolen from my rooms? Have you found them!"

"Some of them," Halvar said. "The ones that were sold to Mendel the Bookseller in the souk are at the Rabat. The one the sekonk got, I gave that back to you."

"And it was not appreciated by my fellows here at the fratery," Leon grumbled. "It reeks of sekonk." He wrinkled his nose.

Halvar handed him the scrap of paper that had fallen from the ballad when Leon unfolded it. "Take a look at this," he ordered. "Can you tell me anything about it? Such as, who belongs to the bit of man on one side, and when you wrote what's on the other?"

Leon took the scrap between finger and thumb and held it up to the light.

"I can't say for sure," he admitted after scrutinizing both sides. "This could be almost anyone. It's not as if I keep a record. There's something I wrote about little girls on this side, so I think this piece might be from that last page, the one that got torn out, not the one that was carefully cut."

"Written before or after you got to Manatas?"

"Written just after, I should think." Leon edged back to his painting. "What difference does it make?"

"It could be the reason a good man committed a heinous murder."

"That's not my concern," Leon said. "I've got work to do, Hireling. Go away, and let me do it."

Halvar stood back and regarded the faces of the men depicted on the wall of the refectory.

"Interesting," he commented. "I've seen some of these people in Manatas and Green Village. The one in the middle is the Redeemer, of course. Don Felipe would be flattered to know you're still using his image. That's Cormack MacCormack, the Bretain ironmonger, and that's his son Padraig. The big fellow next to the Redeemer is Donal, the bouncer at the Gardens of Paradise, and this youngster looks a lot like Benyamin ibn Mendel. I see you've put the big Afrikan blacksmith Malik in there, and even poor Otter Tail." He squinted at one more image, at the end of the table. "Now, there's a face I wouldn't think to see in one of your paintings. That's Tenente Ruiz."

Leon shrugged carelessly. "I paint what I see. I draw images from life."

"I didn't know you knew Ruiz."

"He was at the Rabat when I first came to Manatas." Leon added another line to his drawing.

"And this fellow, all the way at the other end of the table, the one who's going to betray the Redeemer, the one with the bag of coins, that's Jacques Tavernier," Halvar pointed out. "You spent the last year at the Mermaid Taberna. Did you have any dealings with the servers, Henri and Robert?"

"Who cares about servers?" Leon sneered.

"Someone killed Robert two days ago," Halvar informed him. "Dumped his body in the brickyard, took out his heart, and burned it."

"Ugh!" Leon shuddered. "Whoever did it must be mad. Well, Halvar Danske, it wasn't me. I have been right here. Abbas Mikhail won't let me leave this compound." He carefully measured some powdered black stuff into a dish and added a few drops of water to make ink, dipped his improvised brush in the mixture, and turned back to his work.

"I don't think you did it. I think you know who did."

"What difference does it make? This Robert was just a server in a taberna."

"He was also a Parigi assassin, probably responsible for killing the pawnbroker Manolo," Halvar said.

"So if he's dead, it's one less criminal to worry about in Manatas. Whoever killed him did you a favor, saved Manatas Town the cost of a trial and execution."

"It was not done according the law," Halvar said.

"What do you know of laws, you Danic dunce?" Leon turned to face him. "Do you think because you attended a few classes with Don Felipe that you know anything about laws? Don Felipe hated having you there, you know. He called you Fidus Achates, the Faithful Dog, set there by his mother and grandfather to watch his every move."

"It was the Old Calif, Don Carlus, who hired me to guard his grandson after I saved the boy's life in a tavern brawl, and I did just that," Halvar stated. "I am still the Calif's Hireling, doing what he tells me to do. I have been paid in gold reales to bring you back to Al-Andalus, along with the silver and goods from the Feria, and that is what I will do.

"Like they say, 'You buy the Danes, the Danes stay bought.' Our slogan in the Company was 'Semper Fidelus,' Faithful always. We do what we're paid to do, no shirking, no shuffling, no shifting off to a better paymaster. I've been bought, I stay bought, and I'll keep at you until I get you onto that dhow. Your letter said you wanted to go back home, didn't it?"

"A very long speech for a man who doesn't speak Arabi," Leon jeered. "And I don't want to go back, not just yet. I have things to do, places to go."

"I learn fast," Halvar said. "I remember, too. I can see it now, you and Don Felipe on the docks. He cared enough for you to give you something for your voyage. A fine rosewood box with a handgun in it, crafted by a gunsmith from Pistoia."

"I suppose you were the one who found the gunsmith," Leon sneered.

"I was," Halvar said. "Don Felipe said he wanted you to have protection from savages and wild beasts."

"And there are none of them here," Leon retorted. "Manatas Town is safer than Corduva in that regard."

"Whatever happened to that pistoia, Leon?"

Leon's face went blank again. "I don't recall."

"I didn't see anything like that box or the pistoia that was in it when I checked your rooms at the Mermaid Taberna. It wasn't among the things Tavernier sold to Manolo, and he would have sold it if he could. A thing like that is too dangerous to keep, to easy to identify. So where is it, Leon?"

Leon shrugged. "I may have left it at the Rabat when Sultan Petrus decided he thought more of the opinions of bigots like Mullah Abadul than of the advantages to having me near his child. I may have thrown it away."

"Did you give it away?"

"What does it matter? Go away, Hireling. I have work to do."

"I'll be back," Halvar promised, and left Leon to his painting.

Chapter 26

HALVAR STOOD OUTSIDE THE REFECTORY AND CONSID-
ered his next move. There were questions to be asked, people to see,
and less and less time to do it before the Feria ended and with it, whatever small authority he had over Manatas and its inhabitants.

One of the fraters interrupted his thoughts.

"Don Alvaro? I am come from Frater Iosip. He sent me to bring
you to our dead-house. You wished for him to examine the dead
man from the brickyard?"

"I did."

He followed the frater across the compound to a shed that was
almost the exact replica of the one in which Dr. Moise conducted his
business at the Rabat. It reeked of death; its furnishings were sparse,
consisting of a rough table in the center of the room, shelves along
the sides that held mysterious jars and bottles of unnamable po-
tions, and a rack of sharp instruments. A lantern hung from the ceiling beam to focus light on the table.

The only difference was a crux over the door, whereas Dr. Moise
had painted an inscription from the Prophet's Holy Book on the
wall over his instruments.

The man on the table in the middle of the room lay on his back,
naked, covered only by a small cloth over his privates. Frater Iosip
had removed the insects and their maggots to reveal the gaping
hole in the chest. Halvar swallowed hard and stepped forward for
a better look.

"What can you tell me about this man?" he demanded.

"He is most definitely not Islim or Yehudit," Frater Iosip stated. "But you knew that. As to what killed him, all I can say is that it must have been aimed at his chest. There are no wounds anywhere else. Bruises, marks of having been thrown over the escarpment, and the marks of animals that tore into his flesh, but that happened after he was dead. Old scars, yes, there are those, on his back where he had been whipped badly at one time, and this one across his forehead that took off his eyebrow, but these are from some time in the past. They are quite healed."

"What about that hole in his chest? What made that? What kind of knife?"

"Hard to tell. There are cuts made after he was dead on his inner organs, where the heart was removed, but the edges of the wound itself are ragged. If I did not know better, I would say he had been in the way of a musket, but that, of course is impossible. As far as I know, the only muskets on Manatas are the ones here in Green Village, and this man was not killed here."

Halvar tugged at his mustache as he digested this information. Frater Iosip went on with his analysis.

"His shirt and trousers are Franchen-style, to be sure. There are spatters of blood on the shirt, but none on the trousers. No coat, no hat. None found at the brickyard, either."

"Where are his shoes?"

"Not here. Nor did we see them at the brickyard," Frater Iosip forestalled the next question.

"No shoes, no coat, no hat," Halvar muttered.

"As you said, he was killed elsewhere, brought to the brickyard, dumped over the escarpment, and left for the animals."

Frater Iosip wiped his hands on a cloth laid out on the examining table. "We will bury him with Bretain Kristo rites. Not Roumi!"

"I don't think he cares one way or another now," Halvar said.

"I wish I could tell you more," Frater Iosip said. "I am not one to cut into him, so I cannot tell you what he ate, or when. I leave that for the unbelievers and scoffers at the Madrassa in Manatas. All I can tell you is that whatever killed him was enough to blow this hole in his chest."

"A musket or pistoia," Halvar summed it up. "Which, according to Sultan Petrus, is not allowed in Manatas Town."

"That doesn't mean there isn't one."

"I suppose some of the Franchen captains have muskets on board," Halvar said. "And I know of one person who has a pistoia in Manatas Town. The question is, did any of these people have reason to kill Robert Mortmain? If they did, how did they know where he was? And why kill him at all?"

"Those questions I leave for you to answer," Frater Iosip said, adjusting his spectacles. "I hear the bell calling me to prayer. I wish you success, Don Alvaro. This was a shameful death."

"No death is ever good," Halvar muttered.

"You shouldn't be chasing about up-the-hills," Iosip scolded. "Your shoulder is still sore. Sit down so I can replace the bread poultice."

"I don't have time," Halvar protested.

"You will have less time if you don't!" the frater warned him.

Halvar allowed the fierce physician to apply a new bandage to his wounded shoulder. He was still muttering to himself when he left the fratery.

He strolled back to the common, where he found Padraig Mac-Cormack, waiting for him with Mollie hitched to a small cart.

"Selim found me in the Feria. My father let me have the pony and the cart, and told me to take you wherever you wanted to go," Padraig explained.

Halvar eyed the large redheaded lad then pulled the offensive lampoon from his pocket.

"Before we go anywhere, laddie, I want you to tell me about this. I've heard the ballad. Not the grandest poetry in the world, but enough to get folks laughing. The picture tells the rest."

Padraig flushed under his freckles.

"It was a joke," he stammered. "The words aren't mean, just funny."

"I suppose so, unless you're the one being made fun of. Seekers of Truth shouldn't mock their elders. It's not mannerly." Halvar folded the paper and put it back under his coat.

"How did you know it was us?" Padrag quavered. "Me and Benyamin and Selim?"

"Had to be. You three were there when I faced the sekonk, along with the Scavengers. The Scavengers don't read or write, but you write Erse, and Benyamin writes both Erse and Arabi. Trouble with being clever is, you want to show how clever you are. Whose idea was it to make the copies and sell them at the Feria?"

Padraig glanced toward the lights that were beginning to glimmer beyond the iron fence of the Gardens of Paradise.

"Fru Glick heard us laughing while we were writing down the verses, and she thought they were funny. Then Selim drew the picture, and Fru Glick asked if we would let her make the copies."

"On the printing press she keeps in the attics?" Halvar hinted.

Padraig nodded. "We all know it's there."

"So you let her have the verses."

Padraig's guilty grin faded.

"She offered us a bargain. If we let her print the copies, she'd pay us, for the verses and again for every ten sold, a white wumpum. My father is always telling me I should pay more attention to business and forget about attending Madrassa. He thinks my making verses is useless."

"How much have you made off this business venture so far?"

"Fru Gluck gave each of us three white wumpum, and I've got six more for the ones got sold today. We didn't mean to make you angry," Padraig said. "But it was funny, seeing you with the sekonk..."

"Damage is done," Halvar sighed. "I don't take offense. Just be careful who you mock, laddie. There are some folk in Manatas Town who aren't as forbearing as I am." *And Dani Glick has her revenge for what happened in the bath. What did Old Sergeant Olaf tell me?* "Never make a woman angry; they'll always get back at you."

Padraig nodded toward the pony cart.

"Where do you wish to go, Don Alvaro?"

"Back to Manatas Town," Halvar decided. "I want another word or two with those Scavengers. That Emir knows a lot more than he's telling."

"Shalom!"

"Salaam, Dani Glick." Halvar strolled to her, noting the progress made on the odd-looking booth behind her. "Making improvements to your Paradise?"

"Only for a week," Dani said. "It's our Harvest Festival time. What have you found out about our mysterious man in the brickyard?"

"Only that he was killed by whatever blew the heart out of his body, and that he'd been badly whipped at one time. A thief, an assassin, not much of a man by all accounts," Halvar said. "So. Dani Glick, what would happen if I were to go up to the very top story of your great house? Would I find your printing press?"

142

"You don't dare enter this house unless you are invited," she told him. "If you go where you are not wanted, Donal will remove you from the premises. The law of Green Village is Bretain law, not Sharia."

"And if I get a writ, a legal paper that authorizes me to examine your Gardens of Paradise?"

"You get such a writ from the one designated by the sachem Gray Goose-Feather as Master of Green Village, who happens to be Donal. He, of course, is Master because the sachem's council has taken the advice of their women, who trust me to keep him in line."

"The women?" Halvar had never heard of women being openly in control of public matters. Even Lady Zulaika, the formidable mother of Don Felipe, kept her manipulations hidden under the veils of the harem.

"It's how the Locals govern themselves," Dani explained. "The sachem may be a man, but it is the women who choose the sachem. They want the wisest, bravest of the warriors to keep them safe. The Mahak don't understand why someone claims to own land they don't farm, and since the women farm the land, the women own it, and they determine who rules it. They've chosen me to run the men of Green Village. I suppose they thought that if I survived being held by the Huron and escaping in the snow, I could do anything."

"I think you can do whatever you set your mind to," Halvar assured her. "If you wanted to run a printing press, you would find a way to do it. And you may be sure that I will do everything I can to find it."

"Oh, I'm sure you will," Dani said with a wry twist of her lips. "But what do you intend to do about it?"

"Depends on whether what you're printing is going to harm Don Felipe. But that's not why I'm here. I'm here to bring Leon di Vicenza back to Al-Andalus, together with the silver from the Feria. Don Felipe needs both of them if he's ever going to keep Imperator Lovis out of Al-Andalus."

"What if you're too late?" Dani shot back. "We have our sources of information here in Green Village. We know what's going on back in Oropa. Al-Andalus is finished, Halvar Danske, and your little calif, Don Felipe, is as good as dead. What happens then?"

"I'm sworn to protect Don Felipe," Halvar said slowly. "Until I see his dead body before me, I keep my word."

Dani Glick made an exasperated noise.

"Then you're a fool, Halvar Danske."

"Maybe so," Halvar retorted. "But I am a loyal fool. I am going to get Leon to Al-Andalus, and I am going to get Don Felipe his silver."

"Don Felipe's silver is one thing, Leon is another," Dani said. "Getting the silver back to Al-Andalus depends on the winds and tides, and whether or not your ship sinks, and assuming that the will of Adonai or Chesu or Ilha is in your favor. Leon, on the other hand, is his own man. You'll have to do a lot of persuading to get him out of that fratery where he's taken refuge."

Halvar grinned nastily. "I may not have to do too much persuading. He's taken up painting again, but only the Redeemer and his Mother Mara know how long he'll keep at it before he's distracted by something else. And he's going to get tired of wearing Beggars' Order robes and sandals once the winter cold sets in, and the constant praying will get on his nerves. Oh, yes, Dani Glick, Leon will be begging me to get him out of the fratery and onto that dhow by the end of the Feria."

He strode back to Padraig and the pony cart. The sun was halfway through its daily journey, and he had a lot to do before darkness closed in on Manatas once again.

Chapter 27

THE SCAVENGERS' PIT WAS AS NOISOME AS EVER. NOW that he was not distracted by sekonks, Halvar observed that the Scavenger's settlement consisted of an assortment of buildings lined up in the shadow of the Manatas Town wall, some built of mismatched stones cemented with mud and clay, some of boards that showed signs of charring, some in the Scanian style of logs notched together to form a square cabin. Emir Achmet sat on an imposing Oropan chair, presumably rescued from that same fire as the boards, in front of an Andalusian-style house whose bricks were plastered over with lime-wash.

He exuded shabby dignity in a kaftan that was once elegant but now showed its age, his turban decorated with a cheap brooch. Behind him hovered two women, their faces modestly veiled; before him was a low table with a battered copper mokka-pot, a set of brass mokka-cups, and a bubble-pipe.

Achmet rose when he saw Halvar and salaamed with extravagant politeness.

"Don Alvaro! Back again! To what do we owe the honor this time?" He motioned toward the trench. "The sekonks have been removed."

"I want to take another look at this place," Halvar said, hopping off the pony cart. "I didn't get much chance yesterday."

"It is not much to look at," Achmet said, surveying his modest domain. "We are poor folk here. We provide a most necessary service to our town, and we allow the good followers of Islim and the Prophet the opportunity to fulfill the commandment to give alms to the poor and destitute."

"You don't seem too destitute," Halvar commented, gazing at the emir's impressive house and more impressive girth.

"All made from materials others discard, I assure you. Wood from houses damaged by storm or fire, bricks that others will not use."

Halvar paced along the footpath between the trench and the pits.

"Your beggars have their place in the world," he said. "What about the thieves?"

"Thieves?" Achmet was horrified. "None of my people would steal! To remove a few unwanted items from an abandoned house, to take a neglected item from one who cannot value it, this is not stealing."

"The Law thinks otherwise," Halvar reminded him. He continued his search. "But that's not my business. It's up to Sultan Petrus and Tenente Ruiz to enforce the laws of Al-Andalus."

"And well they do it, too," Achmet said with an oily smile. "Now that Tenente Gomez has gone to a just reward, Tenente Ruiz has taken measures to see that all is kept within the bounds of Sharia."

Halvar stopped at the end of the trench.

"Padraig," he called. "Bring your pony over here!" He pointed to a patch of coarse grass where the wall ended.

Mollie had other ideas. She jerked her head away from Padraig when he tried to hold her bridle and whinnied loudly as she approached the place.

"That's all I wanted to see," Halvar said as Padraig calmed the pony. He squatted to take a better look at the ground. "There's blood here. It's soaked in, but there hasn't been rain since the storm, and it's still here."

"Here?" Achmet echoed, edging away from the spot.

"Robert Mortmain, the Franchen assassin. His body was found at the brickyard, but he was killed here, at the Scavengers' Pit."

"But how did he get from here to there?" Achmet sputtered.

"Your own men, Rachev and Osman, claimed to have seen something evil just after the storm," Halvar reminded him. "And the donkeys had got loose. My guess? Someone put the body into a donkey cart, hitched up one of the donkeys, and hauled the body away before daylight. He didn't latch the paddock gate properly, so the other donkeys got out, and those two rascals had to catch them He strolled back to the settlement. "I want to have another word with Osman and Rachev."

"They are out on their own business," Achmet protested.

"Find them!"

"To what end? Osman is daft. He was badly treated in Al-Andalus, lost his hand, and was transported here with Rachev when the Old Calif decided to empty the jails to make room for new prisoners. You can't believe him. You said it yourself—they are liars."

"Osman saw something the day after the storm," Halvar said firmly. "A ghoul, with no head, bending over the dead man."

"I tell you, they are not here!" Achmet all but shouted, glancing at something just behind Halvar.

Halvar turned to find the men in question ambling up the path. When they caught sight of him, they made as though to run, only to find their way blocked by Firebrand and two Mahak warriors armed with small hatchets.

He's done it again, Halvar thought. *You don't see those Mahak until they're right upon you!*

"What is this? You have the Mahak working for you?" Achmet sputtered.

"We do not like having dead Oropans thrown on our lands like refuse," Firebrand said. "You will take him back!"

"We didn't do it!" Rachev declared.

Osman cowered behind his taller, thinner partner.

"I told you, it was the ghoul!"

Halvar looked them over.

"I see you've changed your coat, Rachev," he observed. "It's a fine one, too." He stroked the sleeve that ended well below Rachev's fingers, noting the braid on the cuff. "Franchen style, good wool, well-cut. And Osman, your hat is new. Franchen, too. Made of beaver-fur."

Osman put up his one good hand to touch the offending hat.

"It's useful, keeps the sun out of my eyes," he protested.

"I *found* the coat," Rachev insisted, pulling away from Halvar's hands.

"Where?" Firebrand's voice was hard with menace.

"Inside Ismail's old house," Osman quavered. "He died of the ague, and no one wanted to have his place until it was properly cleaned out."

"Someone was there during the storm," Rachev corrected his friend. "I saw a light."

"It was the ghoul," Osman insisted. "He stayed in Ismail's house. I saw him. He had no head. He came out of the house to the donkey paddock."

"Take off the coat, Rachev. I want a good look at it." Halvar held out one hand.

"It was left behind," Rachev grumbled. "The one who had it didn't want it."

"Because he'd been killed," Firebrand snapped. "By you!"

"Not by us!" Osman yelped. "We didn't do it, the ghoul did it. We saw him bending over the body, didn't we, Rachev? He had no head!"

"What you saw was a man with a very tall hat," Halvar said. "And he'd been inside one of these huts. Where did you find that coat?" His voice rose to an insistent bark.

"Why didn't you sell it, you greedy bastards!" Achmet roared in anger. "You know the rules! Sell what you can, hand the money in, I make sure all share in the profits."

"It's a fine coat, and I need one for winter," Rachev whined. "We sold the shoes. Here's the wumpum." He handed a string of white beads to his leader, who pocketed the offering with the air of one who must put up with fools.

"The coat, Rachev!"

Rachev slowly slid his arms out of the sleeves and handed over the garment. Halvar examined it carefully, while Firebrand eyed the three Scavengers, daring them to try to run.

"There's something inside the lining of this coat."

"What has this Oropan coat got to do with the dead man in the brickyard?" Emir Achmet asked anxiously. "What could be inside it?"

Halvar peered at the hem then inserted a finger into a small gap in the stitching. The Scavengers gasped as he withdrew a folded paper from the lining.

"It's been wet through—it's still a little damp in the corners." Halvar unfolded the paper to reveal what had been a drawing and was now a smear of ink. "Whoever wore this got soaked in the big storm."

"What was it?" Achmet asked, trying to peer over Halvar's shoulder.

"Nothing, not anymore," Halvar said, refolding the drawing and shoving it into his breeches pocket to join the bit of Leon's artwork and the ballad-sheet. "It's the coat I'm interested in. And the shoes and hat." He was relentless. "You took them, didn't you?"

"Yes, I took the shoes and the hat, too," Rachev confessed. "I tried the shoes, but they had high heels, so I couldn't wear them. Osman needed a new hat."

Halvar smelled the coat.

"No sekonk on this," he said. "But it smells of black powder."

"And this tells you...?" Firebrand asked.

"It tells me what killed Robert Mortmain, and why the killer had to burn the heart," Halvar said slowly. "But I still don't know why the man was killed in the first place."

"Burn...?" Achmet's face turned gray. "The heart was burned, you say? You found it?"

"But you knew that, didn't you? You were the only one the killer could count on to help him get the body into the donkey cart."

"I?" Achmet's face turned from gray with fear to red with anger.

"If I look into your strongbox, will I find Bretain pennies?" Halvar asked. "For that was the price of Robert's sanctuary here during the storm. He came here, he asked for help, you gave it, and then betrayed him to his killer."

"I did not betray him!" Achmet protested. "And I did not kill him! I have no pistoia, no musket! You may ask any of my people!" He looked about wildly for support and found it only in Rachev and Osman. The rest of the Scavengers were gone from the pits.

"You will tell us who did!" Firebrand stepped forward, his hand on the war-club at his waist.

Before the terrified man could speak, a squad of six Town Guards marched up the path to the pits, headed by Tenente Ruiz in full regalia, pistoia at his belt, bludgeon swinging at his side.

"Achmet the Scavenger, whom some call Emir!" Ruiz announced. "You are to come to the Rabat with me to give evidence about the murder of the Franchen, Robert Mortmain!"

"But I did not do it!" Achmet yelled.

"You do not deny that he was here." Ruiz advanced on Achmet.

"He might have been," Achmet reverted to his usual oily obsequiousness. He turned to Halvar. "He came on the night of the big storm, soaked to the skin, as you said. Could I turn him away? I could not, in all good conscience, and by the Prophet's command to take in the stranger. I gave him food and drink, I allowed him to use the house left by the death of one of our number, I had a fire lit for him."

"How long was he here?" Halvar asked. "He didn't leave during the storm?"

"Who would go out in such a downpour? The wind fairly took the roofs off the houses!" Rachev noted.

"I told you the roof leaks," Osman complained. "After the storm, I looked out, and I saw the ghoul, and the donkeys got loose."

"So you said," Halvar mused. "I want to see this hut where Robert stayed."

"Why bother?" Ruiz snapped. "Enough of this nattering! Achmet called Emir, you are charged with harboring a fugitive from the Sultan's Justice. You will come with me to the Rabat for further questioning."

He nodded to his men, who lowered their halberds.

Achmet shrugged. "I see I have no choice. If you insist, I will go to the Rabat, but I swear by the Prophet's beard, I did not kill that man." He turned to Rachev. "You will see to things in my absence. Go to the Muskat, you know what to do there." He turned back to Ruiz. "You wasted no time, Tenente. You are a worthy successor to Tenente Gomez."

With that, Achmet was surrounded by the Town Guards, and they set off down the path toward the Broad Way and the Rabat.

Halvar followed at a slightly slower pace than he had taken earlier that morning. Beside him, Firebrand mused over what he had seen and heard.

"I don't understand you Andalusians. What has that slimy emir to do with Tenente Ruiz?"

"More than you know," Halvar said. "What's more important is that we make sure Achmet gets both in and out of the Rabat alive. I have a few questions for Tenente Ruiz concerning his investigations."

"I will come with you," Firebrand decided. "To make sure this Achmet does not escape."

Together they marched down the Broad Way, bringing up the rear of what was becoming a rowdy procession through Manatas Town.

Chapter 28

THEY PROCEEDED SOUTHWARD ALONG THE BROAD WAY, gathering followers as they went. The arrest of so notable a figure as Emir Achmet the Scavenger set tongues wagging in the mokka-shops and brought traders out of their offices. Halvar could sense eyes peering out from behind beaded curtains and wooden shutters in the houses where Andalusian women were sequestered.

He suddenly realized he had lost track of the calendar. It must be Frigg's day, what the Andalusians called Gathering Day, *It's the Islim Holy Rest Day, when they present themselves at the muskat for prayer and to hear the imam or mullah discourse on the Prophet's teaching in the Holy Book.*

Sure enough, there was Mullah Abadul, tall and grim, in his long robes and high turban, standing in the door of the Grand Muskat, ready to deliver his weekly sermon. Around him stood other imams, including the testy little imam from the waterfront muskat, Hassan.

The crowd in front of the muskat included well-dressed merchants, students in their shabby coats and trousers, and Scavengers in their beggars' rags. Behind the men were women, some in full burka, some led by Eva Hakim and her Sisters of Fatima, their green hijabs making them conspicuous in the crowd.

The press of people in front of the Grand Muskat brought the procession to a halt.

"Make way!" Ruiz barked out. "Make way here!"

"In the name of Ilha, the all-merciful, may his name be praised!" the muezzin intoned.

"I said, make way!" Ruiz repeated.

"What is this, that interrupts the service of the Prophet?" Mullah Abadul glared at those who dared disrupt his oration.

"This man is being taken to the Rabat to be questioned in the matter of the death of the Franchen, Robert Mortmain," Ruiz announced. "He is a murderer and a thief!"

"That has yet to be proved," Halvar put in.

"It will be," Ruiz retorted. He faced Mullah Abadul. "I arrested this man in the name of our Sultan Petrus, who represents the Calif Don Felipe of Al-Andalus!"

"On what evidence?"

"There was blood at the Scavengers' Pits. The dead man's clothing was found there, in the possession of two of the Scavenger Emir's henchmen."

Halvar winced as Ruiz strutted defiantly in front of his squad. This wasn't the way he'd do things, but, as Ruiz so often said, it wasn't his place to object.

"The Prophet will not welcome those who spill innocent blood into Paradise," the Mullah stated. "If the man was killed at the Scavengers' Pits, then the one in charge should answer for it."

"The Franchen was no innocent! He was an assassin, and an infidel Kristo," Achmet retorted. "I am good Islim. And I didn't do it!"

In the crowd, the Scavengers began to move towards the muskat. Halvar noticed that some of them held baskets filled with debris from the streets.

"I don't like this one bit," he muttered to Firebrand. "There are too many of those Scavengers and not enough Guards."

"To kill an infidel is not so bad as to kill one of the Faithful," Mullah Abadul conceded.

"He came to me in the storm. Does not the Prophet tell us to give aid to the weary traveler? To provide for the hungry? Do not my people allow all good Islim to follow the Prophet's teaching to give alms to the poor?" Achmet waved his arms at the assembling Scavengers.

"You do such a service," the Mullah agreed.

"And this Mahak and this Kristo Dane are my accusers!" Emir Achmet pointed at Halvar.

"Will you let them take me to the Rabat?"

Halvar tried to take control of a situation that was getting out of hand.

"This man is being taken to the Rabat for questioning," he announced. "That is all."

"I am accused of murder!" Achmet shouted. "By infidels and pagans! Will you let an innocent man be taken to the Rabat?" He looked intently at the crowd, silently directing certain individuals to take their places.

"Is there proof of this man's guilt?" Mullah Abadul glared at Halvar.

"There is proof that murder was done at the Scavenger's Pits," Halvar stated. "And that the fugitive, Robert Mortmain, was taken in by said Scavengers. The body of Robert Mortmain was found somewhere else."

"In what way does this implicate the Emir of the Scavengers?"

Halvar tugged at his mustache in frustration. The last thing he wanted was to conduct his investigation in public, under the eyes of a crowd led by this fanatic mullah.

"He was there. He sheltered a man who was a known assassin," Ruiz put in. "Let us pass! We will take him to the Rabat, where he can be properly questioned."

"Tortured, you mean!"

Halvar tried to find the source of the cry. He caught sight of the large Franchen hat that Osman had appropriated. If Osman was in the crowd, could Rachev be far behind? He spotted other Scavengers moving forward, pressing the others ahead of them.

"How was I to know he was a murderer? Do I have the gift of second sight, that I should look into a man's soul?" Achmet's voice rose to a screech. "I took him in, I gave him food and fire, and this is how I am repaid? Does the sultan, in his Rabat, think that I, a poor Scavenger, have no say in my own future? The Prophet said that all men must be judged fairly! I am being accused by pagans and Kristos! Will no Islim speak for me!"

The muttering grew louder. The Scavengers in the crowd surged forward.

Ruiz and his Guards took up positions around Achmet, their halberds at the ready.

"Away with the infidels!" someone in the crowd shrieked, and a stone flew over the heads of the guards.

It was the signal for an attack. Knives and cudgels, fists and feet, even donkey dung was used as a weapon as the Scavengers tried to overpower the Town Guards surrounding their leader. Halvar had his dagger out, slashing a path through the mob to reach

Achmet before his Scavengers did. Firebrand lashed out with his war-club, laying one man low, while Ruiz jabbed his sword at the nearest Scavenger. Halvar dodged a clod of dung, only to be hit with another one between his shoulders that sent him staggering forward. Behind him, he heard shouts and screams.

Suddenly, shockingly, there was silence. Ruiz and his men were left with their halberds pointing at empty air, and Halvar's newest coat was covered in slime and donkey dung. He wiped muck off his mustache and surveyed the street.

Mullah Abadul had gone back into the Muskat, the loungers back to their mokka-shops, the students back to the Madrassa. The bodies of two Scavengers and one other man were left unmoving on the street while others stirred feebly, groaning from their wounds.

For a riot, it was well-organized, Halvar thought as he assessed the situation. Only two dead, and those from stones, not from the Guards' halberds.

The third man looked like a merchant, dressed in a kuton kaftan and turban.

"There will be a reckoning," Halvar muttered grimly. "Ruiz, get your men back to the Rabat, and have someone pick up those two. Find their families, let them know what happened to them. We'll have to go back to the pit later, after I have another word with that pawnbroker, Jehan."

He stalked down the Broad Way. There were things going on in Manatas, he now fully understood, that meant trouble for Al-Andalus; and Sultan Petrus would have to answer for the disorder.

Chapter 29

HALVAR SEETHED ALL THE WAY BACK TO THE RABAT, tramping stolidly beside Ruiz; Firebrand had slipped away again, to report to his sachem. He waited until the squad was through the gates to unleash his fury.

He followed Ruiz into the Guards' barracks, where the newly appointed tenente had a small private room, a luxury denied the other guards. He watched as Ruiz divested himself of pistoia and sword, before exploding with pent-up rage.

"What were you thinking, Tenente?" he shouted at the Andalusian. "To march in and arrest that Scavenger Emir, and then to parade his sorry arse through the town? To shame him in front of his own people? Or were you trying to show all Manatas just who was now Tenente of the Town Guard?"

Ruiz stood, hands on hips, his head thrown back, defiant.

"Who are you to criticize me, Hireling? Do you think you are the only one in Manatas with the ability to solve crimes?" he retorted. "It was clear to me that the Scavengers were guilty."

"Just how do you reason that? What led you to the Scavengers?"

"I read young Selim's report, about the doings at the Scavengers' Pit yesterday. I sent my men out to the souk to see if there was anything there that shouldn't be. They found the Franchen's shoes, at the stall of a certain Yehudit vendor who specializes in used clothing. "The vendor confessed he'd got them from Osman and Rachev, the Scavengers. It was enough for me. I took my men, and there they were, those two thieves, in the stolen coat and hat. Where would they get them, if not from Mortmain?"

"That doesn't mean they killed him, only that they found his coat, hat, and shoes," Halvar countered. "And it doesn't excuse your foolishness, giving that mullah an excuse to start another riot. Lovis's agents have been busy in Al-Andalus pitting Kristo against Islim, and factions against factions, starting riots against the calif the better to take over during the disorder."

"That's politics, and it's in Al-Andalus. This is about murders, and it's here in Manatas." Ruiz straightened his tarboosh. "As you have said so often, Don Alvaro, you are not here to solve murders. You are supposed to be looking after the Feria and chasing Leon di Vicenza. I don't see much success in either effort."

"Leon's in the fratery," Halvar conceded. "And the Feria's not in my hands right now. I leave it to the tallymen to make a correct accounting. Once that's done, I'll take ship and get the silver back to Don Felipe. As for solving murders, you were the one who asked for help with Manolo's death, and the sachems called on me to take care of the body in the brickyard."

"And now that's all settled," Ruiz said. "Robert Mortmain killed Manolo, and the Scavengers killed him."

"Why?"

"For the hat and coat and shoes, of course. What does it matter why they killed him? Mortmain is dead, and the Scavengers did it."

"Which ones? Achmet? Perhaps he took care of the body for the killer, but he didn't do the deed himself. Osman and Rachev? Witnesses, perhaps, but not killers, not a one-handed man. And there's that story Osman told me, about the ghoul."

"Lies, fancies. A man befuddled with hemp or drink, wakened from sleep—"

"By what? A noise, he said, like thunder." Halvar stopped shouting and tugged at his mustache. "And the girl at Green Village—"

"What girl?"

"A whore. She also saw something odd that morning, right after the big storm."

Ruiz shrugged. "Women can't testify in court, no matter what they saw. No, Don Alvaro, it's clear to me the Scavengers were responsible for Mortmain's death, and they will pay for it. I'll see Achmet hanged."

"Those Scavengers may be thieves, but they're also cowards. They don't steal big, and they don't risk their necks. Osman's al-

156

ready lost a hand, Rachev's missing fingers. Kill a man for his clothes? I don't think so, Tenente. There's more to this than a simple robbery. And it doesn't explain where Leon's notebooks come in."

"The notebooks?" Ruiz looked puzzled. "Oh, those. I suppose Mortmain took them to Mendel to get money to bribe the Scavengers into getting him to Green Village, where he could find passage back to Kibbick with the rest of the Franchen traders."

Halvar shook his head. "I don't think so," he said. "I want to have another word or two with Jehan."

"What for?" Ruiz sneered. "The man's gone mad. I spoke with him this morning while you were off with that Mahak, and all I got from him was Roumi Rite gibberish."

"You're Roumi Rite yourself, aren't you?"

"I was educated at the Waterfront Chapel," Ruiz admitted. "And I attend the Holy Meal at the chapel. But Jehan's ramblings are useless. He's convinced his father's death was necessary, that the old man was going back to his Yehudit ways, and that they'd both face the fire when Lovis took Manatas for himself."

Halvar tugged at his mustache. "He thought the Franchen were on their way here?"

"Apparently." Ruiz shrugged, dismissing any notion that the pawnbroker's ravings made sense.

"Then I really want to talk with him," Halvar decided. "Take me to his cell, Tenente. I want you there as witness. If there's treason here in Manatas, I'll have to let Don Felipe know about it when I get back to Al-Andalus."

"If you get back," Ruiz murmured.

He led Halvar to the prison in the lowest story of the large central tower of the Rabat. A guardsman lounged at the entrance to the row of cells.

"Nothing to report, Tenente," he said. "Not a peep out of him since you left."

"Let us in," Ruiz ordered.

The guardsman unhooked the ring of keys kept hanging from a peg driven into the bricks of the Rabat wall and strolled down the corridor. He chose one key and carefully turned it in the large lock.

Halvar took one look inside the cell.

"Too late. He's dead."

"What? How...?"

The guardsman and Ruiz both rushed into the cell, where Jehan lay, his head at an odd angle.

"Someone got in here and killed him the same way Manolo was killed," Halvar said.

"But that's impossible!" the guardsman sputtered. "I was here all the time! No one's been in or out but Tenente Ruiz, and he said Jehan was alive when he left."

"He was breathing," Ruiz said. "And you heard him, Shaul. When I left, you heard him. He was muttering to himself, you heard him."

"I did that," Guardsman Shaul agreed. "He had to have been alive then."

"Well, he's not alive now," Halvar said. "Send for Dr. Moise. I want to know exactly how he died, and how long he's been dead."

"I suppose we'll have to tell that Local woman of his," Ruiz said, shifting uncomfortably from foot to foot.

"More to the point, we'll have to tell the sultan," Halvar pointed out. "He's not going to be happy about this."

"He's going to be less happy about the riot in front of the Muskat." Ruiz sighed. "We'd better go face him, Don Alvaro. Old Silverleg blows up, but he calms down again fast enough. We just have to ride out the storm."

Chapter 30

SULTAN PETRUS WAS IN HIS AUDIENCE CHAMBER ON THE upper floor of the central tower of the Rabat. The peppery old soldier stamped up and down, his ivory peg-leg ringing against the floorboards, kicking cushions and small tables out of his way. An Afrikan servant cowered in one corner, while young Selim observed the scene from behind the large chair at the head of the sultan's table, where packets of paper held down a large map.

As soon as they appeared in the doorway, Petrus lit into them, his voice loud enough to be heard in the courtyard below.

"Tenente Ruiz, I thought you knew better than to arrest Emir Achmet without my approval!" he roared. "I appointed him, I should have been informed!"

"I did not think it necessary to take you from your other duties for such a small matter," Ruiz said, no doubt hoping to soothe his master.

It didn't work.

"I am not so busy that I can't be told someone as important as Emir Achmet is going to be charged with a serious crime!"

"A Scavenger? Important" Ruiz sneered.

"A vital part of this community!" Sultan Petrus roared. "Until I got those Scavengers under control, this place reeked of donkey dung and worse. Achmet keeps things going! He has the scavengers organized, he makes the streets safe."

"He also keeps petty thievery down," Halvar observed. "Your former Tenente, Gomez, told me how well Achmet's people kept thieves away from the Feria. I suspect he and Emir Achmet had a little agreement going, that your Emir of the Scavengers made sure thievery was petty and no one got robbed who couldn't afford it."

Sultan Petrus tugged at his beard.

"That is not the point. I want to be informed when you make an arrest, Ruiz! I did not appoint you to your post so that you could run Manatas yourself, as Gomez tried to do."

"As you say, Excellent Sultan." Ruiz bowed. His face was bland, but Halvar could see tension under that thin mustache, and the clenched jaw that meant words being choked down.

"There's something else," he put in. "The pawnbroker's son, Jehan ibn Manolo. He's dead, killed in his cell."

"What? Murder here, in the Rabat?" The Sultan again looked ready to explode. "Ruiz, I want no torture here! It never works, I don't care what they say in Corduva. Confessions made under torture are worthless! The accused will say anything to make the pain stop, and half the time it's wrong."

"And the other half?" Ruiz asked.

"You don't know which half is wrong and which isn't," Sultan Petrus told him.

"Jehan wasn't tortured," Halvar said. "His neck was broken, the same as Manolo."

"That's impossible!" Ruiz said. "Robert Mortmain must have been dead by then. It's in young Selim's report." He dragged the youngster forward. "Show them, boy!"

Selim opened his notebook to the appropriate entry.

"That's right. According to the brickmaster, the body was found yesterday, and the two medical men said it had been dead at least two days."

Halvar tugged at his mustache, his forehead wrinkled in thought.

Sultan Petrus stopped pacing to look at his offspring.

"Got all that down in writing, did you?" he said, a note of approval in his voice.

Selim nodded. "I made a record of everything said and done at the brickyards," he said proudly. "And at the Scavengers's Pit the day before, when Don Alvaro was looking for Manolo's killer."

"I've had a look at that report," Ruiz said. "It's accurate. With drawings, too. A good job, lad."

"Selim's right handy with his pen," Halvar added.

Selim fairly glowed in the light of his elders' praise.

Sultan Petrus collapsed into his chair, his fury spent.

"Tenente Ruiz, I want you to find out what happened to this pawnbroker, and why he was killed."

"That's obvious," Halvar said. "When we took him, he must have recognized someone who had been on the waterfront that night, just before the big storm broke."

"Someone who was doing something he shouldn't have?" Selim piped up.

"Or someone who was working with Mortmain, and Jehan knew it," Halvar said. "Jehan had to be silenced."

"But...who? And who knew how to do it?" Selim asked.

"I'll have to think this over," Halvar said.

"While you do, I'll have Dr. Moise look at poor Jehan, and then get the body to the Waterfront Chapel," Ruiz said. "With your permission, Excellent Sultan." He bowed to the sultan.

"Get the wretch out of here," Sultan Petrus ordered. "I want to talk to Don Alvaro alone. Selim, think about what I told you!"

Selim and Ruiz bowed again and left Halvar to face Sultan Petrus by himself.

There was silence for a whole minute. Then the sultan said, "What is going on here, Don Alvaro? I heard you were looking into those allegations by Leon di Vicenza claiming I stole money from the Feria to build the Manatas Town Wall."

"Whose idea was it to build that wall, anyway?" Halvar wanted to know. "It doesn't seem to be doing much good. I found at least two ways to go around it, and the guards at the gate in the middle are more of a hindrance than a help. They sleep when they're supposed to be on night duty, they let anyone in or out, and they hate having to do the job, so they do it sloppily if they do it at all. It's not much of a defense against small beasts, those sekonks and opassoms and araghouns that eat at the Scavenger's Pit."

"Especially the sekonks!" Sultan Petrus let out a crack of laughter.

Halvar nodded. "You've heard."

"And seen the verses. Clever, my Selim."

Halvar would not be deterred

"But the wall? That cost money, and time, and it's all for nothing, as far as I can tell."

Sultan Petrus shifted uncomfortably in his chair.

"There was a palisade when I got here, put up by my predecessors to keep out the wolves and bears and other large beasts, and to mark the boundary between the territory ruled by Al-Andalus and that of the Locals. All I did was enlarge what was already there, and reinforce it so it would withstand the wind and rain.

"The stone was quarried locally. The bricks were castoffs. And the manpower? Scavengers, beggars, thieves set to useful work instead of being hanged or sent into the wilderness to starve. We don't waste anything here in Manatas, Don Alvaro. Not even people. I am proud of my work here. I will leave Manatas Town better than I found it, with the Prophet's help, may his name be blessed."

Halvar nodded. "You seem to have done a good job of it, Excellent Sultan, even with Tenente Gomez nipping at your heels. I'm not here to spy, but I'll put in a good word for you when I get back to Al-Andalus."

"If you get back," Sultan Petrus corrected him. "There's news from Al-Andalus, from the latest dhow to get through. Imperator Lovis is up to some new tricks. He's got ships out looking for our dhows, stopping whatever they can, confiscating cargoes, taking our seamen, and stranding the officers without food or water on the nearest island, to starve or die of thirst."

"Nasty, but that's Lovis for you," Halvar commented.

"He can't last forever." The sultan sighed.

"What happens when he goes? He's been on the throne since I was a lad, and that's nearly twenty years."

"He's got two sons, Enrik and Carlus," the sultan said gloomily. "Enrik is leading the army in Al-Andalus—latest word is he's taken Madrid and is setting himself up there. Carlus is in charge of Parigi while Imperator Lovis is in Rouma consulting with Episcopus Innocente."

"Where is Don Felipe?" Halvar leaned over the table, wishing he could read the twisting Arabi script before him.

"No one knows for sure. The last anyone saw of him, he was in the fortress at Jebel Tarik with Lady Zulaika. My First Wife Lady Maryam sent me these letters."

"I hope all is well with your family," Halvar said to be polite.

"Maryam has the care of the estate, and my eldest son is with her. When she wrote these, the estate wasn't in any danger—we're too high in the mountains for an attack to be worth the trouble—but she's trying to make alliances with other families, to protect what we have. A marriage would cement ties between our family and one in the south where Lovis's troops haven't managed to infiltrate."

"A marriage?" Halvar echoed. "Selim?"

162

Sultan Petrus shrugged. "I leave such things to Lady Maryam. She knows who's who and what's what, and she's better at politics than I am. If it wasn't for her, I wouldn't even be here. She got me posted here. She even got Ayesha to keep me company, a sop for an old man."

"But you're no old man!" Halvar jerked his head to indicate the harem on the floor above them. "Your new daughter will be the delight of your life and, with the blessings of Ilha, more to come."

Sultan Petrus's stern expression softened.

"True. It would serve Lady Maryam right if I came out of this better than she." He straightened in his chair. "Don Alvaro, when you get back to Al-Andalus...if you get back...you may tell Don Felipe that I held Manatas together for Al-Andalus."

"Manatas Town, or the whole island?" Halvar looked at the map on the table, a rough outline of the island on which they stood. "It seems to me there are at least three different standards here. There's Al-Andalus here in Manatas Town where Sharia law rules. There's Bretain law in Green Village, which is set apart from Manatas Town. And the Locals have their own laws and rules and customs, and they have their own ways of enforcing them. If Robert Mortmain hadn't been killed at the Scavengers' Pit, he'd have taken refuge in Green Village, where you couldn't touch him. Those brickmakers owe their rent to the sachem, not to Al-Andalus or Green Village. This doesn't make sense for such a small island as this one."

Sultan Petrus nodded agreement. "Quite so, Don Alvaro. I met with the sachems of Mahak and Algonkin today to sort this out, before the Grand Divan."

"In that case, Excellent Sultan, may I have your leave to go and find something to eat? It's been a long day, and I still have things to do before I'm ready to call this matter of Manolo's killer settled."

"What about this Franchen assassin, this Mortmain? What about *his* killer?"

"I think I know who did that. I even know how. I'm not too sure why, and I don't want to arouse suspicions until I do. With permission?"

"Oh, do what you have to do, but don't kill anyone else doing it."

Sultan Petrus waved Halvar out. As he stepped onto the landing, Halvar heard the thump-thump of the ivory leg going up the private stairs to the harem.

Chapter 31

HALVAR STOOD OUTSIDE SULTAN PETRUS'S DOOR AND considered what he should do next. A growl from his midsection reminded him he hadn't eaten anything since the sausages at the Feria. A meal was definitely called for.

A voice brought him out of his reverie.

"Don Alvaro! I've got the report ready." Selim had been waiting for him to emerge from his conference with the sultan.

"Have you, indeed? Who else knows about it?"

"I went over it with Tenente Ruiz," Selim said. "And my father, of course."

Halvar thought this over as he maneuvered down the twisting stair to the courtyard.

"Where can I get something to eat?" The Local woman was still there with her maiz-cake and mokka, but he needed something more substantial to fuel his thought processes.

"The barracks cooks usually have something on the fire," Selim told him. "Ever since Leon left, I'm supposed to take my meals with them."

"Not in the harem?"

"I used to." Selim squirmed uncomfortably. "But Mullah Abadul didn't like me going there, and besides, I can't stand watching my father fawning over Ayesha, and with Sharona gone…"

"Come along, laddie, and fill your belly. I want to hear this report of yours. Has Ruiz told you anything to add to it?"

They strolled across the courtyard to the tower that held the barracks. The muezzin's call echoed within the stone walls of the Rabat, and Selim obediently knelt in praise of Ilha the All-Merciful while Halvar clutched his amulet. That done, they presented themselves at the refectory, where two large Afrikan men were assisted by two larger Local women serving the guardsmen. A fireplace kept the room warmer than Halvar had been all day.

Two long tables sat between benches, ready for the evening meal. The sultan's personal guards were gathered at one of the tables, tearing into roasted fowls and bowls of maiz-mush, while a squad of Town Guards sat at the other. The Sultan's Guards glanced at Selim and Halvar then turned back to their meals. There would be no offers of friendship from that lot, Halvar decided.

He accepted an earthenware platter of fowl and mush and a mug of chicory-laced mokka from the cooks, then followed Selim to the corner of the table farthest from any listening ears.

"Not very chummy," Halvar commented.

"They're not happy to be here," Selim said with a shrug. "My father's own people went back to Al-Andalus with last year's Fall Feria tolls. This lot came in the spring, and they think they're better than anyone else here in Manatas because they're pure Andalusian. They don't mix with anyone, they revere Mullah Abadul, and they keep the Prophet's law very strictly."

"Not loyal to the sultan?" Halvar tried to identify the species of the bird he was munching on. Duck? Goose? Gobble-bird? Whatever—it was stringy and tough, but it filled the empty stomach, and it was halal.

"Loyal to Al-Andalus." Selim dismissed the Guards with another shrug. He hitched closer to Halvar. "Don Alvaro, I've made a chart of the events of this past week." He opened his notebook. "See, I've put the days of the week here, and what happened on each day. It doesn't make sense, though."

"How so?" Halvar peered at the page, on which Selim had created neat columns, each headed with a squiggle of Arabi.

"I worked backwards from the day of the big storm," Selim explained. "That was four days ago. Today is Gathering Day..."

"In the Dane-march, we call it Frigg's Day," Halvar interrupted him. "Yesterday would be Thor's Day, and the day before that Woden's Day, and the day before that Twy's day."

"That was the day of the big storm," Selim said.

"And the Yehudit's Day of Repentance," Halvar added.

166

"Right. And what do you call the day before that?" Selim added the information to his chart.

"That's Moon's Day, and the day before that is Sun's Day. That's the Kristo Holy Day of Rest. The Yehudit Shabat is what you call Il-Isbit, and we call Saturn's Day. Don't know why we took an Old Roumi god for that one, you'd have to ask Leon; he'd tell you all about it."

Halvar forestalled any more questions he couldn't answer by pointing to Selim's chart.

"All right, laddie, tell me what you've written here. Moon's Day, that was when I was flat on my back, thanks to that harpy with her poker and all the other things that happened to me when I first came here to Manatas." He shrugged his shoulder experimentally, feeling a stab of pain under Frater Iosip's bandage to remind him he was not fully healed from his wounds.

Selim read his notes. "Second Day, the storm starts at night. Manolo is killed; Hannes Zilberstam's dhow docks, and he goes to the pawnbroker; Robert Mortmain takes Leon's books to the pawnshop, then goes to the Scavengers. Third Day, the day of the big storm. No one goes outside except the Yehudit, who have to go to their study house to pray to Adonai and repent their sins. Fourth Day, the Scavengers see the ghoul, Mendel the Bookseller gets Leon's books, the brickmakers find the body. Fifth Day, Manolo's body is found, we are called to investigate, we find the book in the pits, you get sprayed by the sekonk."

"And you and your fellow Seekers of Truth write a poem about it, and you make a picture of it, and Fru Dani Glick pays you to allow her to print copies of it under the roof at the Gardens of Paradise," Halvar put in. "For which I do not thank you."

Selim's eyebrows seemed to meet over his snub nose as he bent over his chart.

"What I don't understand is, if Robert Mortmain was killed in the morning, right after the big storm..."

"Woden's Day."

"If you say so. On Woden's Day, someone all muffled up comes to Mendel before dawn and sells him Leon's notebooks. At the same time, someone lets the donkeys out of the paddock at the Scavenger's Pits, takes Robert Mortmain's body up to the brickyards and leaves it there for the brickmakers to find later that day. How can this killer be at the souk and up-the-hills at the same time?"

"He wasn't," Halvar said. "Achmet was the one who got the body away from the pits while the killer got rid of the notebooks."

"But he kept one of them," Selim reminded him.

"So he did. Robert carefully removed one page, but someone else tore out another and threw the book into the trench."

"Where the sekonk started to eat it." Selim squelched a giggle. "You'd think he'd toss it into the river."

"He probably thought he had," Halvar decided after considering it for a moment. "He was in an almighty hurry. He had to do a lot in a short time, it was still dark, and he didn't see where the book landed. He'd hoped it would go into the dung pit if it didn't get to the river, but he missed that pit and it landed where the sekonk found it instead."

Selim entered the information on the chart

"When did all this happen? And how did Mortmain know what was in those books in the first place? And if he did, how did he know if it was important or not?"

Halvar tugged at his mustache and frowned.

"What about Moon's Day? When I was laid up, and the Mermaid Taberna wasn't guarded? Mortmain was holed up in Leon's rooms upstairs. He could have used the time to look over those books. He was a server at the taberna, he knew full well what went on upstairs and what kind of visitors Leon had, even if they came up the outside stair. He had all of Moon's Day to look at the notebooks."

"And he saw the naughty picture of Calif Don Felipe," Selim said. "And he carefully cut it away."

Halvar tugged harder at his mustache to speed up this caravan of thought.

"Now, why would he do that? How did he know who it was in that picture? There hasn't been a coin struck with Don Felipe's face yet, and the Afrikan mullahs are always howling about making images of living beings. Unless..."

"Unless?" Selim prompted him when the silence had drawn on for several moments.

"The image was signed," Halvar said slowly, remembering. "I was there when it was made. All the young men in that picture signed it."

"In Arabi?"

"The Bretains wrote in Ogham, but Don Felipe signed in Arabi."

"Robert didn't know how to write or read Arabi," Selim said, "but Jacques could read it as well as Franchen."

"Then Mortmain wasn't alone on Moon's Day. There must have been someone else in the Mermaid Taverna with him, someone who could read Arabi, who told him what the image was. When he realized it could be used to blacken Don Felipe, Mortmain cut it out of the book and carefully put it into his coat. Only the coat was wet through, and the image was ink, and the ink smeared."

"So it's useless?" Selim thought this over. "What about the other one, the one that was torn out? And why wrap the heart in it?"

"Considering what was on that page..." Halvar chose not to finish that thought.

"Was it that awful? It just looked like the tip of a toe to me."

"It wasn't a toe." Halvar glanced at Selim, a glint in his eye. "It was another part of a man's body, and it might lead to some questions the owner of that part wouldn't want to answer."

Selim's dark face turned darker as comprehension dawned.

"Leon made an image of everyone and everything he saw. Could he have made an image of someone's parts without their knowing about it?"

"He must have done it while the someone was asleep. The subject of his art didn't know about it until he saw it in the notebook at the Mermaid Taberna, and he tore it out in a hurry. He wrapped the heart in it and told Achmet to get rid of it. Probably told Achmet to take the body and the heart and throw them in different places so the wild beasts could destroy them before they were found."

"Only Achmet was lazy and just tossed the body behind the ovens and threw the heart into them, thinking it would be burned when the brickmakers started their fires." Selim finished the chain of events.

"Shows you that you can't trust those Scavengers to do what they've been told." Halvar considered what the chart indicated. "One thing I've noticed about you Manatas folk, he continued. "You all have your own little patch and don't go anywhere else. If someone's used to the waterfront, they never go past the warehouses. The Yehudit at the souk don't go to the Feria, the ones on the east side of the island don't go to the west. Green Village folk don't go past the Broad Way to the Locals' camp, the Locals don't go to Green Village. Mahak and Algonkin don't go to each other's villages. The only ones who go everywhere are the Scavengers."

"And the Town Guard," Selim reminded him.

"Oh, yes, the Town Guard," Halvar said. "Which reminds me, have you seen Tenente Ruiz? I have a few questions for him."

"I saw him leaving with the Local woman to take Jehan's body to the Waterfront Chapel"

"I thought I told him to let Dr. Moise check that body out before it was buried." Halvar finished his mokka and slammed the mug down.

"I don't think Tenente Ruiz obeys your orders," Selim said.

"Tenente Ruiz is getting a swelled head," Halvar muttered. "I thought he was ready for the job."

"You may have been mistaken."

Halvar looked at his self-appointed assistant.

"I think I've been mistaken about a lot of things," he confessed. "But this is the worst. When I make a mistake, it's a great one." He stood up, made sure his dagger was firmly in its sheath and ready to his hand, and nodded at Selim.

"You make a neat copy of that chart and add what we said to it. It's going to be useful at the Grand Divan."

"You're going after Tenente Ruiz. I'm going with you."

"It's too dangerous. Your father—"

"I want to see how this ends," Selim insisted as he gathered up his notebook and writing materials. "You'll need a written account."

Halvar motioned to the Sultan's Guards.

"Two of you, come with me."

"What for?" one of the Andalusians demanded with a sneer.

"To take down a killer," Halvar told them. "And to defend Al-Andalus."

Chapter 32

THERE WERE STREAKS OF GOLD AND RED IN THE DARK sky above the Great River, the last embers of the dying day, as Halvar made his way through the alleys back to the waterfront. Two guardsmen marched behind him, armed with halberds; Selim brought up the rear.

They went past the house once used by the Taverniers; another tenant had already claimed it. No living space in Manatas Town remained empty for long; there were always people looking for somewhere to live, and space was scarce within the wall. How long before some merchant would try to breach the peace and build a house outside the wall in Mahak territory? Halvar wondered.

Not his problem, but there would be trouble if the Locals thought they were being invaded.

The reek of a latrine penetrated his nostrils. He was behind the Mermaid Taberna, skirting the infamous outside stair where the server Henri had met his end. The alley opened onto the plaza, beyond which small boats bobbed at the piers of the East Channel.

Hannes Zilberstam was again doling out soup to the waterfront workers—seamen whose ships had just made port and brawny longshoremen who unloaded the barges that carried the goods from the ships in the harbor to the merchants on shore. Torches lit the plaza, turning it into a place of shadows between the flickering glare.

Halvar ignored the stares and muttered comments that followed him and his party across the plaza. He turned northward, past the pawnshop, now dark and shuttered, along the path beside the East Channel. The small chapel had been built between the fence that encircled the blacksmith's domain and the warehouses that marked the boundaries of the Waterfront District.

Unlike the plain wooden structure at Green Village, this chapel was of sturdy brick overlaid with plaster in the Andalusian style. It might have been a muskat, but the inscriptions above the door were in the Old Roumi letters that were as square as Rune. Halvar could even make out the words: TO THE GLORY OF THE HOLY SPIRIT, SANCTUS SPIRITU.

He stepped into the sanctuary and blinked. The light of lanterns and candles revealed painted images of the Redeemer, his Mother Mara, and the circumstances of his life: his birth, his miracles, and ending as it always did with his execution on the Crux. That image was painted with startling realism over the altar, where Prester Nicodemus was ending his evening service. His congregation was small—three or four Local women and twice as many men in the broad-brimmed hats that marked them as Franchen.

"It is done. Go in peace," the prester intoned. He looked up from his book and frowned at Halvar. "What do you want here? This is God's house, not to be defiled by armed men."

"We're looking for Tenente Ruiz," Halvar said.

"Why do you think he is here?"

"He said he was bringing the body of Jehan ibn Manolo, the pawnbroker, here for burial. If he is here, I want him. He has some questions to answer regarding another death, that of Robert Mortmain, a Franchen, whose body was found at the brickyards up-the-hills."

Prester Nicodemus stepped away from the altar, bowed to the Crux, and turned back to Halvar.

"This Franchen, he was of my congregation?"

"He was one of those who worked in the Mermaid Taberna," Halvar stated. "Jacques Tavernier, his wife Lizette, the server Henri, and this Robert, they all came here from Kibbick and were Franchen, so I suppose he was one of yours. He's at the fratery in Green Village. Abbas Mikhail is going to put him in the ground there."

"In heretical soil!" Prester Nicodemus was more upset about the theologically incorrect disposal of one of his flock than he was about the man's death. "This must not be!"

"That's not important." Halvar strode through the chapel. "It's Tenente Ruiz I want. Did he come here?"

172

Prester Nicodemus looked at the two guardsmen, who lowered their halberds to point the axe-heads towards him.

"Tenente Ruiz came here," he admitted. "He brought the remains of our faithful servant Jehan for burial in our sacred ground."

"And where is he now?"

"He went with the Local woman, Morning Star, to the burying ground." Prester Nicodemus edged away from the guards.

"Where is that?"

"At the end of Maiden Lane, between the East Channel and the smithy. But it is holy ground, and by orders of our most holy father, Episopus Innocente, you must not remove a man seeking sanctuary within holy ground. It is a sin, a deadly sin, and you will burn in Sheol if you violate that order!"

"Episcopus Innocente is no father of mine," Halvar gritted out. "I will burn or freeze when I go, whether I want to or not. I need to get Tenente Ruiz away from Morning Star. That woman's in danger!"

"Danger?" Prester Nicodemus squeaked.

"Tenente Ruiz is responsible for at least three murders and may well be ready to add another to his list."

Prester Nicodemus stood, dumbfounded, muttering prayers in Old Roumi as Halvar strode out of the chapel.

"Follow me," he ordered the two guardsmen. "Selim, bring that lantern. And stay behind me. I don't want you to get within range of that pistoia he carries!"

"What about you?"

"I can take care of myself. Let's get him while there's still some light to see by!"

Chapter 33

HOWEVER, BY THIS TIME THE SUN HAD SET, THE SLIVER of moon had not risen, and the only light came from the taverns and cribs that lined the unpaved alley that led from the chapel to the looming darkness of the Manatas Town wall. From the sounds that drifted out of the wooden shacks, business was brisk. Halvar smelled raw alcohol and hemp, both in lavish supply, in defiance of both Sharia and Sultan Petrus's orders.

The East Channel must be at low tide, he thought, and his nose wrinkled as he smelled seaweed and rotting fish. Somewhere overhead a bird called out, flying back to its roost.

The flickering light of the lantern sent weird shadows dancing across the road. Halvar slewed his head around at the sound of something in an alley between two of the houses.

"Just an araghoun," Selim whispered.

A round, furry creature something like a small bear, with a pointed snout and fluffy tail, waddled out of the alley, intent on its own business.

"It eats garbage. It doesn't stink like a sekonk, but it can bite."

"Good to know," Halvar muttered. The araghoun was too small to worry about; he was after larger prey.

A woman in a filmy kuton skirt and blouse staggered out of one of the cribs, supporting a large man in the canvas trousers and jacket of a seaman. By the look of them, both had partaken liberally of the refreshments offered in the taverns.

Halvar grinned under his mustache. This, at least, was familiar territory to him. Whores were universal, and no business of his, as long as they stayed in their own houses and refrained from robbing their clients too badly. Sailors would go to whores and spend their money gambling and drinking. At least they weren't arguing about religion!

"Where's this burying ground?" he asked aloud, peering through a mounting mist rising off the East Channel.

"Just ahead," Selim said. He held the lantern higher, so Halvar could make out the bulk of the Manatas Town wall.

The road ended abruptly at an iron fence that set the Roumi Rite burying place apart from the rest of the town. Halvar focused on the dot of light from a lantern at the farthest end of the burying ground, almost under the wall itself.

There was Ruiz, with Morning Star and an older man who held a spade in one hand and a lantern in the other.

"It's late for a burial," Halvar commented as he joined the grim group, taking a halberd from the hand of the nearest guardsman. Selim followed, holding his lantern carefully to illuminate the scene. "You're in Shaitan's own hurry to get Jehan underground. Didn't even wait for Dr. Moise to have a look at him."

"Jehan has to be buried by morning," Ruiz said smoothly. "By Sharia, all deceased persons must be buried within twenty-four hours of their death."

"And you obey Sharia." Halvar looked about him. "But you are Kristo, Tenente Ruiz."

"I still obey the laws of Manatas."

"Do you, Tenente? I'm here to take you to the Rabat for questioning on the matter of your part in the death of Manolo the pawnbroker, and to bring you to trial for the murders of Jehan ibn Manolo and Robert Mortmain."

Ruiz looked past Halvar to the two men behind him.

"Are you going to allow this Dane, this Hireling, to accuse me?"

"They're the sultan's men, not yours," Halvar pointed out. "And as you keep reminding me, I have no authority here except that of the sultan. So, I'm going to bring you to him and lay out the case before him, and let him decide what to do with you."

"Oh, really?" Ruiz sneered. "Why would I go on this murderous spree? What reason would I have to kill the pawnbroker, or the assassin? And Jehan?"

"You killed all of them because they'd seen something, knew something that would destroy you, Tenente Ruiz. They knew that you'd been lovers with Leon di Vicenza. The proof of it was in that book you tried to destroy."

"*What?*" Selim exclaimed

"You killed my man!" Morning Star hissed. She reached under her shirt for something.

Before she could draw her knife, Ruiz grabbed the lantern from the hand of the gravedigger and threw it at Halvar. Then he turned and fled through the graveyard towards the end of the wall.

"Get him!"

Halvar followed, stumbling over hidden roots and stones, steadying himself with the butt of the halberd, trying to reach the end of the wall before Ruiz could get to the clam beds and claim he was in Mahak territory, out of the reach of Al-Andalus. He heard the crunch of boots on the dry leaves that covered the burying ground. He braced himself against the wall, gasping with the effort of running.

There was a sudden spark and the reek of burning kuton—the wick that lit the black powder that propelled the lead bullets from the pistoia in the hand of Tenente Ruiz. The outline of the man was a dark spot against the pale glint of the rising moon on the water of the East Channel behind him.

"I *thought* you'd have your pistoia with you," Halvar panted. "A nice piece of machinery, that handgun. Very expensive, too. I wondered where you got it."

"A gift from a friend," Ruiz said, edging backwards to the very end of the wall. He raised his arm, taking aim, seeking a target in the gloom.

"A very fine gift, from a very good friend," Halvar expanded on Ruiz's comment, stepping forward carefully, halberd shaft probing for loose earth or roots that might catch in his feet. "You know, Tenente, those handguns aren't all that common, even in Oropa. The troopers have muskets—the Franchen and the Bretains make them two or three at a time; but they are given to the soldiers to clear the field of pikemen. I know all about that. I've gone against them.

"But a small piece like that one…you know, Tenente, that's very fine work, indeed. Not too many can make them. In fact," Halvar said, taking another step towards Ruiz, "the only one I've seen up close belonged to Don Felipe, our calif."

"Your calif," Ruiz sneered.

"Yours, too, Tenente Ruiz. You serve the sultan, and he serves the ruler of Al-Andalus, or had you forgotten?" Halvar took yet another step forward. "Now, that handgun, it was a thing of beauty, made with a rosewood butt, inlaid with ivory, carved with the name of Ilha in Arabi letters, and decorated with fine calligraphy inscribed on the barrel. Don Felipe had it made special, for someone he truly loved as a teacher and a master and a friend. Can you guess who that was?"

"I can't imagine," Ruiz/snarled. His hand began to shake with the weight of the pistoia.

"He gave that handgun to Leon di Vicenza as a parting gift the day before Leon left for Nova Mundum." Halvar answered his own question. "I know, because I was there when that pistoia was made, and I know where it went. I didn't see the box it came in in Leon's rooms, and it's too valuable for someone as greedy as Tavernier to miss when he cleared out Leon's belongings."

He held out his hand. "Tenente Ruiz, will you let me look at that handgun of yours? Because if it's the same one I saw in Al-Andalus, I'd like to know how you got it. Was it a gift from Leon, to one of his own...dear friends?"

"I have my finger on the trigger," Ruiz said. "I can send the lead ball through your belly instead of through your shoulder."

"And that would be very unpleasant," Halvar agreed. "I've had your lead in my shoulder already. It's painful, but some who are so wounded survive. And there are witnesses." He jerked his head backwards. "I've got young Selim and two of the sultan's guards with me. Selim won't lie for you, nor will the sultan's men. You're wasting time, Ruiz. Shoot me now, and be done with it!"

"If I do, I'll run to Mahak lands. You can't touch me there!" His voice was shrill.

"You aren't ready to shoot yet. Not the way you were with Robert. You're not angry enough."

Halvar took another step towards Ruiz, his voice casual, his eyes on the pistoia.

"*You* took Robert to the Scavengers. He'd never have found the place on his own, not in that storm. He stayed in his hut for a day to ride out the storm, maybe looking at the images in Leon's notebooks, the ones he brought with him from the pawnshop. Then he left the hut, just before sunrise, to take the footpath to Green Village.

"But you were waiting for him, and shot him there, directly in his heart; the shot that killed him left little burns and bits of black powder on his shirt. Then you had to get the heart out, because it held the bullet from the pistoia, and if someone found it, it would point right at you.

"You cut out the heart with your sword and wrapped it in the page you tore out of the notebook. Then you and Achmet got the body into the donkey cart. You told the emir to get the body far away, up-the-hills, to where the bears and wolves would tear it apart and it wouldn't be found, while you went back to the souk, to get rid of Leon's books.

"You knew Mendel wouldn't ask questions, he'd grab what he thought he could sell.

"Then you went back to the Rabat and put on your fine new coat, sure that Robert was never going to be found, and that you were safe. Trouble is, you can't trust a Scavenger. Achmet didn't bother to take Robert any farther than the brickyards, and the brickmakers found him a lot sooner than you liked."

Halvar moved carefully, judging the distance between himself and Ruiz. One more step, and he'd be able to hook that pistoia out of his hand...

Ruiz stood, entranced, as Halvar approached, the gun in his hand lowering at each word. His finger tightened on the trigger without aiming.

The sound of the blast sent a flock of birds soaring upwards, startled out of their roost by the noise. The bullet whistled past Halvar's foot, shattering bits of stone from the wall behind him.

"Not a good idea, using a handgun," Halvar said. "Takes time to replace that bullet, more to light the pan. One miss, Tenente, and you're done!"

He held the halberd in two hands, feinted with the blade, then struck out with the end of the pole to knock the pistoia from Ruiz's hand. The handgun went skittering into the darkness, leaving Ruiz with empty hands

"That club you're carrying at your belt is better, but messier. Of course, a knife or sword works the best."

"You would know, Hireling," Ruiz rasped out. He unhooked the bludgeon that hung at his waist and raised the club for a smashing blow.

Halvar whirled, parrying the attack. He felt the tug of the bandage on his shoulder, dropped his guard, and Ruiz landed a hard blow on the wounded shoulder.

Halvar hissed at the sudden pain as his arm went numb and he dropped the halberd.

"Pistoias aren't accurate at a distance, Tenente. You tried to kill me on the path to Green Village a week ago and only got me in the shoulder instead."

Ruiz snarled. "I wanted to blow your interfering head off!"

"Instead, you got me angry," Halvar said. He drew his dagger. "It got me thinking about you, Tenente Ruiz. A very clever young man, second to Tenente Gomez, who was not very clever. Gomez was brutal, he was tough, but he couldn't read or write. He needed you, Ruiz, to run his errands, do his bidding. But just who was bidding whom? And where did your ideas come from? Were you the first Seeker of Truth? Leon's student, along with young Selim, and the girl Sharona?"

Ruiz slashed out again. Halvar dodged and parried, again feeling the wall behind him.

"When did you realize that Leon had drawn an image of you?" Halvar waited for sensation to come back to the numb arm. "Was it when you saw an image of Otter Tail?"

Ruiz took a sharp breath. "Obscene!"

"Accurate," Halvar said. He gripped the dagger tightly. "I can understand how it was, Tenente. A youngster, not quite twenty, cooped up in the Rabat for the winter with a persuasive sort like Leon? He can be really charming. I know. I've seen him with the students at the Madrassa. He had Don Felipe in his spell, too."

"But not you," Ruiz sneered. "Not a Dane, oh, no."

"I'd seen his like before," Halvar said. "And I couldn't be cozened because I didn't speak enough Arbi. So, no, Ruiz, I wasn't taken in by Leon di Vicenza. I'm not taken in by him now. He can influence people, but it's you who did the dirty work, Ruiz, not Leon, and it's you who'll pay the price for it at the Divan."

"Not if I get out of Manatas first!" Ruiz shouted. "I'll go to Green Village and get asylum there!"

"Then what? The Mahak may have something to say to the one who encouraged Gomez to take the hammer to poor Otter Tail. You got rid of two rivals that way, didn't you? You plan long, Ruiz. What's your final goal? To rule Manatas yourself?"

"You talk too much, Hireling!" Ruiz swung his club again. Halvar dodged to avoid the blow and slipped on the wet sand of the clam bed. He fell heavily and rolled away from the next blow as Ruiz forgot all finesse in his fury, laying about him with no regard for aim. Somewhere in the back of his mind was the thought that he'd ruined yet another coat.

Ruiz raised his arm for the killing blow then stared at nothing and collapsed. Behind him, Firebrand stood with bow ready to shoot another arrow to match the one that now protruded from Ruiz's middle.

Chapter 34

"WHAT DID YOU DO THAT FOR?" HALVAR SCRAMBLED TO his feet. "Selim! Hold that light steady! Someone get the lad, he's going to faint again!"

One of the guards retrieved the lantern while the other held the youth upright.

Firebrand stood over Ruiz.

"I was aiming for his heart, but I got him lower down. He's still breathing."

"Not for long," Halvar said grimly. "Selim! Stop that sniveling and run for Prester Nicodemus. I want to hear a confession of guilt."

Selim trotted back toward the chapel.

Halvar knelt beside the dying man.

"You're bleeding inside," he told him. "You haven't got long. Tell me, Ruiz, am I right? Did you kill Robert Mortmain?"

"He laughed at me," Ruiz spat out. "He saw the image that Leon drew, and he called me a name. And I had the pistoia..." He stopped to breathe. A trickle of blood ran down his chin, staining the well-trimmed beard. "Achmet and Gomez were partners. I knew he'd do anything for money."

"And you could always arrest him," Halvar finished.

Ruiz grinned feebly. "You got in the way, Hireling. You were always in the way. Everything would have worked beautifully, but you were always there. You wouldn't even die when you were shot."

"The Redeemer and Thor may have other uses for me," Halvar murmured.

More lanterns bobbed toward the burying ground. Prester Nicodemus hurried forward to anoint the dying man and pronounce the Last Blessings. Halvar rose and stepped aside to let the cleric kneel beside Ruiz. Firebrand joined him with Selim close behind.

"He would have killed you," Firebrand observed.

"He could have tried," Halvar countered.

"It's horrible!" Selim quavered. "All of it! Why did he do it? Why did he have to kill all those people?"

"Because he was afraid of what they would say or do," Halvar explained. "Ruiz had just risen to be tenente. He had to put himself forward, to command respect, and he'd never get it if he was known as Leon's lover. Leon must have done the drawing while Ruiz was asleep, just as he made an image of Otter Tail. It will tickle that sly fox's vanity to know that something he did cost three lives. Leon's got a lot to answer for."

"But Leon didn't kill anyone," Selim protested.

"No, he didn't. He just gave Ruiz that pistoia and fed him a lot of philosophy, nonsense about Truth and Justice, what the students at Corduva argue about in tabernas and mokka-shops," Halvar retorted. "Then Leon got besotted with Otter Tail and left friend Ruiz to stew in his own juice, as Old Sergeant Olaf used to say."

"That's why he killed Robert? And Jehan? Out of jealousy and fear of what people might say?"

"And he'd probably have found a way to get rid of you, Selim." Halvar patted the youth's shoulder.

"Horrible!"

Prester Nicodemus finished his sad task.

"Where is Jehan's earthly body?"

"Back there." Morning Star, who had just arrived, led the group back to the burying ground, where the gravedigger still rested on his shovel, waiting for more orders. She regarded the remains of her former spouse, sighed heavily, and said, "We will take my Jehan back to the chapel for a proper Roumi Rite blessing before we put him into the ground. I am now owner of the pawnshop. Go, Firebrand. Tell Sachem Mahmoud of the Algonkin that justice has been done. I will not demand blood vengeance."

"Good thing Ruiz has no kinfolk to take revenge on *you*, Firebrand," Halvar murmured as they turned back towards the lights and sounds of Maiden Lane. "According to Sharia, you are not guilty of murder. You killed to save my life, and that's what I'll tell the sultan when I report to him."

"And Selim?"

Halvar smiled in the darkness. "Selim is not going to be a problem, Firebrand. I know all about Selim." He smiled at the youth, "Come on, Selim. I think it's time you and I had a talk before I take you back to your father."

"Where are we going?" Selim quavered.

"To the Mermaid Taberna. We can have mokka, and there's a nice place we can chat where we won't have a lot of ears listening to what we're saying."

Halvar strode along Maiden Lane, past the Roumi Rite Chapel and the pawnshop to the waterfront plaza, with Selim trotting behind him. Across the plaza, the lights of the Mermaid Taberna shone through the open door, inviting weary travelers to enter.

Firebrand frowned. "I don't like that place," he declared. "I will go to my sachem now."

"And I will bury my man properly tomorrow," Morning Star added. "I will take the shop as my portion."

"You can go home to the Algonikin village," Firebrand suggested.

"I have no place there now. I am Roumi Rite Kristo. I will have the shop for my son to take." Morning Star placed a hand protectively on her middle.

"Another halfling," Firebrand muttered with an air of disgust. "Too many of them. We will be nothing if this keeps on."

Halvar eyed the two Locals.

"What happens to the pawnshop will be decided by the sultan at the Grand Divan," he stated firmly. "Right now, Firebrand, you go back to your sachem and tell him the business of the body at the brickyards is finished. We got the one who killed Robert Mortmain, that's all you wanted."

"True. But there is more to it than you said."

"There is," Halvar said. "But it doesn't concern the Mahak. It's about what's going on beyond the sea." He gestured toward the dark bay where the cargo ships bobbed at anchor. "And it concerns the sultan and his own family."

"Selim?" Firebrand looked sharply at the youngster. "What's he got to do with anything?"

"He's one of the keys to this mystery," Halvar said. "Leon is the other. And Leon wouldn't be here if it wasn't for Selim. So, now, Mahak, I'll have a chat with Selim and get things sorted out before the Grand Divan."

With that, Halvar turned to the guards and explained.

"Selim and I are going to have mokka at the Mermaid Taberna. You two go and report what happened at the Kristo burying ground to the sultan, and tell him I'll be along shortly with Selim. You can take the lantern with you, I won't need it."

He watched the guards cross the plaza and climb the little hill that led to the Broad Way.

"Now, laddie," he told Selim, "you and I are going to have another talk. And this time, you are going to tell me the truth."

Chapter 35

HANNES ZILBERSTAM WAS STILL AT HIS STATION DOLING out soup and mokka when Halvar and Selim entered the Mermaid Taberna. The air was thick with smoke and the greasy smell of the soup that bubbled in the cauldrons set up in the huge fireplace, whose heat intensified the odors of meat and tabac.

"Landsman!" Hannes greeted his fellow Dane. "Gods be with you!"

"And with you, Hannes." Halvar glanced at the stairs on the far side of the main room. "Tell me, have you decided to use those upstairs rooms for yourself? Or do you plan to rent them to passing merchants or captains laying over for the winter?"

"Haven't made up my mind," Hannes said. "Them stairs are troublesome, it's true. I haven't even been up there since you was here."

"Don't rent them yet. I'm thinking of taking them myself if I can't get a ship out before winter sets in." Halvar scanned the room for an empty table and found one in the corner near the stairs. "Over there, laddie. Pot of mokka for the two of us," he ordered.

Selim turned to flee, but Halvar caught him by the sleeve of his silk kaftan and hauled him to the bench. The tall Dane blocked the slender youth's escape with one arm and glared fiercely at the two men on the other end of the bench until they moved off. The halfling server deposited two clay mugs and a pot of mokka on the table, waited for Halvar to hand him wumpum, and hastened away, leaving Selim trapped between the wall and Halvar's bulky body.

"Now, laddie," Halvar began, pouring the mokka, "or maybe I should say lass?"

"What?" Selim gulped.

Halvar sighed," It took a bit of time, but after a little thought, it was clear enough that you were a girl and not a lad. Whose idea was this masquerade? Leon's?"

Selim took a sip of mokka and made a face at its bitterness.

"This needs sugar," she complained.

"Not likely here. Is it Selina?"

"Salomay," Selim whispered. "A very wicked girl in the Kristo Holy Book, according to Lady Maryam."

"And I suppose she'd know," Halvar said. "But I'll keep calling you Selim, because that's how I know you. So, when did you decide to be a boy and not a girl?"

"It started as a joke," Salomay said. "Back home, on the estate, I wore boy's clothes when I went riding. Lady Maryam didn't really care what I did or didn't do, because she and my mother were at odds anyway, and Lady Maryam had the estate to run, while my mother went on campaign with my father.

"After he came home from Italia, my mother was starting the Sisters of Fatima, and setting up Houses of the Green Crescent in Corduva and Madrid and Savilla, until she took the Indian plague and died, and Lady Maryam said it served her right for neglecting her husband and child.

"Then word came that the Old Calif wanted to see my father, that he had a special task for him, a new post, here in Manatas. Only, I think it was the young calif's mother, Lady Zulaika's, idea, because she got my father a new wife, Ayesha, to go along with the new posting. Since Ayesha wasn't much older than me, my father thought it a good idea that I should come along with them to Nova Mundum. At least, that's what they told me."

She took another sip of the bitter mokka.

"And Leon was sent with you," Halvar summed it up.

"His sister, Eva Hakim, was supposed to be the head of the harem servants, and he was supposed to be my tutor," she explained. "That's when my father thought it would make more sense for me to be a boy, because people might wonder why he would take so much time to educate a girl."

188

"Lady Zulaika wanted to get Leon out of Al-Andalus," Halvar said. "Sending Sultan Petrus to Manatas was as good an excuse as any. Everyone knew he had a young child, but it was supposed to be a boy. He had three other sons, why not a fourth?"

Salomay nodded. "My oldest brother runs the estate, or thinks he does. Lady Maryam really does. My middle brother went to Madrassa and got a post at court. And my youngest brother decided to go to sea, and no one's heard from him in years. They're all Lady Maryam's sons, years and years older than me. I was born a year after my father met Lady Fatima. Lady Maryam always called my mother 'the camp follower' because she was the daughter of a Turkish general and went on campaign with her father. That's how she met *my* father."

Halvar waited for her to put the rest of her story together.

"So, you came here to Manatas, and everyone thought you were a boy," he said when she didn't.

"Leon thought it a great joke. He said people see what they want to see. No one really looks at any child, they only see the clothing. So, if I wore trousers and kept my hair under a turban, no one would think I wasn't a boy, and he and I could go into the town or Green Village or the Mahak territories, and no one would care."

"And it worked," Halvar said. "Until it didn't."

"Until things changed," Salomay said dolefully. Her narrative picked up speed. "I'm not sure how. Maybe it was because Ayesha was old enough to want to have a baby, and my father noticed that she wasn't skinny anymore. Maybe it was when our old imam, who was Sufi, had to go home, and Mullah Abadul, who is Sunni and very fierce about anyone who isn't, came with a whole lot of strict rules about what could and couldn't be done. Maybe it was when Otter Tail came to work with Malik the Smith, and Leon fell in love with him.

"But it all fell apart, and the only one I could talk to was Sharona, but she was kept away from me because Mullah Abadul said that a boy shouldn't be allowed into the harem after he was of an age to get children, and that I was old enough, so I shouldn't go up to Ayesha's room anymore.

"Then that horrible man Gomez started to make my father do things like promoting Achmet the Scavenger to emir. Leon had to move to the taberna, because Mullah Abadul was preaching about man-lovers, and how terrible they were, and how they were going to burn in Sheol. Then came the letter from Lady Maryam." Selim stopped, breathless.

"The one about the marriage?"

"I won't do it!" Salomay cried, drawing the attention of the nearest soup-eaters to their table.

"Marriage isn't so bad," Halvar said, glaring at their neighbors, who turned back to their bowls.

"I know Lady Maryam! She's probably got me tied to some horrible old man with three wives already." She lowered her voice but not her intensity. "I'd just be a servant to the other three. And I'm not like Ayesha, I can't be stuck in the harem all the time. I don't want to be penned in!"

"What do you want to do?"

"I want to go to madrassa. I want to learn philosophy, and law," Salomay said.

"And art," Halvar added, with a grin. "You drew that cartoon of me and the sekonk."

"It wasn't really very good."

"Good enough to get folk laughing," Halvar assured her. He looked around the room, conscious of the eyes that were studiously avoiding looking at that corner. "Well, 'Selim,' I think it's time we got you back to the Rabat."

"What are you going to do?" she quavered.

"I'm going to report to your father," Halvar said. "Then, I'm going to do what I was sent here to do. I'm going after that wily rascal in Green Village."

Chapter 36

HALVAR HAD THE FEELING HIS LIFE HAD COME FULL CIR-
cle. Here he was, back in the sultan's rooms, reporting on yet another murder while Sultan Petrus reclined in his chair and Salomay stood, shamefaced, next to her father.

"So you see," he finished his narrative, "it was Ruiz who killed
Robert but Achmet who took the body away, out of Manatas Town
to the brickyards. Ruiz probably planned to accuse the Scavenger
Emir at the Grand Divan, and it would be his word against that of
a known rogue."

"Mmmph!" Sultan Petrus grunted. "What am I going to do about
you, Don Alvaro? In the space of two weeks you have removed both
of the tenentes of the Manatas Town Guards, caused two riots, and
killed five people."

"He didn't kill Ruiz," Salomay stated. "That was the Mahak, the
one they call Firebrand. He didn't want to kill Lizette Tavernier,
either. Ruiz joggled his arm, I saw him do it."

"And it was Ruiz who got Tavernier," Halvar finished the tally.
"Tavernier knew what went on in those upstairs rooms. Ruiz must
have used the outside stair to visit Leon, until Leon met Otter Tail,
and cut Ruiz off."

"I never suspected," Sultan Petrus muttered.

"He wasn't like Leon, flaunting himself about. He was Roumi
Rite Kristo, fighting with his inner self."

"What made you suspect Ruiz?" Salomay asked. "I thought you
liked him."

"I did. I thought he was a clever lad, better than Gomez to lead a Town Guard." Halvar tugged at his mustache. "I was wrong. It was all a pretense, like the play-actors who come around to tell tales in the Dane-March.

"But there were signs, things that just didn't sit right. He knew a lot more about Leon di Vicenza than he should have, and he wasn't as diligent as he could have been in looking for Robert Mortmain. He'd been at those discussions at the Mermaid Taberna often enough to tell me what they were about."

"But you didn't do anything about him," Salomay said.

"I wasn't sure, not until I realized what had killed Mortmain. Ruiz had the only pistoia on Manatas that I knew of."

"We'd better go back and find it tomorrow at daybreak," Salomay said.

"We?" Halvar's eyebrows rose. "When did you join the Town Guard, girl?"

Sultan Petrus harrumphed. "That's another matter, Don Alvaro. You've discovered something I've tried to keep secret. When did you first suspect that 'Selim' was not all that he seemed?"

Halvar tugged at his mustache. "There were a few things. Like, why would a soldier like you, who is no fool about the ways of men like Leon, allow his own son to be tutored by someone who made no secret of his private affairs? Why was your son accompanied by one of the harem attendants, instead of another lad?

"I noticed that even when Salomey was in the taberna as a server, she clutched that shawl around her not to hide what wasn't there, I finally realized, but what was. You're developing a fine bosom, girl, and the kaftans and silk jackets won't hide it much longer. Mustache or no, you won't grow a beard.

"And a woman moves differently than a man, the way she throws her legs about when she runs. And when you saw the, um, part, you didn't know what it was at first. Any lad would have known right away. You didn't until I pointed it out to you.

"There was one other thing—that picture of Leon's."

"What picture?" Sultan Petrus asked.

"Leon is painting the image of the Redeemer and his followers having the Holy Meal. He's got everyone he knew in Manatas in it—Otter Tail, Benyamin, even Tavernier and Ruiz. For all I know, he was ready to include Gomez. But not Selim. Why? Because Selim wouldn't have been there; the Redeemer's followers were all men or boys. When did Gomez suspect that Selim was Salomay?"

192

Salomay's eyes filled with tears. "He was horrible. He must have been peeping when I went to the hammam. He went to my father, said he knew that I wasn't a boy, and he'd tell Mullah Abadul the sultan was hiding a great secret. Mullah Abadul was already angry with my father about Leon's being my tutor; that was why he made Leon leave the Rabat."

"I've heard the mullah's preaching," Halvar said. "He's a rabble-rouser, true enough."

"There's worse," Sultan Petrus added as Salomay paused to sniffle, "If the Mahak found out I had misled them, there would be a break between Al-Andalus and the Locals."

"Over a thing like that? What difference can it make whether your child is a boy or a girl?"

"You saw what happened at the brickyards when Frater Iosip disagreed with the Mahak shaman," Selim reminded Halvar. "The worst thing you can call a Mahak is a liar. They're fanatical about it. Even their stories always begin with a claim that what is being told is true, that they know because they saw it, or someone told them they saw it."

"If I were revealed to be lying about something as basic as whether my child was a boy or a girl, my authority here in Manatas would be gone," Sultan Petrus said. "The Mahak might change their loyalty from Al-Andalus to Franchenland."

"Even though the Franchen have allied themselves with the Mahak's greatest enemy, the Huron?" Halvar asked, skeptical.

"Politics makes for strange bedfellows," the sultan quoted. "Above all, the Algonkin want to preserve their own trade—whoever can supply them with goods, that's who Algonkin side with. As for the Mahak, they'll fight anyone who tries to take their land from them. I want them with us as allies, not against us as enemies, if the Franchen come."

"You think it may come to that?" Halvar asked. "Then I've got to get that silver back to Al-Andalus!"

"You will have to wait for it a little longer, Don Alvaro. I met earlier today with the leaders of the merchants at the Feria and the sachems of the Algonkin and Mahak. We are all agreed. Because of the big storm, the Feria lost three days' trading: first, getting ready for the storm, then the day of the storm, then cleaning up after it. We are, therefore, going to permit the Feria to continue for one more week.

"At the end of that time, I will hold the Grand Divan to sort out any legal disputes that may have arisen during the Feria. It will likely take some time before the final tally is completed and a ship can be made ready to sail. I think you had better be prepared to spend more time here in Manatas, Don Alvaro. And try not to kill anyone else while you are here."

Halvar smiled ruefully. "If no one else tries to kill me," he promised. "I've bespoke rooms at the Mermaid Taberna. I can move my gear out of the Rabat by tomorrow. Then, maybe, I can get back to doing what I came here to do."

"And what is that?"

"I will get Leon di Vicenza out of that fratery and onto a boat back to Al-Andalus, with the silver and goods Don Felipe needs to keep his lands out of the hands of Imperator Lovis and his Roumi Rite Kristos!"

"Just like you said you would," Salomay said.

"I'll still need someone to read and write for me," Halvar admitted. "With your father's permission, of course."

Sultan Petrus waved his hand in a gesture of futility.

"She's her mother's child, Don Alvaro. All I can do is warn you, she will go her own way."

"And I'll go mine," Halvar said. "I'll get back to the Feria first thing tomorrow and see what the Franchen and Bretain merchants are up to. I hope no one else gets killed in Manatas, because you've got to find someone to head the Town Guards. For all I care, you can let Emir Achmet do it. He's already got his people organized, and like Old Sergeant Olaf used to say, 'Set a thief to catch a thief.' You might let Flores have a turn, though. He's not pretty, but he's loyal, and he obeys orders"

Halvar set his cap firmly on his head, salaamed, and strode out. He had his orders, and he was finally going to be able to carry them out. Leon would be on the ship with the silver and goods for Al-Andalus if it took until the *next* Feria to get him there!

END

Halvar's World

GLOSSARY

AL-ANDALUS	Spain
ALGONKIN	Algonquin/Lenape Indians
ARABI	Arabic
ARAGHOUN	Raccoon
BATATAS	Potatoes
BIRDIE	Homosexual (direct translation of Yiddish *faygaleh*)
BRETAINS	British
BURNWEED	Poison ivy
CHESU	Jesus
CRUX	Cross
CONVIVENCIA	Tacit Agreement Of Tolerance, By Which Islam, Judaism And Christianity Co-exist Peacefully In Al-Andalus
CORDUVA	Cordova
DANE-MARCH	Germany
DANES	Germanic people (includes Denmark)
DANIC	German language (written in Rune characters)
DAY OF BEGINNINGS	Rosh Ha-Shanah

GLOSSARY

DAY OF REPENTANCE	Yom Kippur
EAST CHANNEL	East River
ERSE	Gaelic language (written in Ogham characters)
ERSE RITE	Christianity as practiced in Northern Europe, under Celtic influence
ESCOUASH	Squash
FERIA	Commercial gathering / fair
FRANCHEN	French language (written in Roman characters); a native of Franchenland
FRANCHENLAND	France
FRATER	General term for a Kristo cleric
FRATERY	Monastery
GREAT RIVER	Hudson River
HEMP	Cannabis, marijuana
HOLY BOOK	Bible or Qran, depending on who is speaking
HOLY MEAL	Mass
ILHA	Allah
ISLIM	Islam

GLOSSARY

IVRIT	Hebrew language (written in Hebrew characters)
KRISTO	Christian
KUTTON	Cotton
KIBBICK	Quebec
LOCALS	Native Americans
MACASSIN	Moccasin
MADRASSAH	School/university
MAHAK	Mohawk/Iroquois
MAIZ	Corn
MANATAS	Manhattan Island
MOKKA	Coffee
MOTHER MARA	Virgin Mary
MUNSI	Native American trade language (unwritten)
MUSKAT	Mosque
NGUBA	"Goobers," peanuts
NOVA MUNDUM	New World, North America
OLD GRECO	Ancient Greece
OLD ROUMI	Ancient Rome, Ancient Romans
OPASSOM	Opossum

GLOSSARY

OROPA	Europe; excluding Al-Andalus
PARIGI	Paris
PATRI NOSTRI	"Our Father" / Lord's Prayer
PISTOIA	Pistol
RABAT	Fortress
ROUMI RITE	Christianity as practiced south of the Alps, centered in Rome
ROUND ISLAND	Staten Island
SEKONK	Skunk
SOUK	Shopping Sector / marketplace
STUDY HOUSE	Synagogue
TABAC	Tobacco
"TAKE THE WATER"	Be Baptized
THE PROPHET	Mohammad
THE REDEEMER	Jesus
WEST CASTER	Westchester / New England
WUMPUM	Wampum; Shells Used As Medium Of Exchange For Small Purchases
YEHUDIT	Jews / Jewish

Dramatis Personae
(In order of appearance)

HALVAR DANSKE	Ex-mercenary, The Hireling Of Don Felipe, Calif Of Al-Andalus
PETRUS	Sultan Of Manatas Town, Official Representative Of Al-Andalus
DON FELIPE	Calif of Al-Andalus, currently embattled and missing in action.
RUIZ	Tenente of the Manatas Town Guards
SELIM	Sultan Petrus' child
AYESHA	Sultan Petrus's third wife, currently in the harem with a new baby
JACQUES TAVERNIER	Deceased Franchen innkeeper, counterfeiter and spy
LIZETTE TAVERNIER	Deceased wife of above
LEON DI VICENZA	Artist, engineer, genius, and gadfly
MANOLO	A pawnbroker
JEHAN	Manolo's son, also a pawnbroker
DR. MOISE	Official physician to the Andalusian garrison on Manatas Island
MORNING STAR	Jehan's wife, a Local woman
FLORES	Town Guardsman, second in command to Ruiz
PRESTER NICODEMUS	Leader of the Roumi Rite Kristos on Manatas Island

Dramatis Personae
(In order of appearance)

IMAM HAROUN	Leader of the Sunni Islim on the Waterfront
EPISCOPUS INNOCENTE	Self-styled Pater of all Roumi Kristos in Oropa and everywhere else
LOVIS	King of Franchenland, recently elevated to Imperator by Episcopus Innocente
HANNES ZILBERSTAM	A Danic cook, once a seaman, now runs the Mermaid Taberna
ROBERT MORTMAIN	Mysterious missing server at the Mermaid Taberna
EVA HAKIM	Female physician, Leon di Vicenza's sister
MENDEL	A bookseller
BENYAMIN IBN MENDEL	Mendel's son, one of Leon's "Seekers of Truth"
OTTER TAIL	Deceased Mahak lad, beloved of Leon
PADRAIG MAC CORMACK	Bretain member of Leon's "Seekers of Truth"; son of Cormac
EMIR ACHMET	Head of the Scavengers
RACHEV	A Scavenger missing two fingers (sign of a thief)
OSMAN	Another Scavenger, missing a hand (sign of a very unlucky thief)
DANI GLICK	Yehudit woman, owner of the Gardens of Paradise in Green Village

Dramatis Personae
(In order of appearance)

DONAL   Bouncer at the Gardens of Paradise

CORMACK MAC CORMACK   Ironmonger from West Caster, leader of the Bretains of Green Village

FARRAH   Afrikan bathhouse attendant

BIRGIT   Danic bathhouse attendant

ABBAS MIKHAIL   Leader of the Erse Rite Kristos in Green Village

RAV SHIMON LAYZAR   Leader of the Yehudit in Manatas

FIREBRAND   Mahak warrior assigned to assist Halvar

WILLEM OF COS   An entertainer from the Gardens of Paradise

FAROUK   Afrikan brick-yard owner

SEES-IN-CLOUDS   Mahak shaman

FRATER IOSIP   Physician at the Green Village fratery

KARINA   One of Dani Glick's "girls"

MULLAH ABADUL   Leader of Sunni Islim in Manatas

ABOUT THE AUTHOR

ROBERTA ROGOW wanted to tell stories ever since she could hold a pencil., and to sing before she could walk. After a brief career as professional chorister, coffee-house singer, and actress, she combined her love of literature with her love of music during a 37-year career as a children's librarian in New Jersey, where she could promote literacy and entertain youngsters.

In her spare time, Roberta wrote stories for fanzines incorporating historical characters into fictional situations. This led to paid publication., beginning with a story in the shared-universe anthology *Merovingen Nights*, edited by C.J. Cherryh, in 1987.

Since then, Roberta has written four mystery novels in which the Reverend Mr. Charles Lutwidge Dodgson (Lewis Carroll) teams up with young Dr. Arthur Conan Doyle to solve crimes, and three set in post-Civil War New York City, where a team of waterfront lawyers take on cases that no one else will touch.

Now her love of history has turned in another direction with the Saga of Halvar, set in an alternate universe on what is almost, but not quite, Manhattan Island. *Mayhem in Manatas* is the second book set in her re-imagined Manhattan.

Roberta is a widow. She has two daughters: Miriam Ann Rogow, a travel agent living in San Francisco, who has written the Marti Hirsch mysteries, and Louise Katherine Howard, a computer programmer, who lives near Washington DC.

ABOUT THE ARTIST

Born in Chicago, *WILLIAM NEAGLE* graduated from the University of Tennessee with a BFA. Having done work for the US Department of Energy and other companies, his work has been distributed worldwide. He has done book covers for the writing team of Joreid McFate and for his own novel, *Catching the Ghost*. He resides in North Carolina with his wife and two children.

www.ingramcontent.com/pod-product-compliance
Lightning Source LLC
Chambersburg PA
CBHW030308200626
46816CB00002BA/810